ON A QUIET STREET

ON A QUIET STREET

A DR. PEPPER HUNT MYSTERY

J.L. DOUCETTE

SHE WRITES PRESS

Published 2019
Printed in the United States of America
ISBN: 978-1-63152-537-7 pbk
ISBN: 978-1-63152-538-4 ebk
Library of Congress Control Number: 2019902943

For information, address:
She Writes Press
1569 Solano Ave #546
Berkeley, CA 94707

Interior design by Tabitha Lahr

She Writes Press is a division of SparkPoint Studio, LLC.

"The heart of another is a dark forest, always, no matter how close it has been to one's own."

—Willa Cather, *My Antonia*

For my daughters,
Stephanie and Deirdre

PROLOGUE

The church bells rang out at six o'clock in the morning, the exact moment the Sheriff's Department received the call about a dead woman in a house on Cedar Street.

Sometime in the pre-dawn hours of the first day of summer, Stacey Hart was strangled in her home on a quiet street in Rock Springs, Wyoming.

It was the first homicide of the year and the second time the Sweetwater County Sheriff's Department engaged my services in a murder investigation.

I'm a forensic psychologist, trained to work where the mental health and criminal justice systems intersect. Most of us who thrive in this field are drawn to it because of some dark and unresolved experience in our past.

The process is known as repetition compulsion. We keep going back into the same sad story, hoping to rewrite the ending.

CHAPTER 1

Jack Swailes looked down at the woman he loved. She was lying on the steps to the greenhouse. One of her moccasins had come off and her white shirt was torn at the shoulder. She wasn't breathing.

What he did next would make all the difference. Make a call, or climb in his truck and haul ass out of there? No one would come for hours. He'd be history; his life would be his own again. The way it was before he followed Stacey into the cafe where she hijacked his heart and changed everything.

Her wild, golden hair reminded him of Dante's painting of Helen of Troy. He knew nothing about art; a hooker who worked for his uncle had taped the picture over her bed.

He knelt and kissed the marks on her neck and smoothed the bloody curls. A crazy urge rose up and he snapped a last picture. Her phone blinked where it had fallen near her right hand, outside the circle of blood. Remembering the last thing she'd asked of him, he reached over, picked up the phone, turned it off, and slipped it into the pocket of his vest.

A rolling stone, she'd called him—a guy who wouldn't stick around to put a ring on her finger. But what the hell, she'd belonged to Connor, planned to marry him.

And now this.

What is done cannot be undone, he told himself.

Outside on the wide porch, the air held the night's chill and a clean smell rose from the wet grass. He shivered and rubbed his arms. As much as he wanted to resist, he pulled out his cigarettes and lit up. With the first breath, a slicing pain seized his chest, a heartache he'd never outrun.

He smoked and thought about everything that had happened since he'd first stepped into the house and the way he'd changed it with his hands. After a while, his thoughts came clear: he owed her something.

The phone in his hand was heavy with the weight of his destiny. He dialed the number to summon the sheriff.

CHAPTER 2

Beau Antelope was born to be a detective, a job that kept him tied to the pain of the world.

The Wind River Reservation where he'd grown up had the highest rate of violent crime in the country. He'd figured out early there were two kinds of trouble: the kind that found you no matter how hard you tried to hide and the kind you went looking for. His job was a mixture of both.

When the call came in about a possible homicide on Cedar Street, he drove the three blocks to the scene. A county ambulance and a panel truck with the logo VERY CLASSIC DESIGNS took up the curb space in front of the yellow bungalow. He pulled into the gravel driveway behind a white Prius.

On the porch, a workman dropped a cigarette and stood at attention as Antelope exited the unmarked car.

"Wait here. I'll come back for a statement," he told the man and entered the residence.

In the kitchen at the rear of the house, the paramedics were working on a blond woman with a strong, athletic body that would never move again. A quick scan of the crime scene showed nothing disturbed, except for the woman herself.

Her clothing—in disarray—indicated that she'd struggled and lost the fight. The coroner would determine if it was death by strangulation or blunt force trauma.

Antelope shot the crime scene from every angle with his phone. After the coroner took the body and the forensics team completed their work, he would come back to spend time alone here. If he got lucky, her spirit would offer something to guide his way to the killer.

He watched the workman smoke outside the front window, lost in thought. At the sound of the door opening, he dropped the cigarette, crushed it with the toe of his boot. His right eye twitched as he scanned Antelope's face; a tremble shook the hands resting on the porch railing.

"I never saw someone dead before," he said. "My mind's all kinds of twisted around."

"Let's start with some basic information," Antelope said, pulling out his notebook. "Give me your name and address."

"Jack Swailes. I stay at the Court Motel."

"At Val Campion's place? Is this your rig?"

"It's Val's. He's my uncle. I hired on with him a while back."

"Whose place is this?"

"The woman inside—her name's Stacey Hart. Her man owns the place, Connor Collins. They hired me to get the work done before the wedding in July."

Collins was the Assistant County Prosecutor. The Sheriff's Department would lose control of the investigation the minute word got out that a prosccutor's girlfriend had been murdered.

"Tell me what happened this morning."

"I showed up to work same as always—early, before six. She liked to meet early, before her own job started. But she gave me a key so I could keep my own hours, work late if I want. Her car was here this morning, so I rang the bell. When she didn't come, I went in."

"The door wasn't locked?"

"She doesn't lock it when she's here, only when she leaves."

"I take it those are your tools in there?"

"They are. Can I grab them when we're done here?"

"They'll be marked as evidence. I can't say how long before you get them back. It looks like the tile cutter could be our murder weapon."

Jack shook his head.

"Man, how could something like this happen?"

"It's my job to find the answers."

"I don't envy you, man. It's a sick world we live in."

"You're in the house. What happens next?"

"I called out to her and headed back to the kitchen. I planned to paint in there today."

Swailes took a deep breath and rested his head against the porch railing, eyes closed. "Give me a second."

Dead bodies tend to mess with the mind of the average citizen, Antelope thought.

Swailes lit another cigarette, took a few quick drags, and tossed it away also. "The whole thing rolled out in my mind like the worst movie ever."

"I need you to tell me what you found in there."

"First thing I saw was Stacey on the floor where the stairs go down to the greenhouse. I thought maybe she tripped, so I went over to her. Up close I saw the blood and those marks on her throat."

"Did you touch the body?"

"No, no. just looked."

"When we're done here, head over to the station on D Street and tell the desk clerk I sent you for fingerprints."

"Am I in some kind of trouble?"

"It's standard procedure in a homicide investigation. You found the body, you went to help her, you're sure you didn't touch her?"

"I got down beside her. I could see someone hurt her."

"Any idea who that might be, Jack?"

"You want the truth?"

"Let me set you straight. This is officially a homicide investigation. Anything but the truth, you could be charged with obstruction of justice." Antelope studied the other man's face. "You can proceed with answering my question now."

"Her boyfriend's a jealous guy."

"What do you mean?"

"He gave her a hard time about talking to other guys, the usual shit. Funny thing, though, he didn't give her much attention himself."

"What about you? Was Connor jealous of you?"

"I sometimes got that impression. He had no reason. She had his ring on and I respected that. But some guys don't need a reason."

"So you and the victim were friends, nothing more going on?"

"I worked for her. I know my place. Forget I said anything."

Tires squealed and a black BMW screeched to a halt. Connor Collins ran across the street in sweatpants and flip-flops, remnants of shaving cream on his face, wet hair slicked back.

"A neighbor called. What happened? Where's Stacey?"

He looked back and forth between Antelope and Swailes.

The contractor held both hands up in a don't-blame-me pose then fled the porch, heading to his truck.

Connor moved toward the front door but Antelope got in front of him and blocked his entrance.

"Hold on. I can't let you go in there. It's a crime scene."

"What the hell? It's my house; I'm going in. Is Stacey in there?"

"I need you to step back. The paramedics are with her."

"What did he do to her? Swailes, you son of a bitch, what did you do to her?" Connor took off toward the truck.

Antelope ran after him, grabbed his shoulders, and spun him around as Swailes sped off down Cedar Street.

The two men struggled and Connor lost his footing. Antelope got him face down on the wet grass, his hands pinned at the small of his back.

The prosecutor turned his unshaved face back and forth. "He's getting away."

"Are you going to calm down or do I have to cuff you?"

Collins twisted and groaned, stopped, and went slack under him. "Get off me."

"Are you done? I need your word. There's a street full of witnesses, Mr. Prosecutor."

"I'm all right. Let me up."

Antelope released him, and the two men stood up as a black sedan arrived at the scene and the medical examiner came up the driveway toward them.

Connor's eyes widened. "I knew it. I knew she was dead. Why'd you let the son of a bitch get away?"

It took Antelope a few minutes to convince Connor to leave the scene. When the local news van rounded the corner, it made a bigger impression than anything he'd said. Connor beat a hasty retreat to his car.

This was his cue to exit, too. It was too soon to make any statements to the media. Before he left the scene he instructed a technician to retrieve the contractor's cigarette from the lawn and submit it for DNA processing.

CHAPTER 3

The victim's mother lived in Green River, twelve miles west of Rock Springs off Interstate 80. Eighteen-wheelers dominated the four-lane highway. A thrill ride on a sunny June morning, in winter, with its skin of black ice, the same road became a death trap.

Antelope switched on the lights of his unmarked vehicle and accelerated ahead of the line of traffic. For long-haul truckers, speed meant money, but they got out of the way for police business. Pumped by adrenaline, determined to get the nasty job done, he sped toward the Green River exit ten minutes away.

He took the opportunity to call the sheriff.

"What have we got over there?" Scruggs asked.

"Homicide, female, late twenties. The ME promised end of day tomorrow on cause of death."

"Canvass the neighborhood, talk to anyone who saw anything suspicious last night or early this morning."

"The murder house is the former convent behind the Astro Lounge. We'll need some luck finding anyone awake, sober, or credible. I assigned the best, Garcia and Connors."

Hungry to get out of uniform, the two deputies worked witnesses like dogs on a bone. In a homicide investigation with a family at your neck, persistence was a critical factor. A dead body motivated Antelope, and he only wanted to work with others who saw it the same way. In each murder case he worked, the spirits of the dead haunted his dreams until he caught the killer.

"Who's the victim?"

"We'll have some eyes on us for sure. Her name's Stacey Hart, she was engaged to Connor Collins in the DA's office."

"Damn it to hell and back. Can my luck get any worse? I know her. Pretty girl. She moved in with my Toni a while back. Jesus, Toni's going be hot mess over this."

Antelope understood the sheriff's reaction. The year before, Scruggs' wife had been shot and killed.

After his wife's death, he'd at first sworn off women and thrown himself into his work, determined to reestablish his credibility. But it hadn't taken long for him to get back in the saddle. A few months later he'd met Toni Atwell, a former nun, and it had been love at first sight for both of them.

"How can I get in touch with Toni?" Antelope asked.

Scruggs sighed. "Just what I need. Another dead woman."

"We need Toni's perspective on the victim. Are you going to give me her number, or do I have to track her down?"

Up ahead, the morning sun lit the steep rock cliffs a dazzling copper red. As he entered the Green River Twin Tunnels, Antelope lost the call. Exit 91 put him on W. Flaming Gorge Way. The GPS showed the Harts' place on the left, a mile past the Sweetwater District Court.

He hated this part of the job—handing people the worst news of their lives. He felt deceitful and predatory in the presence of a family's grief when all he wanted was something he could use to solve the case.

Sympathy was a luxury he couldn't afford. In murder cases, as in trucking, time ruled; you either moved fast or you lost your edge. The killer didn't want to be caught.

Sometimes families wanted to kill the messenger, and he couldn't blame them. But most of them understood that he was their best hope of getting closure or revenge, whatever they were after.

The Hart family home, a brown shingled raised ranch, sat behind a white picket fence. A rusted Ford pickup sat at the curb. At the end of the driveway, a renovated garage with a yellow door advertised, 'Daycare with Heart.' A small playground with a set of wooden swings and climbing equipment secured behind a chain link fence sat empty.

A wildflower garden, identical to the one at the Cedar Street house, bordered a brick path to the front door. Day lilies and sunflowers swayed in a gathering wind, signaling a storm on its way. From inside the house, Metallica blared at a decibel level too high for the suburban area.

As Antelope opened the gate, a young man with a shaved head came to the screen door. Tattooed arms crossed over a bare chest, black sweats low on his hips. Had Antelope just interrupted his private play time? Did this guy have a woman inside? Whatever the scenario, the fun was over. Nothing, not even sex, would ever be the same again for him.

"This is a restricted area." With a middle finger, the man pointed to a metal sign face down on the grass.

"Kind of hard to see," Antelope said.

"The wind must have got it." He jogged across the small yard, righted the sign, and pounded it into the lawn with his fist. Antelope noticed that he didn't flinch at the impact, although the contact with the metal post must have hurt.

After years in law enforcement, he had to agree: daycare centers needed security. Stranger kidnappings, the nightmare of parents, occurred less frequently than kidnapping by ignorant, angry parents willing to snatch their own kid, destroy their world, for the pleasure of sticking it to their ex. It made him sick, this wanton disregard for children's experience.

"Are you Max Hart?"

"Depends who's asking."

"Detective Antelope, Sweetwater County Sheriff." Antelope held out his ID with his right hand.

Max studied it like a bouncer screening for underage drinkers. "What's your business here?"

Antelope associated this kind of cagey attitude with small-change drug dealers. Time to take the dive off the high board.

"Can we go inside? I have some news about your sister."

"Stacey?" Max's eyes widened. "What about Stacey? I was with her last night."

"It's bad news. Your sister is dead. I'm sorry to have to tell you this."

Max put his hands on his head and walked in circles. An

inhuman sound came from him, a low growl from somewhere deep inside. He raised a fist and swung it hard into the sign, which toppled under the force of his anger. Then he lifted his gaze to Antelope. "What happened? How did she die?"

Antelope noticed the neighbor next door and two across the street had opened their doors.

"Maybe we should step inside," Antelope said.

Max scanned the neighborhood, staring down the onlookers. One by one, the doors closed. "If you don't tell me right now what happened to my sister, that steel post over there is going to be somewhere other than in the ground. You got it?"

Max stood inches from Antelope's face. He smelled of weed and body odor.

"I'm going to forget you said that," Antelope said. "But you need to get a grip. No one's doing anything other than talking here. I don't want to have to arrest you."

Max breathed like a rodeo bull, nostrils flared, spitting with rage. But he backed up a foot, and stood with his hands on hips.

Antelope waited a bit to make sure Max had control of himself before saying, "She didn't die of natural causes." He paused to let this sink in. "She was murdered."

Max rocked back on his heels as if he'd been pushed, then squatted with his hands on his knees, his stomach muscles contracting with the force of his breath. When he stood up, his eyes were dull and vacant. He reached into his back pocket and pulled out his phone.

"Mom, it's an emergency. You have to come home right now. Leave the damn groceries in the cart and come home. I'll tell you when you get here. Just come, right now."

"She's not going to hear this on the news is she?" he asked after hanging up.

"They're on notice to hold off until the family's been notified."

Max picked up the sign and planted it back in the grass, hitting it with more force than the first time. "Come inside before she gets here."

Antelope followed him into a dark living room. Without another word, Max disappeared up the stairs. On the second floor a door slammed with such force that a picture fell from the fireplace mantel.

Shards of glass spilled on the hardwood floor when Antelope turned over a silver-framed photograph of Stacey Hart. He scooped the broken pieces back into the frame and set it on a maple end table.

The music he'd heard outside was coming from a fifty-inch flat screen bolted above the fireplace. Antelope found the remote on the couch and killed the music. In the quiet gloom, he waited for Fern Hart to come home.

Loud footsteps on the wooden stairs. Max stomped into the room, sat in a recliner, and, after kicking out the leg rest, closed his eyes to wait. Antelope positioned himself at the front window.

A blue Kia rounded the corner and jerked to a stop out front.

Fern Hart took in the unfamiliar vehicle and ran toward the house.

She entered the living room and her wild blue eyes scanned the room, frantic, as if she knew what Antelope had come to tell her.

When he delivered his news, her eyes snapped shut—her body's attempt to refuse the unwanted, the unbearable, new reality. When she looked at him again, tears flowed.

Max led his mother to the couch, where she collapsed, her body small and broken beside his. Minutes passed while she cried and Max held her. In his mind, Antelope traveled Highway 191, the often empty, desolate stretch of blacktop that led to the Wind River Reservation. These thoughts put him in the right frame of mind for the situation.

"I'm sorry for your loss," he said.

In an instant, Fern went from desolation to resolve, quick as a safety taken off a gun seconds before a shot is fired. "How did my daughter die?"

"She was found this morning in the Cedar Street house. We're still piecing things together; we're waiting for the medical examiner to determine the cause of death."

Fern sat dead still as the words hit, as her brain made space for the pain. "How did she die?" she repeated. "Tell me everything, and tell it quick."

"The contractor working on the house found her this morning," Antelope said. "It looked like she fell on the steps going down to the greenhouse. There were also signs of a struggle. The Medical Examiner will have the official cause of death within forty-eight hours."

"Someone killed her. What did they do to her?"

"I can't say officially. There was some bruising on her neck, and she hit her head when she fell."

"Do you think he did it, the man who found her, the contractor?" Fern asked. "She liked him, it would be a shame."

"I know you want answers, Mrs. Hart. We all do. And we'll get them. I advise you not to jump to conclusions at the start of the investigation. As soon as we know anything definite, you'll know it next."

She gripped Max's hand tighter, leaned into him. The best thing Antelope could do for her was give her a purpose and a reason to breathe another day.

"When was the last time you saw your daughter?"

"On Mother's Day we had dinner at the Holiday Inn together."

Max shot Antelope a look. "Can this wait, man?"

Fern put her free hand on her son's arm. "I'm alright, Max. He needs our help to find out who did this."

"The sooner I get to work, the better the chances of finding who did this," Antelope said. "The two of you knew her better than anyone else. If it was someone she knew, it's possible you know her killer."

"I can't imagine it's anyone who knew her." Fern shook her head. "Everyone loved Stacey."

Every part of her body trembled and shook—like an aspen in a high wind, Antelope thought, a flurry of protest at being disturbed. Max sprang to his feet and returned with a blanket. He wrapped it around her shoulders, and she stroked the soft fabric.

"Stacey made this for me before she left home. She chose the Blessed Virgin's colors, blue and white. She's a good girl, a religious girl. I thought the Lord would keep her safe."

"When you saw her last month, how did she seem?"

Fern and Max exchanged a quick look.

"Happy. Thrilled about the wedding." Fern broke down again. "My poor girl," she choked out between sobs, "she'll never be a bride . . . and she waited so long, she wanted it so much. Why did this happen?"

"It's been over a month since you last saw her? Seems like a long time."

"She was so busy getting ready for the wedding. And Max hasn't seen her, have you Max?"

"I saw her last night."

"I didn't know you two were talking again. They had a falling out." Fern looked at Antelope.

"He doesn't need to know our business," Max said. "I never stopped talking to Stacey."

"You agreed to take some space."

"You make me out to be a psycho stalker."

"I would have had you take the new gardening magazine to her."

"Christ, what difference does it make now? And I didn't know I'd be seeing her. She texted and asked me to meet her after work."

"You never said."

"It was a drink. Why would I tell you?" Max paced the small room in a tight rectangle, like a prisoner in a cell block.

"You didn't drink, did you?" She looked at Antelope again. "He's been sober five years."

"The tavern serves non-alcoholic drinks. And why are you talking about my issues now?"

"Don't stress, Max." Fern tightened the blanket around her shoulders. "I can't handle it if you get upset now. Why don't you call Dr. Hunt—?"

"Stop running my business," Max snapped.

"She always helps."

"Later."

"Max had an accident a long time ago—a brain injury," Fern explained. "He has some issues."

"He doesn't care about my medical history," Max muttered. "This is about Stacey getting murdered."

Antelope wondered if the outburst he'd witnessed out front was due to the brain injury.

"Will you sign a release so I can talk to Dr. Hunt?" he asked Max.

"I don't have a problem with that."

"I appreciate it. Where did you and Stacey meet last night?"

"Johnny's Good Time Tavern."

"What time did you meet?"

"After work, she gets off at five. Why?"

"I need to know her activities, everything in the days leading up to the time she was found. It's a place to start. Any particular reason she wanted to see you last night?"

"It was drinks. TGIF—no big deal."

"And how was Stacey last night? Did she give any indication that she was worried about anything?"

Max snorted. "If my sister ever worried about anything, you'd never know it."

"What can you tell me about her relationship with Connor?"

Fern Hart looked straight at Antelope and pointed a finger, five pounds of silver jangling.

"They were college sweethearts. He was her first boyfriend. How is poor Connor? Does he know?"

"He took it hard," Antelope said carefully. "It's a shock for all of you. One more question and I'll leave you alone. Was Stacey having a problem or conflict with anyone?"

"My daughter never had a problem with anyone," Fern said firmly.

"Is there anyone I can talk to—a friend who Stacey would have confided in?"

"Her best friend, Kelly Ryan, lives around the corner. You can't miss it; it's the big blue Victorian the corner of Sage and Terrace. I can call her and let her know what's happened. She'll take it hard, and it's better if she hears it from me. I don't think she's seen Stacey for a while, though. They had a little falling out. Kelly has always been a little jealous of Stacey, right, Max?"

Beside her, Max shook his head. "I have no idea what you're talking about. Not my business."

"If you give me the address I'll stop there now," Antelope said.

"It's 2 Sage Drive. And have you talked to her roommate? Such a lovely woman, Toni Atwood's her name."

"I got the impression she lived with Mr. Collins," Antelope said.

"Not before marriage. Stacey wouldn't live with Connor until they married. I know a lot of young people do it these days, but it's very much against my beliefs. We're a Catholic family. I asked her to respect my wishes, and she did. She lives with Toni Atwell—she's a former nun—in a small house in Rock Springs. Toni will tell you the same thing I just did. Stacey never had a problem with anyone."

Max put his right hand over his eyes and banged his head against the back of the couch. Fern took both his hands in hers. "Stop, Max, please."

He pulled his hands away and stood up. "Don't do that. I've asked you not to touch me."

"I'm sorry." Fern grew tearful again. "I just hate to see you hurt yourself."

"Stop pushing the fairy tale of how everybody loved Stacey," Max said. "She's dead, Mom, murdered. *Somebody* had a problem with her."

CHAPTER 4

Outside, black thunderheads rolled in from the south to darken the day. Before Antelope made it back to the car, sheets of freezing rain hit the ground with a loud fury. Hailstones pelted the roof and hood in a wild staccato beat. He was soaked to the skin, and when he started the engine, a blast of frigid air sent a shiver up his spine—like a goose had walked over his grave, his mother would say. It was an idea he wanted to shake off but couldn't because of where his head was at, what he'd just had to do.

Shielded from the weather and the grief of the house, he waited for the storm to die out.

Ten minutes later, the rain stopped as abruptly as it started. Muddy water coursed through the viaducts and flooded the narrow streets. A double rainbow over the interstate brightened his spirits and reminded him of how as a kid he'd walked for hours to find the pot of gold. Back then, he'd believed every magical story he heard. Who was he kidding? He still believed. He wondered if Stacey's family would give nature's artwork a special meaning: Stacey saying good-bye.

■ ■ ■

Hidden behind a strip mall off Exit 92, a hole-in-the-wall joint called the Black Tiara served the finest Mexican food in Wyoming. It opened for lunch six days a week. On weekends it operated as a speakeasy and exotic dance club.

He placed an order to go and waited in the dining room, where the soothing sounds of a Mexican guitar played. A few minutes later, he left with a warm sack of spicy burritos. He planned to check in with Scruggs after lunch.

Before he swallowed the first bite, his cell phone rang.

"I was in meetings all morning and came out to a truckload of texts from Toni," Scruggs said. "You can imagine her state of mind."

In the last six months, the sheriff had evolved into an emotionally sensitive male. In treatment for serial cheating, he'd gotten in touch with his feelings and learned to express them. Some of the guys had even reported hearing sobs in the bathroom from time to time. Scruggs was a changed man. Antelope wasn't sure which version he preferred.

"I plan to speak with her when I finish up here in Green River."

"The woman's torn up and devastated. Take my advice and give her a day to pull herself together."

"Since when does the Sheriff's Department maintain a boutique interview schedule?"

"Since my gal's on the witness list. No surprise you never married, Antelope. You don't understand the first thing about women. And don't even go there; I'm not in the mood. What have you got so far?"

"Stacey's brother's a nut job. Brain injury makes him go off half-cocked sometimes. When Mrs. Hart said he and Stacey had some trouble, he became defensive. He sees Pepper Hunt for counseling—gave me permission to talk to her."

Dr. Pepper Hunt was a forensic psychologist who had assisted on another homicide earlier in the year. Antelope was starting to think it would be helpful to bring her on for this one, too.

"Contractor who found the body was twitchy," he said. "When Collins accused him of having done something to Stacey, he bolted. I'll catch up with him later. Kelly Ryan's next on my list. She's a friend who might know more than the mother, who claims everyone loved her."

Scruggs grunted. "Those types don't get murdered."

"Except this one did. I hope Toni can give me the straight story on her. We need more than a one-dimensional sketch."

"Let's not forget they both work jobs where they could pick up enemies. Have someone check on people Collins sent away recently—family members looking for revenge, recent parolees carrying a grudge. And Stacey worked at the YMCA, something to do with domestic violence and the Safe House. There could be a crazy ex who wanted to even the score because she helped his woman escape."

"We'll need manpower on this one."

"Take who you need—and get on it, quick. We don't want the trail going cold. Humor me, though. Give Toni a day's grace period."

"Trust me; I'll leave her in one piece. I know how to handle a witness. Time is crucial in homicide. You taught me that."

"Don't bust my balls, Antelope. Go easy on her. I'll pull the shift reports and see what the neighborhood canvass yielded. If anything jumps out that I want you to snag pronto, you'll hear from me. If not, I'm off the clock until 8:00 a.m. I plan to take Toni out for a few pops, settle her down before she has to deal with questions."

"Do me a favor and make it an early night. I need her clear-headed."

More than once, Antelope had witnessed the former nun downing shots and keeping up with the regular sport drinkers at the Saddle Lite Saloon. He'd also heard rumors that she'd left the convent because of an alcohol problem. One would think alcoholism was less of a problem than the thousands of cases of Catholic priests sexually abusing children, but he supposed the standards were higher for women.

"Don't worry about Toni," Scruggs said. "She can hold her liquor."

CHAPTER 5

We rode back to the barn at a gallop to outrun the thunderheads racing across the sky and made it through the barn doors as the deafening downpour hit.

Safe in the barn, Soldier was nervous at the scatter-shot of hailstones on the tin roof. I finished wiping him down, gave him a carrot treat, and nuzzled him good-bye with a promise of another ride soon.

Then I ran out through the heavy downpour and realized I couldn't see clear enough to drive. I pulled out my phone to check the weather forecast just as it started to ring.

"What are you doing?"

Detective Antelope's customary greeting no longer annoyed me. At first I'd seen it as adolescent, intrusive, and way too intimate for the relationship the two of us had. We'd worked a case together. We'd tried to be friends. But he'd pushed it, so I'd put up a wall and stopped it before it could go anywhere.

Why should I tell him what I was doing? The question assumed he had a right to know, which was why it had put me on the defensive. But I had to admit, it was an excellent way for a detective to start a conversation. It gave him the upper hand right from the start. Plus, Antelope is one of the good guys—and a great detective. So I'd given up and gotten over it.

"I'm waiting out the storm, dripping rainwater all over my Jeep."

"Where are you?"

"At the barn, I just got back from a trail ride. Why, what's up?"

"Some bad business. A woman was murdered on Cedar Street this morning and you have a connection to the case."

"Tell me."

"In the process of notifying the family, her brother disclosed that he's a client of yours. He volunteered to sign a release. I know you can't talk to me until he signs it, but I thought I'd give you a heads up it's coming. It's Max Hart."

My heart sank. "Stacey Hart was murdered? I know Stacey."

"I'm sorry. I didn't know. What's your connection to her?"

"I teach a class on sexual abuse prevention through your department. Stacey worked at the Center for Families and Children. What happened? What can you tell me?"

"A contractor working in the house found the body early this morning. Looks like blunt force trauma to the head, but there were bruises on her neck, too. Waiting on the medical examiner for cause of death."

"This is terrible news." My first thought was what it would do to Max. He would be devastated.

I hadn't seen Antelope since the day we drove to Ocean Lake, the place where my patient Kimi Benally had died. After that long and strangely intimate day we'd shared, I'd thought I might hear from him. It had been mid-January then, smack in the middle of a cold, hard winter—the definition of lonely. But I hadn't heard from him again until now.

I'd wondered more than a few times what I would have done if he had reached out. He's a handsome guy with a mysterious soul. I could do worse than Detective Beau Antelope, if I wanted romance—which I didn't.

When we'd worked Kimi's case together, he'd made it clear he wanted something beyond a professional relationship. When I shut things down—pretty hard—he didn't try again. I respected him more for respecting what I wanted.

Six months is a long time, however, and my defenses were in place again.

"You think the contractor did it?"

"He's number one on the list right now."

"Any other thoughts?"

"She was too young to die, for starters. So what do you say, Doc, are you up for getting your hands dirty with another murdered girl? It's a criminal case, so outside the scope of your current contract. I'm sure there's enough in the budget to make it worth your while."

"You make it hard to resist."

"This stuff doesn't bother you? I mean, it gets kind of gritty when you get close to murder—you found that out last time. A lot of the shrinks around here won't touch a murder case, or any violent case, for that matter."

When you discover the bodies of your husband and his mistress, shot and killed in the office you shared, your perspective changes, I thought grimly. "You know my story," I said. "I'm hard to shock."

"The sun's coming out over here in Green River. I need to get back to work, but I'll be back in Rock Springs in time for appetizers. Want to meet me at Bitter Creek Brewing?"

"What time?"

"Shoot for five."

"I'll be there."

He hung up without saying good-bye.

■ ■ ■

I met Beau Antelope a few months after moving to Wyoming. We both have reasons to be cautious about the people we let into our lives. He admitted he ran a background check on me, the way he does with all potential friends, after our initial meeting. A few things came up that caused him to think twice about me—the Grand Jury Hearing for my husband's murder, for one. They determined then that they did not have enough evidence to charge me for the crime, but still . . .

"I meet all kinds in my work. I can't be too careful," he said.

For me, a simple background check didn't work. The kind of treachery I feared wouldn't show up on an arrest record.

Law-abiding citizens who harbor villainous hearts were the ones who terrified me. Unfortunately, there was no way to know who they were until you got close enough to feel the stab wounds. Safety came from being alone.

CHAPTER 6

Her red eyes and a pink nose made him think of spring bunnies on the reservation. Kelly Ryan came to the door in a blue silk robe with a pack of Newport 100s tucked in her cleavage. Her pretty face was swollen from crying, but she tried for a brave smile.

"Come in. Fern told me. I can't believe it. Who'd want to hurt Stacey?" She lit a cigarette and fanned the smoke away.

"The Sheriff's Department will make every effort to find out," Antelope said.

"Excuse the mess. I'm cleaning up from breakfast."

The first floor was open plan and had a wall of windows at the back. A bowl and spoon, a box of Cheerios, and a banana skin at one end of a long kitchen island were the only signs of life in the spotless kitchen. Kelly Ryan felt the need to apologize when things were less than perfect, a trait Antelope found annoying.

The same vintage as all the other 1950s post-war cottages and bungalows in the neighborhood, the renovated home looked new. The white walls, charcoal carpets, teak cabinets, pink granite countertops, and stainless steel appliances in the kitchen transformed it into a showplace.

She smoked the way his mother did—head thrown back, eyes closed, deep breaths—drama queen moves, a mix of sacred and pornographic that turned him on. He gave himself a mental slap on the head and remembered why he was standing in Kelly Ryan's kitchen.

"Tell me about Stacey."

She leaned and opened a window to fan the smoke outside and he caught a glimpse of the small breasts inside her robe. She saw him look and took her time before adjusting it.

"I need ice cream. Sorry, I eat when I'm stressed. Classic chick move, right? You like Cherry Garcia? Albertson's started carrying it. Care to join me?"

"No thanks."

"Oh, right, I bet they won't let you. Don't worry, I won't tell anyone."

"I have a few questions. I won't take up much of your time."

"I'm in no hurry," she said, opening the freezer door. She kept talking as she rummaged for the ice cream. "My parents took my son on vacation, an RV trip down to Utah. They'll be gone for two weeks. They bust their butts all year at Ryan's Southwest Dry Cleaning—Green River's Best for Your Best, that's their slogan. They handle all the dry cleaning for the Sheriff's Department." She shut the freezer door, Cherry Garcia in hand. "I'm sorry, I'm a little scattered with everything. You're not here to talk about dry cleaning. I'll shut up and you can ask your questions."

She ate ice cream straight from the carton, which she held cradled in her arm like a baby. Resting there it made a kind of shelf for the sculpture of her breasts. His mind came back to sex again. He made a mental note to watch himself around Kelly Ryan.

"When did you see her last?"

"About a month ago, I think. I wanted to stop by and see the progress on the house, but at the last minute she asked if she could come here instead. She said she needed to step out of her life for a little bit. She came over and then we ended up taking a drive out to Little America, we love the pie there."

"How did she seem to you?"

Kelly savored a mouthful of cherries and went someplace in her head. Out in the garden, the cheerful sound of birds singing brought her attention back. She shook her head. The long spoon dangled from her fingers and dropped into the empty carton. "Something was off." She ran the spoon around the bottom of the carton and caught the last bits of fruit and melted cream, then dropped everything into the sink before taking the final bite. She lit up again and executed the same slow, soulful drag, drawing out the pleasure and the poison. Since he'd stepped into the house, she'd had something in her mouth.

"I'm restless, let's sit on the deck," she said.

The wooden steps felt damp from the noon cloudburst. Her bare feet, toenails bright as poppies, brushed the top of the pale, wet grass.

"Feels good," she said.

He relaxed beside her, enjoyed a moment of contentment in the sun before his left brain booted up an image of Stacey dead in her kitchen.

Kelly finished her cigarette and lit another one from the stub.

"I know I'm hopeless. I want to quit before it ruins my skin. Not today, though. Today is not the day to give up my number one coping mechanism. I only have one other way to deal, and it's not ice cream. Sorry, TMI. You want one?" She offered him the pack.

"I'll pass."

"No ice cream, no smokes. No vices for the detective?"

"None I'll admit to."

"Touché."

Antelope refocused. "What made you think Stacey was off that night?"

"I don't know the right way to describe it. Wound a little too tight. Somebody else, you wouldn't notice it, but Stacey was usually so happy and sweet . . ."

"How long have you been friends?"

"Fern didn't tell you?"

"Tell me what?"

"They told you about Max's accident?"

"Mrs. Hart mentioned an accident, a head injury."

"That's an understatement. He almost died, in a coma for six months with serious brain damage, and when he woke up he couldn't remember a thing, not the accident or anything before it. Max will never be okay. "

"You knew him before. How is he different?"

"My whole life, he was best friends with my brother, Tim. Max was a quiet little nerd back then. Well, he still sort of is, sometimes, but also he can be a hothead. The accident changed him. They were together that day. They fell eighty feet off a rock down in Flaming Gorge. Tim died."

"I'm sorry," Antelope said.

Kelly acknowledged his words with a quick nod. "It was supposed to be a special graduation trip for the three of them . . ." She shrugged. "What happened to our brothers brought me and Stacey together. We ran with different crowds in high school. Then these freaking tragedies landed on us and we had something in common, we related. We handled it different, though. Stacey got out as fast as she could, but me, I'll be stuck here forever. The tragedy broke down the walls and we each found a kindred spirit. I'm going to miss her."

"What keeps you here?"

"You know what glue does? It holds things together. My parents, my family, my son's the glue. His birth gave them a reason to go on. I can't take him away from them."

She reached for another cigarette, changed her mind, and stuffed it and the lighter into the crumpled pack. She held it out to Antelope. "Here. Hold these for me. I'm going to be sick if I smoke another one."

In one magic-trick motion, she twisted her hair in a coil and fixed it in place with a strand of yellow grass, transforming herself into a geisha.

"What did you talk about?"

"Not about the wedding—her usual topic—or the house. She was on edge. I should have called her again. I suck as a friend."

"You didn't see this coming."

"I'm about done with things I don't see coming, asteroids smashing my life to pieces while I sleep." She reached for the cigarettes cupped in Antelope's left hand, fingers cold as ice. "Give me those before I tear my hair out."

The tip of one of her manicured nails pressed hard enough

to puncture skin; it left a tiny half-moon in his flesh. Her touch set off fireworks in the air between them. He surrendered the pack.

"They say the earlier you start smoking, the harder it is to quit." She tapped a cigarette into her hand and lit up. "I started at twelve when I stole my first one from my brother. After, I black-mailed him for more. I threatened to tell our parents if he didn't share with me. Being an altar boy, he had a reputation to protect."

"My gut tells me you know something that might help me do my job. Your friend was murdered today. Murder motivates me. Tell me what you and Stacey talked about."

"I don't think it had anything to do with her getting killed."

"You lost me."

"Hold on. I'm getting there." She inhaled and held the smoke in for a long time, like it was pure oxygen. "She suspected Connor was cheating. Someone saw him go into a motel with another guy in Salt Lake City."

She fanned her face with the cigarette pack and cool air brushed Antelope's cheek.

The sun beat down with a full head of steam; it had to be 90 degrees and there wasn't a shade tree in the yard. Overhead, a jet out of Salt Lake streaked contrails across the sky.

"Who saw him?"

"She didn't say—like it was some kind of confidential infor-mant. I told her to put a tracker on his phone if she wanted really wanted to know."

"Sounds like she didn't trust what this person said. What would she have done if she'd caught him cheating?"

"What would you do? Stacey would've called off the wed-ding." For a long time, Kelly sat quiet beside him. Then she looked at her watch and turned her head away. One tear dropped onto her cheek and she swiped it away. "Promise me it didn't get her killed."

He made a lot of promises in his work he never intended to keep, and still others he found reasons to break—to move cases to a solve, to lock up folks who shouldn't be free—always with the satisfaction of severing the rattler's head before a strike. He slept well with those broken promises. But in his gut, he knew it would be different if he broke a promise to Kelly Ryan.

"If it means anything, I think you did the right thing trying to help her."

She stood up and tossed the pack of cigarettes overhand into the rain-soaked grass.

"Another thing I'm going to have to live with. Fuck it." She turned and went into the house.

As Antelope followed her inside, he remembered there was something he'd meant to ask her. "You said three of them went down to Flaming Gorge. Who else went?"

"Connor. The three of them were inseparable; he and Max still are."

"Thanks for your time. You've been a big help."

He was at the door when she said, "Wait . . ."

"What?"

"Maybe it's not important."

If he'd learned anything in his years investigating crimes, most people underestimated the significance of their observations. Often the smallest piece of the puzzle held the solution.

"You never know," he said, "better safe than sorry."

"Fern said Stacey was strangled."

"We don't have an official cause of death yet. The Medical Examiner will let us know."

"Stacey and Connor weren't as straight-edge as everyone thinks. He choked her during sex. She'd almost pass out, but her orgasms were super intense. Don't let him know I told you. He might kill me."

■ ■ ■

The skies opened up again on the way back to Rock Springs and the sheets of rain slowed traffic. Outside the Green River Tunnels, an eighteen-wheeler hit a flooded area and jackknifed across both lanes. Two hours passed before the rig got turned around and the road reopened.

Heavy rain continued to fall. Thick ropes of gray water coursed down the windshield. The wipers were no match for the force of the weather. Most of the way back, Antelope drove with his head out the window, raindrops hitting his face like nails. The world wept for Stacey Hart, who would not walk its surface again.

At the city limits a clear, violet twilight broke through the storm clouds. At the first Rock Springs exit, Antelope got off the highway and turned right down Dewar Drive toward Broadway. Time to meet Pepper Hunt.

CHAPTER 7

The Bitter Creek Brewing Company was located in a renovated four-story brick building. When I arrived, Antelope was at a table in the far corner, staring out the window, lost in thought. When working a case, Antelope, a cerebral type who valued both logic and intuition, went into his own world. In that way he was different from most detectives, who tend to focus on the physical world of evidence and clues.

He smiled and stood up when I got to the table.

"Good to see you, it's been too long," I said.

"I ordered a bottle of the red. Can I pour you a glass or do you prefer something else? They've got an extensive wine list. I'll put it on the county tab." He handed me a menu.

I slid my wine glass across the table to him.

I intended to be agreeable and flexible. The last time we'd worked together, I'd kept things rigidly professional. No friendships for me, and definitely no romance. But Antelope had followed my lead and never once crossed the line I'd drawn in the sand. I felt less tense with him now, but still, as I scanned the menu, I couldn't think of anything but consulting on the case.

No matter how hard I tried to get away from it, violent crime fascinated me. In the first months after I became a crime victim, I wanted nothing to do with my chosen field. Shocked and stunned into a dull paralysis, I couldn't work at all. I took off to Wyoming thinking my work as a psychologist was done.

But I needed money, and I only knew how to do one thing. So I started a new practice in Wyoming.

It was in the first case, working side by side with Antelope, that my excitement came back—the thrill of working at the edge, close to danger. After staying quiet for so long, at once my heart beat again, like a wild, bucking stallion.

I liked the hard cases. Antelope did too; a shared passion that made him dangerous. We'd bonded over the work, but I'd broken the bond when he got too close.

Now, though, I'd figured out that I didn't have to worry about Antelope. If I took care of my side, stayed aware of my own thoughts and feelings, moments of easy playfulness were possible during our time together. Ours was a professional relationship, but it could still be enjoyable.

"The sheriff wants to bring you on the payroll in a permanent consultant position, with a contract and negotiated hourly rate," Antelope said. "He thinks we're spending too much time and money hiring people for a one-off who don't have what it takes to do the job. He liked your work on Kimi's investigation. This case is personal for him—again—and he trusts you. If you know the man at all, you know that's big for him. Think about it before you say no."

"Send me the contract. I'll take a look."

"That went better than I thought."

"I haven't said yes."

"I'm surprised you're willing to consider it."

"Why?"

"I thought you liked doing your own thing. Private practice, being your own boss."

"I do like it. But I never hired another secretary after Marla. It can get lonely being in the office alone all day; the only people I talk to are the patients I'm treating, and that's not an equal relationship. I'm used to working in a court clinic with other psychologists. I enjoy the back and forth with other clinicians—conceptualizing cases together."

"Sounds like it could work. No shortage of action in the Sheriff's Department."

"I'll think about it overnight and give you my decision in the morning."

"Take all the time you need. Here come the appetizers. I ordered one of everything."

A waiter balancing an enormous silver tray carefully arranged eight small plates on the table.

After he walked away, I asked the question that had been on my mind since I sat down: "How did it go in Green River?"

He looked away and something passed over his face, a shadow of fleeting sadness. He was a detective and he worked homicide investigations, but he wasn't hard. Murder got to him.

"It was tough. Max and her mother both took it hard. At least it's over. When we finish here, I'm doing a second interview with her fiancé. He was at the crime scene this morning, briefly. It was all about him reacting. I've got a lot of questions for him."

"Is it possible he did it?"

"He seemed pretty broken up. But yeah, he's number two on the list."

"But he would be, right?"

"He lost it when he saw the contractor. Flat-out accused him right there and tried to get physical. The contractor is missing in action, so maybe he's right about him. Why else would he take off? I'm curious to hear your thoughts on her brother. He's one of three impulsive men who were close to the victim. He's number three on the list."

"If you think a man killed her, the top motives for male murders are concealment and jealousy, followed by hate, revenge, and thrill. You didn't mention any female names, but women kill for different reasons. Women kill when their security is threatened for financial gain, or when they believe they are killing for love."

"Tell me about killing out of love?"

"An example would be an assisted suicide or when a mother kills a child because of misguided beliefs due to mental illness or because she plans to kill herself and fears the child won't survive without her."

"I've only met two women in Stacey's inner circle."

"Does either of them stand to benefit financially from Stacey's death?"

"Not on the surface, but I'll keep an open mind."

"What about the men? Do any of them have a motive?"

"You said the top two are concealment and jealousy? I had to pull Collins off Swailes this morning."

"Do you see evidence of concealment or jealousy with Max?"

"Nothing jumps out. You can tell me tomorrow when he signs off on you talking to me."

CHAPTER 8

When Antelope left Bitter Creek Brewing, he drove across town to the Preserve, the modern apartment complex where Connor Collins lived. Six apartment buildings surrounded a large in-ground pool and patio on a large parcel of land. The compound had an unobstructed view of open land and White Mountain in the distance. Wildflowers bloomed on the desert floor. Connor's building faced the mountain on the west side.

As he pulled into the parking lot, Father Todd Bellamy came out of the building. Antelope made a mental note to contact the priest.

Collins had the penthouse apartment. When he pressed the doorbell, a tired voice came through the intercom. "Yeah?"

"Detective Antelope, can I come up?"

A buzzer sounded above double glass doors. Inside the lobby of polished wood, large copper pots held arrangements of sagebrush and lavender. The sweet aroma carried him home.

When he stepped out of the elevator on the penthouse floor, he found Collins leaning against the doorjamb with his eyes closed. Barefoot and unshaven, the county prosecutor was drunk. He startled awake when Antelope cleared his throat.

"I'm wrecked," Collins said. "Come in."

The large, square living room, furnished with high-end designer furniture, reeked of cigarettes and alcohol. On top of the polished parquet floor, oriental area rugs in shades of muted green and brown reflected the desert floor, which was visible from the western windows.

Connor motioned to a pair of white leather couches. He sank into one of them and finished off the scotch in his glass. "Did you pick him up?"

"I'm here to ask you questions, Mr. Collins, not the other way around."

"You're wasting your time. Swailes did it."

"Have you been drinking all day?"

"Damn straight. You would be too if someone murdered the woman you loved."

"Make some coffee. Take a cold shower. I need you coherent. I'll wait."

Connor went for the scotch, but Antelope moved it out of reach. "Time is of the essence. I'm the one who'll find her killer. Don't get in my way. If you give me reason, we'll take this interview to the station."

A half-hour later, Collins returned, clean-shaven, in pressed jeans and a white dress shirt.

He placed two cups of black coffee on the table and lit a cigarette. "Ready when you are," he said as he exhaled a stream of smoke.

"I need a timeline. When did you see Stacey last?"

"We met for dinner last night. Our usual thing, pizza and beer at Johnny Mac's Tavern. We're creatures of habit, some would say boring, but it worked for us. We ended the night early, both beat from the week. About eight o'clock she left for her place."

"What's the address?"

"Thirty-five Wardell Court, a tiny little place she shared with another gal, Toni Atwell. Used to be Sister Antonia back in the day."

"Did you talk with Stacey again after she left?"

Collins looked away, considered the question. Antelope thought it shouldn't be hard to remember a phone call with a fiancée. Under the circumstances, though—shock, grief, and too much to drink—maybe he should give the guy a break.

Maybe. But something about Connor Collins bothered him. It wasn't rational, just a gut feeling that Collins was hiding something. He made a mental note to keep a check on his reactions, make sure they didn't affect his investigation.

Collins looked at his phone and turned the screen so Antelope could see. "Looks like she called me to say good night—a thirty-six second phone call at 1:17 a.m., must've woken me out of a dead sleep. She never liked to go to sleep without saying good night and I love you."

"I'm confused. You left the bar at eight o'clock because everyone's beat but it's one in the morning when she goes to go to bed?"

"I passed out right here and woke up this morning with my laptop open on my chest. Stacey's a chronic insomniac. Trust me; 1:00 a.m. is on the early side for her."

Collins threw his phone down. "The last time I'll ever hear her voice and I don't remember the call."

"You got more coffee?" Antelope asked.

"Good idea."

Collins left for the kitchen and his cell phone vibrated. Antelope noticed the call came from Father Bellamy.

"You had a call," he said when Collins came back.

His host set the coffees down and reached for the phone, but put it right back down. "It can wait. Everything can wait until I'm ready."

They drank coffee in silence for a minute, then Antelope launched in. "Tell me about your relationship with Stacey."

"She was the love of my life. I can't see my future without her. We got together the summer after I graduated from high school. I'm best friends with her brother, Max. They probably told you all about the accident. We thought we were going to lose him. Stacey was a basket case and needed a lot of support. I wasn't doing too well myself but I did my best to be there for her. I guess it sealed the deal."

"How were things between you?"

"It's been a rough patch. My job eats up every waking minute. With the wedding plans and the house renovation, we didn't have a lot of time together. It was all going to be fine, though, after the wedding. I don't understand why you're wasting time with me. I told you, Swailes is our guy."

"What makes you so sure?"

"Right from the get-go he wanted her. I could tell by the way he looked at her. Guys know these things. You can feel it when some guy wants to make a move on the woman you're with. If I'd known how they met, I never would have hired him. But Stacey didn't tell me until recently. I was pretty steamed when she told me."

"How did they meet?"

"She met him in the hardware store looking at paint samples and they struck up a conversation. He planned it right from the start. If I'd known, he never would have gotten near the house, or her."

"You sound angry."

"I *was* angry. But Stacey was so trusting, bordering on naive; I couldn't stay angry with her. She trusted everyone. I warned her, but she never listened."

"What made you think he was interested in her?"

"The way he looked at her, flirted with her in front of me. He wanted her, no doubt in my mind."

"Would she have told you if he'd made a move?"

"I asked her to tell me, and I trusted her."

But she didn't tell you how she met the contractor she convinced you to hire, Antelope thought—*a lie by omission.*

"You trusted her?"

"Absolutely, with my life." Collins made the sign of the cross over his heart. Then he leaned forward in his seat. "I better tell you the rest of it."

"What?"

"We didn't go our separate ways last night because we were tired. We fought about Swailes. I told her to fire him the next time she saw him. She wasn't happy about it, but she agreed to do it if it meant so much to me. The fight killed the mood for the night."

"You think Swailes killed Stacey because she fired him?"

"When a guy like Swailes loses his meal ticket, don't put anything past him."

"He wants her, and then he kills her when she fires him?"

"This is how I figure it went down: She fired him. What did he have to lose? He made a pass at her. She told him no. He got rough and tried to force it. Stacey would fight him, I know that for sure. He lost it and killed her. Maybe he didn't mean to—a crime of passion. If he can't have her, he'll make sure nobody else can, either."

CHAPTER 9

As soon as the detective left the apartment, Connor started drinking again. His phone showed fourteen calls and voicemail messages. A lot of people wanted callbacks but he didn't have it in him. Couldn't they figure out he was in no shape to talk? Stacey hadn't been gone a day. Christ, how would he make it without her?

The priest had called twice. What could he want? He'd just been here. But better not ruffle any feathers. The man could be persistent. He didn't want him to get worried and drive over here and wake him up in the middle of the night to check on him.

He dialed the number and Bellamy answered on the first ring. "How did everything go with the detective?"

"I laid it all out for him, told him everything he needs to know to wrap this thing up."

"And what did he think of your theory about the murderer?"

"He's very interested in talking to Swailes. I made a strong case, and especially with him taking off, it looks very suspicious."

"You don't want to have to deal with an investigation going on indefinitely. It could be very stressful."

"Stressful is not the word I'd use for my situation. I'm half-crazy over here. I'm mad as hell at her for getting involved with him and setting this whole thing in motion. I blame her. And I miss her. And I want her back. It happened so fast. Yesterday I had a normal life. I want my life back. Things will never be the same without Stacey. I should have trusted her. I never should have—"

"Stop," Bellamy commanded, "don't say another word. Don't do that to yourself. You're overwrought—and who wouldn't be after what you've been through? Any thoughts you have tonight are bound to bring more pain and guilt and regret. Do yourself a favor. Shut off your brain. Go to bed."

"Okay, okay, that's smart advice. I feel like shit."

"Call me in the morning. There are plans to be made for the services."

Connor hung up without saying good night. Those words, "the services," about did him in. He turned off his phone and plugged it into the charger.

His heart felt heavy and raw with Stacey gone. His eyes filled and a wave of sadness rose in his chest—a swell of darkness that threatened to drown him. If he opened his body up to tears, it would end with him howling like a mad man.

The future, the next few days, was a dense thicket of old trees with gnarled roots and a roof of twisted branches.

And how would he face her mother? Stacey had told her about his anger and his need to control every freaking thing in his world. Fern would figure it out and she would blame him. The thought brought a stabbing pain to his eyes. He couldn't think about it now.

He carried his bottle and glass to the bedroom; they were the only friends he wanted tonight. He needed the comfort of his bed.

He stripped naked and poured a three-finger nightcap. The whiskey went down fast and burned his throat and eyes. His head was a concrete sphere, too heavy and ready to topple. He slipped between the cool sheets—freshly washed after the cleaning lady's visit the previous day—and pulled all the bedclothes over his head. The light from the bedside lamp was a warm gold glow outside his cocoon.

He refused to sleep in the dark. When Stacey stayed with him, she always wore a sleep mask to block out the light. Ever since he'd lost his parents—in an auto accident, when he was five years old—the dark had made him think of them locked up in their black, airless coffins.

In the drawer of the bedside table, the silk mask smelled of lavender and sage and something else uniquely Stacey. The smooth cloth pressed to his mouth, made him long for her soft lips and fierce kisses.

His last thought before sleep was a comfort; his breathing slowed as the idea took root. He hadn't lied to the detective. Antelope had never asked if he'd left the apartment last night, so there had been no reason to offer any information. His legal training was clear and unequivocal: don't answer a question that hasn't been asked.

CHAPTER 10

Val Campion sat on the hood of his gold Lincoln Town Car, smoking a Cuban cigar and enjoying the stars as they showed themselves one by one in the purple sky. Music and laughter escaped from the club and lifted his spirits. Sometimes he needed to be alone with his thoughts. The police had come about the dead woman.

It had been a long time since anyone had questioned him. He lived as he pleased and answered to no one; he was an outlaw, under the radar.

He'd known about his nephew's involvement with her before Jack had told him. He made it his business to know what went on in the lives of those he loved. Jack was a fool. He'd set himself up for trouble with this business with the girl.

Did he think she'd leave her world for him? We are what we are, Val thought. *Change is hard. Lovers think love solves everything and it solves nothing.*

Life had taught him different. If you wanted misery, you chose love.

He stayed free of women and their traps. His rule—*Don't commit to one woman*—made it easy. Having more than one woman kept him from being dragged around by the nose, heart, and balls by any of them. *If you have just one woman,* he thought, *you think you can't live without her.*

Jack had forgotten about the rule when he met this woman, and that had made him vulnerable and dangerous. Before the woman came along, Jack had his pick of the dancers, and why hadn't it been enough? Greed led to trouble. If Jack had followed his advice, the woman might still be alive.

The only way to protect himself and Jack was to stay close to the situation. One of his dancers was in the middle of the whole mess. He would make his move tonight, after the club closed down. But first he would enjoy watching her dance.

He heard the voices of the audience through the open window. On Saturday night they always drew a sizable crowd. His favorite attraction—a marketing idea he'd come up with himself, Legs and Eggs—brought customers in for a morning breakfast show.

The Astro Lounge kept a low profile in the community. Though it was alternately referred to as a bar, lounge, nightclub, and dance club, everyone knew it was a strip club, even the schoolkids who passed by on their way to Bridger Elementary School.

CHAPTER 11

The news of Stacey Hart's murder didn't slow the Saturday night action in Rock Springs. It was a great night to party. All over town the bars were packed, doors open to the warm summer night; couples laughed; men grabbed at women who didn't object.

Daylight lingered long into the evening in the high desert. Antelope loved these summer nights full of lightness and expectation. The sun set late, well past nine. Fading light cast long, purple shadows along the streets.

When the deputies couldn't locate Swailes, Antelope had authorized a surveillance of the back entrance of his place, hidden at the end of a narrow lane off a side street in old town. His room at the cottage was clean, his clothing and toiletries were there—no sign he'd left town in a hurry.

Antelope pulled into the parking lot of the Burger Bar on Pilot Butte, across from the Astro Lounge. Time to visit Swailes's uncle, Val Campion.

Inside, four security guards, Campion's private security team, manned the premises, disguised as regular patrons. Unrecognizable to most folks in the audience until trouble started and they stepped up, sudden as flashing lights on unmarked cars.

The vibe in the club was dark and decadent with an undercurrent of crime—a sense of something not right, of something sinister about to happen. Antelope felt at home in the Astro, and he wondered what that said about him.

Most bars lured customers in with neon lights and open doors, loud music, and the promise of excitement. The Astro, in contrast, showed a plain face to the world—a beige stucco building, the name painted in plain red. Advertised as "The World Famous Astro Lounge" with the tagline "Serving Mankind," it was known as the best adult club in Wyoming and drew customers from bordering states and beyond.

From the burger joint's parking lot, Antelope downed his double cheeseburger and large order of fries and watched the evening clientele enter the Astro Lounge. From all walks of life and every age group, they had one thing in common: each one wore a hat to shield his face.

The first show went on at nine o'clock. He locked the car and headed for the front entrance. The night had turned cold and he shivered—another goose on his grave. His head ached from the effort of containing the day's sorrow. He longed to crash into oblivion before it started all over again.

On the far side of the smoke-filled room, at a table in a dark corner, he spotted Val Campion. A handsome man with a full head of silver hair, he was tall with a rangy build that made him look younger than the sixty years listed on his Wyoming driver's license. Black designer clothing and expensive Italian loafers set him apart from his customers. Antelope recognized the brand. He had the same shoes at home in his closet. A large diamond flashed in the stage light when Campion lifted a Cuban cigar to his mouth.

Muscles rippled in Antelope's back as adrenaline coursed through his body, a hot liquid sensation. He lived for the hunt of big game. In Rock Springs, Val Campion was the equivalent of a trophy elephant. Campion knew something about the murder; Antelope felt it in his bones and soul.

As he approached the table, Campion watched him, still as a predator. Antelope stood in front of him and blocked his view of the room. Campion stood and repositioned himself to retain his view. The message was clear: he owned the joint.

"Your men came already," Campion said. "Deputy Garcia questioned me."

"I'm looking for Jack Swailes."

"I don't keep track of Jack. He's his own man."

He was lying. Campion ran a tight ship.

"How long has he worked for you?"

"Ask my human resources manager. I don't deal with those things. Jack handles the painting end of the business, among other things. He can give you an estimate if you're looking to spruce up your old place."

"What jobs has he been working?"

"Besides the one for the prosecutor?" Campion shrugged. "I can't say. They kept him busy over there. Why do you want to talk to my nephew?"

"He found the body."

"So I understand. He gave a statement this morning. What more do you want with him?"

"He was involved with the victim, so he had motive and opportunity."

"It was a job. Jack has lots of women. He can take his pick. No reason to lose his head over tits and ass."

"Did you see Jack today?"

"You guys don't talk to each other? I told Garcia, no."

"Where would he go if he wanted to get out of town?"

"If I had a clue, why would I tell you?"

"This is a homicide investigation. You could be charged with obstruction of justice if you withhold information."

"You can't prove anything." Campion narrowed his eyes. "I know this game, just like you. I haven't caught a case in years. You think I'm a small-town businessman in a business you don't like. You underestimate me, Detective."

The disco band started a new set to a round of weak applause. Patrons didn't come for the music. The laugher and conversation died down; the dancer would come on soon. Whistles and catcalls began when Star Bright stepped onto the stage in a white costume covered in sequins and feathers. She flashed a smile and pranced around the stage in silver spike heels, blew kisses into the crowd.

An artful dancer, Star Bright moved on the pole with a touch of class and a touch of evil. The last time Antelope and his ex hooked up, they'd gotten drunk and come out to the Astro together. There wasn't another woman dancing in Rock Springs who could hold a candle to Star Bright.

Antelope had recognized the Native touches in her dance: jingle dances learned on the reservation. With one phone call, he'd found her: Sharnelle Brightwood, birthplace Riverton, Wyoming; Shoshone, nineteen years old. Some lonely nights he replayed her dances in his head.

Campion's eyes followed the fluid sway of Star's narrow hips, as transfixed as his paying customers. Antelope knew he exploited women who took their clothes off for money they needed and never had. He put men who used their power to get sex through intimidation in the same category as rapists who used physical force. In his book, sex required consent between partners of equal status; otherwise, it was wrong.

He didn't judge the dancers. Everyone did what they had to do to survive. No stranger to bad circumstances and bad choices, he recognized parts of himself in the people he arrested.

Campion stood beside him, so close their shoulders touched. He smelled of cognac, cigar smoke, and cheap cologne.

"You have fine taste, Detective," he said. "She's yours if you want her. It's on me. Star likes powerful men."

Antelope pulled out his business card and stuck it in Campion's suit pocket. "When you talk to Jack, tell him we'll find him." He didn't wait for an answer before heading for the door.

As he walked the perimeter of the crowded room, a man jumped in front of him and lunged for the white feather boa that had just been tossed into the crowd. He turned to see Star Bright wave to her audience as she exited the stage.

In that brief moment, he noticed the change. Every shining thing about her was gone, like a light had been turned off. Something had happened in the six months since his last visit to the Astro Lounge. Her spirit was broken.

In the long hallway to the exit, he found a gallery of black-and-white portraits of the dancers. Campion had a discerning eye and chose the talent well. The photographs captured each woman's unique brand of sexiness.

He noticed one woman in particular. With his cell phone, he snapped several pictures to study later in a better light. He recognized the pixie-faced dancer with raven hair and pale eyes, who went by the stage name Kitty Irish, as the woman he'd met earlier: the murder victim's friend, Kelly Ryan.

CHAPTER 12

It rained on and off all day, a disappointing start to summer. The average annual sunny days in Rock Springs, Wyoming number 238. Cambridge, Massachusetts, gets only 201—one of the reasons I'd chosen Wyoming's high desert for my home. But there was no sun today, no clear blue sky or endless-summer-freedom feelings.

I'd planned to spend my day writing up notes and reviewing test results for the psychological evaluations due in court soon, but Stacey Hart's murder consumed my thoughts, leaving little brain space to get work done. After starting on one project that didn't hold my interest, I felt frustrated and moved on to something else equally uninspiring. More frustration.

I gave up on work. I caught up on some reading, looked at some travel sites and tried to decide where I wanted to go for vacation. I lived in a part of the world I considered vacation paradise, which made it difficult to plan. Things would change when winter hit the high desert, along with high winds, sub-zero temperatures, and black ice.

I called Beau Antelope and told him I was willing to sign a contract. It wasn't a difficult decision; from the moment I heard about Stacey Hart's murder, I'd wanted the chance to contribute to solving the crime.

I'd been reluctant to become involved with the last murder case I'd helped him with, which involved the disappearance and murder of one of my patients. After what had happened in my personal life, I'd thought I would never want to work a case involving a homicide again. Since then, however, I'd done some soul searching, and I'd realized that I'd felt more alive while I was working that case with Antelope than I had since before my husband, Zeke, was killed.

Violence and evil, the things most normal people run from, excited me; my adrenaline flowed, my analytical skills became sharp and focused. I had officially turned into a ghoul. What I considered perverse professional interests, the county valued and was willing to pay well to retain.

When I got home I checked my phone and found four missed calls from Max Hart. His sister's death was an enormous loss; I imagined it would take months of intense therapy to process. I called him back, and we scheduled an appointment for first thing Monday morning.

After hanging up with Max, I turned on the evening news. Stacey's murder was the top story, and it was grisly and unnerving.

I wondered if my role as consultant to the sheriff's department would impact my ability to treat Max in psychotherapy. My first responsibility was to patient care and treatment. In case of a conflict, my work as a police consultant would have to be secondary.

I'd find a way to make it work, even if it killed me.

CHAPTER 13

Kelly watched from backstage as Detective Antelope approached Val Campion's table. She was scheduled to be second up after the opening set, but she couldn't go on now, couldn't let him see her here.

What was he doing in the Astro Lounge?

In the bathroom, she forced herself to vomit, loud enough so the other dancers could hear. She told the stage manager she was too sick and weak to dance. It was true. After the detective left, she'd thrown up the pint of Ben and Jerry's she'd consumed. She should have stayed home.

What kind of person goes on with life when her best friend just got murdered? But she'd gotten ready for work without thinking. With her family away, the house loomed too big and too quiet.

She walked out of the club into the dying light of the cool evening. The door slammed shut behind her and silenced the pulsing disco music, the wild sound of raw need.

In the car she blasted the air conditioner, created another layer of soundproofing and insulation from the club's claim on her. She pulled sweatpants and a T-shirt from her gym bag and threw them on over her black sequin dance outfit. She kicked off the killing stilettos and eased her sore feet into her favorite flip-flops. Because of her crazy schedule she carried extra clothing, makeup, and toiletries at all times. No need to go home. She carried everything she needed.

The fear she'd felt earlier was gone; she was free.

She cruised up Elk Street in the Saturday night traffic. In every vehicle, she saw a couple on their way out for a fun evening. Ever since her brother died, loneliness had followed her like a dark shadow. She kept busy to keep it at bay.

When it caught up with her, there was only one person she wanted to see, one person who could chase away the demons.

She drove north—out of town, beyond the business district and into the open miles before Reliance. Her mind cleared; ideas broke into simple black and white. She drove through the darkness, aware of the desert around her, eyes on the white stripe down the center of the two-lane road.

The emptiness of the surrounding land, the infinity of the stars, filled her with dread. A chill came over her, goose bumps rose on her arms and legs, her whole body trembled.

With a sudden clarity, she knew where she wanted to be.

Freezing, she shut off the air conditioner and opened the windows. The night was cool but felt warm in comparison, and the wind coming in made her feel alive.

She made a U-turn and headed back to town.

If he'd made other plans, they could be changed.

CHAPTER 14

When the band started the next set and another dancer appeared in Kelly's place, Val forced himself to stay seated and watch until the buxom blonde finished. The crowd went wild for her as she danced—obvious, lascivious moves too crude for his taste. He liked subtlety and grace, though the patrons of his club were more into the crude seduction of the woman on stage.

His right hand gripped his glass, his only thought, *What the hell happened to Kelly?*

With the sheriffs all over his spot, he couldn't afford to let his guard down—nothing but business as usual. He wanted to keep an eye on the girl. Jack hooked up with her before moving on to her friend Stacey. The boy sure made a mess of things and Val wasn't going to let that come back on him.

He walked backstage, careful to maintain a look of disinterest as he made his way to Olga. She would be expecting him to ask about the switch-up in dancers. Everyone who worked for him knew about his need for control. It made things easy. No one who wanted to stay employed opposed him.

Olga counted the cash tips the dancers handed over when they walked off stage. She sat between the dressing room and the back exit. The pistol on her lap emphasized that she meant business.

Olga looked at him and spoke before he asked: "She got sick all of a sudden, a woman thing, so I sent her home."

He wasn't in the mood to push it. He took her at her word and went back to the bar. He didn't want Olga to know Kelly walking off got to him; he had a reputation to protect. Whiskey would help.

After sitting through the next set, he decided he'd let enough time pass and could leave without raising any suspicion.

If Kelly thought she could keep secrets that meant she under-estimated him. The way things were between them, she owed him the truth and loyalty, and tonight she'd proven to him that she was giving him neither. Things would be different from now on. He knew how to handle his women. He would train this one the way he'd trained all the others.

CHAPTER 15

In the quiet outside the Astro, Antelope heard the blood thump in his temples. Only two things under the sun could shut down the pain: a long sleep or a shot of Honey Jack Whiskey.

He checked the time on his phone and saw a text from Toni Atwell: *Meet at the Saddle Lite.*

Three blocks and ten minutes put him in bed. If he hit it now, he'd clock eight hours. In the cup holder between the bucket seats, he found a quarter. He gave it quick toss and slapped it down. Heads up put him on his way to the Saddle Lite Lounge.

As he drove to the bar, he realized he didn't know much more than he had before going into the Astro. Val Campion, the kind of man who never showed his hand to law enforcement, had given him nothing. He would lay off for a few days; let Campion begin to think they were done with him.

■ ■ ■

The parking lot at the Saddle Lite Saloon was packed, so Antelope drove around back, onto the main road of the trailer park where his Aunt Estella and cousin Diego lived, and parked near the bank of tilting mail boxes.

The moon, a giant white globe high in the sky, lit up the town like it was a football stadium. He didn't want to go inside the smoky, crowded bar when the first night of summer felt so clean and new.

He scanned the parking lot before stepping inside and didn't recognize any vehicles, which suited him tonight; he had no time to spare.

Inside, a country band played dance music. At the pool table, Toni Atwell bent over to lay up a shot. The former nun was dressed like a rock star: white jeans, silver sandals, platinum blonde hair buzzed short and spiked on top.

He scanned the room for the sheriff but didn't see him. Toni was concentrating on the game. From what he'd heard, she played like a pro. There would be serious money on the table.

He paid for two double shots of Honey Jack and found an empty corner table. As he waited for Toni to wrap up her game, he took a drink and waited for the whiskey to work its magic. As soon as it hit his brain, the warm liquid opened blood vessels and massaged away the tension.

The game ended when Toni cleared the table. She shook hands with the loser and tucked the winnings in her vest. Antelope stood up and caught her eye, and she joined him at the table.

"Hello, Detective. Carlton said you wanted to talk to me about Stacey."

"I planned to pay you a visit in the morning. He said you'd be out with him tonight."

"He brought me home early so I could get some sleep, but I couldn't stop thinking about Stacey. So I came back out, bad girl that I am. Is one of those for me?"

He handed her one of the shots he'd intended to drink himself. "There's more where those came from."

She downed the shot and her eyes filled up.

"He didn't want to join you?"

"I didn't tell him."

"You want to do this now? It's your call. It can wait until the morning."

"No better time. You never know what tomorrow will bring. Stacey getting killed brought that home to all of us. It might help me to talk about her. What do you want to know?"

"Just tell me about her."

"You mean who she was behind the polished public relations

spin, the whole sweetness and light thing? You came to me to hear about the real woman, right? Don't get me wrong, Stacey was solid to the core. But anyone worth knowing has a dark side."

"Tell me about hers."

"I could use another one of these." She flicked her glass across the small table.

A barrel-chested man in red suspenders approached with a pool cue in his hand. Toni held up her palm. He stopped in his tracks like a dog halted by an electronic fence, bewildered and still.

"I'll quit while I'm ahead," Toni said. "I'm not at the top of my game tonight."

The man shrugged and walked away. Antelope waved away the twenty-dollar bill Toni offered for the drinks and went to the bar for another round.

When he got back to the table and passed Toni her shot, she raised her glass. "To Stacey."

"And her dark side," Antelope said. He downed the shot. As soon as it hit, he knew he couldn't drink any more if he wanted to remember anything Toni told him.

Toni slapped her empty shot glass on the table. "Ready when you are, Antelope. What's your question?"

"Any chance she could have been cheating on Connor?"

"That's pretty damn straight to the point. What makes you ask? She planned to marry him next month."

"Her fiancé suspects that she had something going with Jack Swailes, the contractor on the house."

"Connor's on the jealous side. Stacey was always checking in with him and letting him know where she was. I would have felt like I was on a leash." Toni made a face. "As for Connor's suspicions, I can say Stacey was on the phone with Jack all the time. She made all the decisions on the renovations at the house, so it made sense they'd have a lot to talk about. I only heard one side of their conversations. I could tell she liked him—always friendly and upbeat, lots of laughing on her end, that's how she was. I didn't sense anything more going on, but I'm not an expert on male/female relationships."

"Would it surprise you?"

"Nothing surprises me, Antelope. I'm a hard case. All my illusions crashed and burned when the Church I loved more than I could ever love a man got broken beyond repair. I'm an ex-nun, that's the definition of disillusionment."

"How did you end up sharing a house with Stacey?"

"I got tired of living in a box at the Evergreen Apartments. A more austere place than the convent, but I couldn't afford anything more. Stacey came back from Laramie after she finished her master's degree and got engaged to Connor, and she wanted to be over here in Rock Springs.

Once she got the job at the college, she convinced her mother the commute would be too dangerous in the winter. Fern wanted to keep her at home in Green River so she could maintain the delusion Stacey was a virgin. The woman lives in a dream world. As an ex-nun, I made the perfect roommate; that smoothed things over with her mother. With Stacey paying half the rent, we could easily afford our little house."

Most of this Antelope already knew. "Tell me about Stacey's relationship with Connor."

"She didn't open up to me about it. We were roommates in the strictest sense. She lived her life, came and went as she pleased. The truth is, she spent more nights with Connor than she did at our place. The whole thing, her living with me, was a cover to get away from home to shack up with Connor. I can't blame her for wanting her own life and the freedom to make her own choices; she was twenty-six, after all."

"Why did they wait so long to get married, any idea?"

"Type A personalities, both of them—ambitious, driven, achievement oriented, goal directed. They wanted to wait until they were both out of school and started on their careers. They're pretty much the epitome of responsibility, and after ten years together maybe the urgency wore off."

"Would you say Stacey was a typical bride to be?"

Toni rolled her eyes. "You seem to think there is such a thing. I'm not sure I know what you mean—happy, excited, stars in her eyes, can't wait for the big day, all that *Bride's Magazine* stuff?"

"Like that."

"I think so, but she was a serious person and a private person. So am I. We didn't have any late-night roomie talks about boys and romance."

"You notice any changes in her mood?"

"I'm a pain in the ass, useless witness, but don't tell Carlton. I rarely saw the woman, especially the last few months once they started work on the house. She spent all her time over there. If anything, the renovations excited her even more than the wedding. Progress on the house made up most of her conversation. Before the work on the house started, she devoted the same attention to detail to the wedding, but once construction got underway . . ." Toni leaned forward. "One thing made me think there was some trouble in paradise, though."

"Tell me."

"The place was all mine on weekends; she always stayed at Connor's. She left for work Friday morning and I wouldn't see her again until Monday after work. About a month ago she came home late on a Saturday night, scared me half to death. I didn't expect to see her in the middle of the night."

"What time?" Antelope asked.

"I think it was two or three in the morning, though I can't be sure. Earlier that evening, Carleton brought me a takeout dinner from the Wonderful House . . . One of his dark moods set in. The pity party annoyed me. You know how he can get?"

Antelope nodded.

"All alone on Saturday night is not a problem for me. I had fifteen years of practice." Toni chuckled. "I opened a Yellowtail Chardonnay, ate my General Tsao's chicken, and watched a movie on Netflix all by my lonesome." She arched an eyebrow. "I'm setting the scene here for you. It's fair to say I was a bit tipsy when Stacey showed up."

"And when she did . . ." he prompted.

"I figured she'd argued with Connor. Why else would she come home? But I never asked her about it. I kept my distance and it worked for us. We finished off the first bottle and Stacey opened another and poured us both another drink. It was a sweet moment: two women drinking wine, without the bullshit men bring. Then she asked me a question that would have sparked an interest if I'd been sober. Bottom line, I didn't pursue it, and in retrospect I regret it. Today, when Carlton told me she was dead, murdered, it was like a spotlight came on and lit up the conversation in neon lights."

"What did Stacey ask you?"

"She asked if I knew the difference between a narcissist and a sociopath."

"Interesting question. What did you say?"

"I told her I happened to be an expert on the topic of narcissists and sociopaths. I worked for years side by side with priests who pass for men of God in the Catholic Church but are hollow on the inside. What I learned from a couple of them in particular is this: Sociopaths are charming and always conniving and setting up the con; they're motivated by self-interest and lacking in empathy. The narcissist shares all those characteristics but has a deep need for validation from others and is motivated to always be seen in the best light. They have fragile personalities; they're easily wounded and, once hurt, will never forgive and forget. It's a fine line between the two."

"What did she say?"

"She went quiet, folded her hands in her lap, and took a long look at the rock Connor spent a fortune on. She drank her whole glass of wine down in one long swallow. Usually, she didn't drink much. She set the glass down and said, 'So the sociopath is more dangerous?'"

"To which you said . . ."

"They both want control. The sociopath will steal your money and ruin your finances. The narcissist will steal your heart and ruin your life. Which one can't you afford to lose?"

"What did Stacey say to that?"

"She said, 'I'll have to think about it.' Then she went to bed and we never spoke of it again."

He'd had a feeling Toni would have the insider view of Stacey.

"What's this guy Swailes like?" she asked.

"Val Campion's his uncle, if that tells you anything."

"The creep who owns the strip clubs?"

"You know Val?"

"Not personally, I know people who know Val."

"Bad pedigree." Antelope shook his head. "My deputy ran a BCI check on Swailes and came up with three domestic violence cases. We put out an All Points Bulletin for Wyoming, Montana, Utah, and Colorado. Whichever way he ran, we'll catch up with him. Not a smart decision to leave town."

"Carlton told me he found Stacey's body. Is he a person of interest?"

"I have some questions for him when we find him. You never met him?"

"Stacey didn't bring people home. Not even Connor. But I knew them both from church—they attended when they were kids, back before I left the order. She kept the different parts of her life separate. I figured it was because her mother controlled her every move. When she got free she wouldn't let anyone control her again."

"Smart woman, but you said Connor always wanted to know where she was."

"As much as Stacey didn't want to be controlled, she needed security, and Connor gave her security. Two sides of the same coin, if you ask me."

"When did you work side by side with a sociopath?"

"It was a long time ago, Antelope. We don't need to go there. I'm sorry I brought it up. I wouldn't have except it fit with the Stacey story."

"The way you talk, it could have happened yesterday."

The band took a break and the room got quiet.

Toni looked at her watch. "I'm ready to call it a night. It's a long story. Let's do this another time."

CHAPTER 16

Antelope felt tired to the bone when he left the Saddle Lite, but the whiskey had killed the migraine, leaving him with a pleasant, light-headed feeling.

He cruised through the blinking traffic lights on Elk Street. The roads would be empty until 2:00 a.m. when the bars shut down and the drunks headed home.

Cedar Street was on the way to his place. The door would be locked but he could be alone there on the porch. He stepped over the yellow tape and sat down on the front steps. He surveyed the quiet neighborhood; not one light on in any of the houses along the silent street.

He closed his eyes; he was almost dozing off when the midnight bells rang out from Our Lady of Sorrows.

A white globe of moon hung above the tall pines and lit up the night in silver fluorescence. Among the polished black stones at the edge of the wildflower garden, something sparkled and reflected the light. Down on his knees, he smoothed the soil away and exposed his find. A few minutes later, he had a video and photographs of the ring, a diamond solitaire in a platinum band, and was holding the ring itself in an evidence bag.

He stayed a few minutes longer to acknowledge the gift, then left Stacey's spirit to rest and drove himself home.

CHAPTER 17

When Max stepped out of the shower, he heard loud knocking—
three fist bangs on the aluminum storm door. He'd trained everyone
he knew not to show up unannounced; he didn't like to be surprised
by unexpected visitors.

Not a naturally friendly guy, he'd made no effort to create a
place visitors would find welcoming. His home was for his comfort
alone; it was his private cave, a place of retreat. The double-wide
mobile home was the last one on the street, set apart from the
others; hard to get to, the way he liked.

Through an opening in the vinyl blinds he saw her, arms
folded across her chest, tapping her foot and biting her lip, impa-
tient and annoyed, a six-pack in her hand.

As she raised her fist to knock again, he pulled the door open.
She fell forward and he reached for her hand and pulled her into
the house. She gasped at his touch and he felt a jolt, like a live wire,
pass between them.

"Is it okay I came?"

"Shut up, Kelly," he said and closed the door behind her.

"You didn't call. I thought you'd call."

"My phone didn't ring, either. And I did call you."

"Why didn't you call again? I don't want to be alone. I mean
. . . I can't be with anyone but you."

"Give me that," he said, taking the beer out of her hands.

He put four bottles in the refrigerator and opened one for each of them.

"You're drinking?" she asked.

"Sometimes; not like before." He avoided her gaze. "I can control it now. Did you eat? I'm thinking about ordering Chinese."

"I'm starving. I didn't eat all day except for some Ben & Jerry's I threw up."

Max kept the number for the Wonderful House Chinese Restaurant on speed dial. He made the call, and while he placed the order, Kelly put on one of his sweatshirts. Her hair was in a complicated knot on her head; she let it fall loose over her shoulders, a tangled mass of black silk.

"Want the heat on?" Max asked her.

"No, it's summer. You don't want a heating bill this time of year."

Her lips were blue and her teeth were chattering. Still half wet and wrapped in a towel, Max felt chilled himself. He turned on the heat and the baseboard unit came to life with small metal clicks. "Have a seat. Let me get some clothes on."

When he came back, she was at the kitchen bar. He tapped her bare foot.

"You want socks?"

"I'm warming up. My friend turned on the heat for me."

"I'm glad you're here."

"This is your man cave. I kind of busted in."

"I don't like surprises. But it's never a mistake when you come here." He smiled. "You look like a mermaid with your hair all crinkled."

"I braided it for work, but I couldn't work."

"It's not your average day."

"The last time I saw her . . . I wish it was different."

Max reached over and tugged her hair. "Hey, we never know."

"You're right, I guess. Still I want a do-over . . ."

"What did you do?"

"You wouldn't get it. Just the usual chick stuff, PMS bitchiness, nothing important."

Max frowned. "For real, what happened?"

"Can I have another beer?" She raised her empty bottle.

He took the empty from her, opened another bottle of Coors, and put it in her hand. "No excuses now. Tell me. You know you want to."

"I feel like shit. I should never have said anything. I don't want you to think anything bad about her, okay?"

"She's my sister and she's dead. I doubt you could say anything to make me think anything bad about her."

Kelly swigged her beer. "She told me she'd developed feelings for the guy who worked on the house and she thought he felt the same about her. Is this news to you?"

"She never said a word. What did you say to her?"

"I didn't take her side. She wanted me to be supportive, you know, excited for her, and I wasn't. It's not like Connor is some anonymous dude. He's a friend too. I felt bad for him."

"That's what's got you all guilty?"

"It sort of crushed her that I wasn't happy for her. Maybe you have to be a girl to get it."

Max rubbed the back of his neck. "You ever think we're cursed when it comes to people dying? We've got to be above the national average for people our age."

"That's random. Also, you're changing the subject."

"My therapist calls me out on that all the time."

Kelly's eyes widened. "Since when do you go to therapy?"

"Six months now." Max picked at the label on his beer. "Don't look so shocked. Real men talk about their feelings."

"That won't sell beer. Why did you decide to go?"

"Some stuff felt too big to deal with alone."

"Does it help?"

"Well, I no longer harbor a constant desire to hurt people . . . until today, today totally fucked with my mental stability. But you didn't come here to talk about my therapy."

"Where's the takeout? I'm starving."

As if she'd snapped her fingers, there was a knock on the door. Max pulled cash from his pocket, paid the delivery guy, and came back with the brown paper bag full of food clutched in his right hand.

They ate in silence for a few minutes, and then Kelly raised her bottle. "Let's drink to Stacey."

Max clinked his bottle against hers, and took a long drink. The electric heat ticked away and the house heated up around them. Steam covered the kitchen windows.

"Have you talked to Connor?" Kelly asked.

"I tried calling him but as usual his voicemail was full. He must be in a world of hurt. All I got was a two-word text, *Tomorrow, bro.*"

"I can't imagine what he's going through. They were getting married in a few weeks."

"It's fucked up," Max said. He went to the refrigerator for another beer.

"What's worse, you think, losing the person you loved enough to spend the rest of your life with, or losing a sibling?"

"All I can say is it sucks either way. And I know it hasn't hit me full-on yet. Stacey dying is going to have its way with me for a long time. You know this territory from when Tim died."

"My life hasn't been the same since. It's not like there are no happy times, but the light went out and I don't think it's coming back on." She pushed her plate away. "I'll be sick if I eat any more of this. Do you think Stacey would want Connor to fall in love and go on with his life? You know how people say the person who died wouldn't want the one they left behind to be sad forever? Bullshit. I'd want somebody to grieve for the rest of his life for me."

"Stacey, though, she would want him to move on," Max mused.

"Do you think they had the real thing?"

He tapped his fork against his plate. "I always thought so. They'd been together forever. I wouldn't put too much stock in her having a crush on another guy. Those things come and go. Why, what are you thinking?"

"You *are* an innocent." Kelly sighed. "There's something else you should know. But it feels wrong to blow your fantasy."

"You started, you have to tell me."

"Someone told Stacey Connor was seen checking into a sleazy motel with another guy."

"No shit, for real? Who said that?"

"The contractor guy, I'm guessing. She wouldn't tell me who it was."

"Same guy she was into?"

"Yeah."

"He could have made the whole thing up to get with her."

"That's what I thought."

"Was she freaked out? I can't believe she didn't tell me."

"I think she was trying to deal with it. She didn't want to jump to conclusions. She put a tracker on his phone, though."

"Jesus, this is getting dark." Max shook his head. "This doesn't sound like Stacey."

"It was my idea. I told her she had to have proof before she called off the wedding."

"She was thinking about ending it?" Max couldn't believe what he was hearing.

"She was a hot mess."

He slumped in his seat. "I can't believe she's dead."

"That's why I came tonight. I couldn't wrap my head around it; I started to feel all lost, out in the black alone. Then I thought about you and how you're the only one who could ever make that feeling go away, so here I am."

His body went still, the way it always did the rare times she talked like this. He concentrated on eating and tried his best to stay in the moment. One of the techniques he'd learned in therapy, mindfulness meditation, required focusing on the physical sensations in his body—but with Kelly that was dangerous, too.

"You have to eat some more, I can't finish this myself," he said, pushing her fork back into her hand.

Kelly laced the fingers of her free hand through his, and when he didn't flinch or pull away, she held his hand on her lap.

■ ■ ■

While Max was washing the dishes, he heard the shower turn on. He pulled his T-shirt over his head and wiped the sweat from his face and chest. He waited for her on the futon, eyes closed, comfortable and drowsy in the overheated room.

For a moment he wanted to be alone in the house so he could drift off to sleep; then he realized that most of his comfort came from Kelly being in the house with him.

The bathroom door opened and he heard her footsteps as she made her way back to him.

"How do you turn the heat off?" she asked. "It's like a sauna in here."

"Leave it. I like it."

"You look like you're burning up and you're half naked."

"I don't mind if you don't."

She sat down beside him and let the towel fall open. Her breasts were cool against his chest. It had been eight years since they'd touched in this intimate way. She opened her mouth to speak and he put a finger on her lips to silence her. Their need was beyond what words could heal.

He'd read once that after a death, humans craved sex as a release from autonomy, a rebellion against death, a manic claim on life—an instinctive and impersonal urge. Tonight, not for the first time, he and Kelly reached out and found each other in grief.

When he was sure she was asleep, he went to the bedroom and retrieved the Smith & Wesson 686 he slept with every night.

■ ■ ■

Max woke to a noise, a scraping sound, and was on his feet in seconds, his pistol drawn and ready.

The door and all the windows were locked and the house was an oven. Soaked in sweat, Max could practically hear his heart hammering in his chest. He turned the thermostat to the lowest setting. In the dark, he drank straight from the kitchen faucet for a long time.

Earlier, her eyes half closed and on the brink of sleep, Kelly had asked a question that had played in his mind all day: "Do you think Connor killed her?"

In need of fresh air, he opened the door. A ghostly mist swirled. At the base of his spine, a tingling sensation rose and spread up and across his back. A primitive fear set in; he felt exposed and watched by someone or something unseen, hidden by darkness. In the narrow lanes of the trailer court, fog swirled and surrounded the houses like a living thing.

He wondered if Stacey's spirit remained, and if she would haunt him day and night for the rest of his life. He locked the door and made his way in the dark to where Kelly slept, grateful to slip in beside her warm body. He felt the length of her at his back while his fingers grazed the barrel of his pistol.

CHAPTER 18

Kelly woke up alone. On the pillow beside her, she found a yellow sticky note on which he had printed, "I locked you in. Lock up when you leave."

Not surprising. She knew him well enough to know that he protected his heart. In the light of day, he wasn't going to show any vulnerability. In the light of day, he'd be covered up in his personal armor of muscle and male distance. He was probably at the gym.

Her own muscles hurt from sleeping on the thin mattress of the futon, nothing more than a foam pad over wooden sticks. They might as well have camped out. She hated camping; that was the one thing that separated her from their gang of friends. She liked comfort. She thought of her queen bed, with its pillow-top mattress and featherbed topper, as she rolled over and stretched out her aching limbs.

The scent of musk and soap on the pillow where Max had rested his head made her think of dark forests, no sun—a fairy tale wood conjured from old stories long forgotten.

Spending time with Max did that, got her mind going in new directions, her own thoughts surprising her. So different from the way her brain usually worked—steady, strategic, one thought following another like cars on an assembly line, engineered by her, nothing unexpected. She came undone in so many ways around this man.

And Max had been there when Tim died and all the light went out of everything. Later, when she read about black holes, she understood the concept easily and resonated with the idea of being pulled into a void. Her world after losing Tim became a vast empty space, one in which she felt untethered and alone.

Broken as she was then, only Max could reach her. In those stricken days, he kept her from feeling deranged and alien.

In a time toxic with sorrow, they'd found a way to walk through the sadness together.

And now, with Stacey's death, the opportunity had risen to do it again. Connor and Stacey were part of that time. Now Stacey was gone too.

All of a sudden, she felt afraid in Max's place alone. Her own thoughts disturbed her. She began to worry she'd screwed up by walking off the job last night.

She hurried out, still wearing Max's oversize clothes, determined to make things right with Val.

CHAPTER 19

Antelope got to the station before the 8:00 a.m. roll call on Sunday morning and was surprised to find the sheriff at his desk. Since his life had fallen apart six months earlier, his boss had slowed down. He rarely showed up for weekend shifts.

A weaker man would be on a lounge under a palm tree, buried deep in tequila. Not Scruggs. When his wife died in January, he'd taken two days off to bury her. The next day, he'd undergone cardiac surgery at University Hospital in Salt Lake City, Utah, followed by two weeks in a rehab facility. By the end of January, he'd put his uniform back on and reported for duty.

"Don't look so surprised, Antelope," he'd said on his first day back on the job. "I just hit the pause button. I'll be here to the bitter end, boots on, ready to draw."

For Antelope, the magic was gone. He tried to keep it from showing, but things were different between them now. Initially, he'd made Scruggs his hero, made of pure gold and heavyweight. As a new detective, he'd cast himself in the sheriff's mold. It was hard to admit that he'd created the mentor he needed—that Scruggs wasn't a superhero, just a flawed human being.

Antelope missed the story he'd told himself about the sheriff— that he was bigger than life, like some kind of tribal elder. He was working to accept that it was enough for them to be two lawmen who worked cases together. Fifteen years of hard-won experience on the job gave Scruggs indisputable credibility in Antelope's mind. Even his cousin told him it was past time to cut the cord. He didn't disagree. But like most things in life, it would have been easier if it had happened the natural way, and there was nothing natural about the cataclysmic fall of Sheriff Carlton Scruggs.

Scruggs held court from the doorway of his office, arms folded across his chest, all the day shift guys gathered around as he filled them in on the murder. When he spotted Antelope, he closed the session down and waved him into his small office.

His desk was piled with slanted stacks of manila folders, all the active cases in the department, everything he was responsible for managing and clearing. He liked it spread out where he could see it and touch it. "I'm a hands-on manager," he'd told Antelope the day he made detective and came under his command.

Despite his heart condition, Scruggs continued his lethal life-style habits. A Krispy Kreme box was open on his desk, sugar and crumbs from his favorite glazed donuts on the bottom. Antelope preferred chocolate-covered donuts, himself.

The sheriff came with a history. Before he came to Sweetwater County, he'd botched a high-profile missing person investigation when he covered up his affair with the victim. Ten years later, another affair and another missing woman with a connection to him. One more mistake and it might be the end of his days in law enforcement.

If that happened, there was no doubt in Antelope's mind that the superhero would exit with a gun in his mouth.

Scruggs squashed the box and dumped it in the trash. "I probably won't have time for lunch, figured I'd stock up now," he said and licked his fingers.

"I'm a cheeseburger man, myself," Antelope said. "It's my go-to meal when I'm on a murder."

"If I've learned anything in this job, it's that we're all creatures of habit." He settled into his chair. "Toni called and said you can catch up with her this afternoon."

"Thanks, I will." Antelope slid into the seat across from him. "We talked last night, but it got late."

"What are you talking about?"

"I talked to her last night at the Saddle Lite."

"What the hell? I brought her home at nine thirty." Scruggs got red in the face and glared. Antelope couldn't tell what got to him the most—his own defiance of the sheriff's wishes, or Toni's.

The moment passed. Scruggs got down to business.

"What do we know about the victim?"

"She was into erotic asphyxiation."

"What the hell? Toni told you that?"

Antelope shook his head. "The friend, Kelly Ryan. She said Stacey got off when Connor choked her during sex. Death can result if the game goes too far."

"The Medical Examiner should be able to tell us what happened, right?"

"Guess we'll have to wait and see. Connor didn't offer up anything when I spoke to him, and it didn't seem the right time to ask. I'll have another conversation with him. Kelly said Stacey used a tracking app to check his whereabouts and look for evidence of cheating. Someone had told her that Connor checked into a motel in Salt Lake City with another gentleman. The app might tell us more. I'll sign the phone out of evidence and give it a look."

"Sex in the city. I'll be damned." Scruggs shook his head. "Good to know I'm not the only fool for love in Sweetwater County. What did Toni have to say?"

"She sensed some trouble between Stacey and Connor; couldn't be specific, but it's consistent with what I heard from Kelly. Stacey asked her the difference between a narcissist and a sociopath. She didn't know if Stacey was talking about Connor or someone else."

"Not much to go on, but at least she's looking a little more interesting. Keep poking around."

"And there's this." Antelope slid the plastic evidence bag across the desk.

"What is it?"

"I believe it's our victim's engagement ring, retrieved from the garden at the Cedar Street house last night."

"How the hell did you find it, and what were you doing there at night?"

Antelope shrugged. "I always go back to murder scenes, and this time it paid off. When I show this to Assistant Prosecutor Collins, he might get honest."

"Bring him in here and get it on video. I'm done with any special treatment for him."

■ ■ ■

Antelope called the Evidence Room to request Stacey Hart's cell phone for sign-out and was told they didn't have it and now that he thought about it, he couldn't recall seeing it at the crime scene. Then he left a message for Connor Collins to call him. His phone vibrated, and a text from Toni settled his schedule: *Any time after 4 at 35 Wardell Court.*

He texted back to confirm the time and place, then called Kelly Ryan.

She picked up on the first ring.

"Hi Kelly, Detective Antelope here. I'm heading over to the Black Tiara. Can you meet me there in about a half hour? I'd like to follow up on a few things with you."

In addition to the Astro Lounge, Val Campion owned the Black Tiara. It would be a good place to question Kelly about the things she'd failed to disclose—namely, where she worked and how much she knew about Jack Swailes.

"I didn't eat breakfast yet, but yeah, sure, I'll have lunch with you. I just need a few minutes to pull myself together, and then I'll head over."

■ ■ ■

As Antelope pulled into the parking lot of the shopping center, Kelly stepped out of a neon yellow Volkswagen convertible. She wore a short yellow sundress with white polka dots and yellow stiletto heels. She gave him a wave and a smile.

He walked to the front door and held it open for her. She walked past him into the cool, dark, uncrowded dining room. In the strong churchgoing community of Green River, brunch didn't get busy until noon.

Kelly led him to the bar and motioned for him to sit beside her. "Hey, Kelly, how you doing?" the bartender asked. "What can I get for you today?"

She smiled sweetly. "Doing okay today, Marco, thanks for asking."

He put up napkins and a bowl of peanuts and took their order: a seltzer for Antelope and a gin and tonic for her.

"They know you here."

"I work here."

"You didn't say."

"You didn't ask."

"There's a lot of ground to cover early in the investigation, sometimes things get missed."

"The tips are great." Kelly tilted her head to the side. "So why are we here?"

"You said you last saw Stacey a month ago?" Antelope asked, intentionally ignoring her questions. "I would have thought you'd see each other more."

"Everybody's busy. Our schedules didn't leave us much down time."

"Did something happen between you and Stacey? An argument?"

"Fern told you, right?" Kelly snorted. "She blamed me. In her eyes, Stacey could do no wrong."

Antelope maintained a poker face. "I wanted to get the straight story from you."

"Stacey got all self-righteous when she thought Connor cheated on her. The next week, she tells me she's got feelings for another guy! What's the difference? I can't stand hypocrites. She didn't like hearing the truth."

"This is Jack Swailes you're referring to?"

"Yes, he worked at the house."

"Did she admit to being involved with him?"

"You mean romantically?"

"That's what I'm hearing."

"Even if something had happened, it would never have lasted."

"You seem pretty sure."

"I tried to tell her, but she wouldn't listen—a real innocent, totally naïve. Connor was the only boyfriend she'd ever had, and he treated her like a queen. No hookups for Stacey; no heartbreak, either. She asked for trouble when she started up with him. I told her. The two of them couldn't have been more different from each other."

"Sounds like you know the guy."

"I was going by what she told me."

"Opposites attract in romance, don't they?"

"So they say. I'm trying to imagine someone who would be your opposite." She fluttered a hand. "Don't mind me. I get this way when bad things happen. Stacey didn't know anything about men and what they can do."

"Not like you."

Kelly blushed and looked away, finished her drink.

"Were you involved with Jack Swailes when he hooked up with Stacey?"

"What are you talking about? Marco, another one of these," Kelly said and pointed to her glass.

"Time to get honest, Kelly. I know you dance at the Astro Lounge. Val Campion said Jack had his pick of the dancers. I'm guessing he picked you."

"Jack's a man-whore who wouldn't let any woman tie him down, not even Stacey."

"Did you tell Stacey about you and Swailes?"

Her eyes filled up and she reached for the gin and tonic Marco had just set down in front of her. After swallowing a huge gulp, she said, "There was nothing to tell. And how would I have explained how I knew him? Nobody knows I work at the Astro. I'm not ashamed of it; I just don't want to be judged."

"Were you jealous when Stacey told you about her and Jack?"

"You don't get it. Jack and me, we were not together." She raised her chin in defiance.

"It's a serious mistake to hold back information in a homicide investigation."

"My friend was murdered. I was in shock."

"Fair enough. I won't arrest you for obstructing the investigation. But if you hold anything else back and I find out about it, I won't be able to make the same call. You're on notice. Are you hearing me?" Antelope gave her a hard look. "Let me decide what's important and what's not. It's my job."

Kelly nodded.

"It was Swailes who gave her the idea Connor cheated on her, right?"

"That would be like him," Kelly said.

"To start trouble between Stacey and Connor?"

"Yeah, to make himself look better to her. He needs all the help he can get. Do you think he killed her?"

"It's a possibility. All I know is he ran off and that looks bad for him. Do you happen to know where he is?"

She put her hand to her mouth and whispered, "Jack's gone?" Her eyes filled with tears again—surprise, a genuine response, not acting, Antelope thought.

"He didn't get in touch with you?"

"No. I called him yesterday when the news said a workman found her but his phone was turned off."

"I need to follow up on this thing with Connor in Salt Lake. It would help to know which of the 515 hotels he was seen at. Jack is running scared. If you let him know we're looking into this, taking it seriously, maybe he would give you the name of the place if he thought it would get the spotlight off him. Can you work with me on this?"

"I can ask." Kelly's tone was doubtful. "He's not the easiest person to deal with, especially if he thinks it's a trap."

"Tell him if gives up the name, it's good for him. But bottom line, if he wants to help himself, he should get back here and cooperate with the investigation. And don't agree to meet with him. He's a person of interest in your friend's murder. This is the real deal, Kelly. Don't take any chances. He might not be who he seems to be. The man could be dangerous."

Kelly got very still. She looked frightened and trapped. He

hadn't meant to terrify her into cooperating—but no, he realized, her eyes were looking past him. He turned to see what she was focused on.

Val Campion stood in the doorway. A gust of wind caught the door and sand blew in from the desert and swirled around the room. Kelly covered her face.

Campion looked at Kelly, laughed, and turned away without speaking. The young woman beside him grabbed onto his arm and followed him into a back room.

Val Campion, a man with a cruel streak. Did his nephew take after him? For whatever reason, Stacey had been drawn to Jack, and now she was dead. Could it be as simple as that?

CHAPTER 20

At five minutes after four, Antelope parked under an old cotton-wood tree in front of 35 Wardell Court, the house where Stacey Hart had resided with Toni Atwell. The compact white cottage, with its bright blue front door and shiny brass knocker, stood out among the other homes in the modest neighborhood. A half-mile from the Cedar Street house, this was an older, more ragged section of town where smaller, shabbier houses stood close together. But this house had fresh paint, and trimmed rose bushes bordered the manicured lawn. Someone cared about the place.

Toni came to the door before he knocked. He thought she must have changed out of the clothes she wore to her job at the women's shelter; she wore a bright red silk kimono and gold slippers.

"Your timing is perfect," she said. "Come in, make yourself comfortable. I've got coffee brewing." She pointed to a pair of royal blue wing chairs in front of a white brick fireplace.

Antelope took in his surroundings. Toni's home was a bright space with white walls, flowering plants in ceramic pots, and primary colors in the artwork, pillows, and rag rugs.

In his work, he got to see the inside of many homes. He believed the way people decorated and kept their living spaces said a lot about what they valued. Only rarely did he find himself comfortable in other people's surroundings, but here he did. The furnishings and the care evident in this house created an unexpected feeling of serenity—even during a murder investigation.

Toni returned from the kitchen and handed him a thick mug of steaming dark coffee.

"Carlton tells me you're a double espresso guy. So am I. For my birthday he gave me the new Starbucks Venti machine. He claims he bought it to save himself some money. I've never dated anyone who knew how to choose a gift, but he's got a real knack for it. How about you, Detective, do you enjoy buying presents for the women in your life?"

"That opportunity hasn't presented itself."

"Clever answer." She chuckled. "You managed to give me no information whatsoever."

"You have a nice place here. Is the artist local?" He pointed to the watercolor above the tiled mantel.

She smiled. "I painted that one. Most of the things you see are from artists in Wyoming and Colorado. I make several trips a year to area art shows. Since I left the religious order, I am free to indulge my love of color. My greatest joy. Don't tell Carlton. He thinks it's sharing a bed with a hot sheriff."

"Are you ready to tell me about your decision to leave the convent?"

"Message received. Fun time's over."

He waited while she drank her coffee. She set the empty cup on the floor and folded her hands in her lap. He could see remnants of the demure and serious nun.

"Let's get down to the business you came for. It's a sad saga, hard for me to talk about. I loved the Church and I still do, though it will never be the same for me again."

"Tell me your story."

"You know how when you're going through something and it sucks you ask yourself, *How much will this matter years from now?* because you think it'll help put the current thing in perspective? That little trick is bullshit. It's been sixteen years and I'm here to say, it still matters."

"Did you leave the convent then?"

"I left ten years ago, but the story starts long before. I tried to hold on to my vocation, I did. You may not remember, but it was sixteen years ago, January 2002, when the *Boston Globe* broke the story about priests being tried for the rape of children. As the months went on, the stories kept coming. It hurt the Church hard; both religious and lay people reeled in disbelief. Across the country, parents got scared and started asking their kids questions. And the numbers got bigger. Other people responded with denial and believed it couldn't happen in their parish." She sighed. "It saddens me to admit I shared those thoughts. Out here in Wyoming in our small-town church, I truly believed we were safe from the evils of the world. I never imagined the evil could thrive within the walls of my own church. I entered the religious order because I wanted to be part of this massive force for good in the world." She cocked her head. "Stop me if I'm getting too wordy for you. I have a tendency to embellish."

"I'm interested, keep going."

"I need a refill, how about you?"

"No thanks, I'm still working on this."

She picked up her mug and disappeared into the kitchen, obviously in need of a break. Antelope thought it must have been difficult for her to voluntarily sever her connection with work that gave meaning and purpose to her life.

She sat back down and continued. "My first job after I took my vows in the order was at Our Lady of Sorrows parish school. Todd Bellamy had started there a year before as pastor. A breath of fresh air, everyone said; young, vibrant, straight out of the seminary. Truly, the way he engaged the young people in the parish was great; he was an outdoor enthusiast who got the youth group involved in nature activities and hiking and camping trips. My faith in the Catholic Church, the priesthood, and human nature returned. I committed myself to doing the Lord's work through my vocation." She took in a shaky breath. "After I'd been here about a year, a parishioner shared some dark history with me. It was no idle gossip or secondhand rumor; the story involved her family directly, and I didn't doubt the disturbing information she shared. I went to Father Bellamy and he confirmed what the woman had told me. Before I could ask about the secrecy he told me I couldn't speak to anyone about it.

Antelope's curiosity was eating at him, but he held his questions for the time being.

"Needless to say, I didn't react well." Toni stared down into her coffee. "I felt disgusted and disappointed. It was the beginning of the end for me and the Roman Catholic Church. But I followed his order because I didn't have a choice, and I've never spoken to anyone about it since. What I'm about to tell you is part of the sordid history of Our Lady of Sorrows, known to only myself and the parties involved." She lifted her eyes to meet Antelope's. "Fern Hart disclosed to me that Father Gerard Kroll sexually abused her son, Max, and his friends Timothy Ryan and Connor Collins, during the time they served as altar boys. The abuse went on for several years, until one of the boys confided in a parent."

"Do you know the extent of the abuse?"

She shook her head. "I don't know all the details. The Harts and the Ryans reported the situation to the Bishop in Cheyenne. Connor's parents were killed in an auto accident when he was very young and he was being raised by his maternal grandmother. Being of a different generation, she couldn't bring herself to challenge anything done by a priest. The Bishop responded by removing Kroll, sending him to a different church, and offering a financial settlement to the three families."

"Sounds like the usual approach," Antelope said.

Toni nodded. "And now I'm telling you this, I remember another time Stacey got angry at Connor. She found the financial records detailing the payout from the Church. Connor gave no indication during the whole time they dated that he'd received a settlement of any kind, never mind of the sum involved. You'd think given the serious nature of their relationship, he would have trusted her with that information. Stacey did too. She felt very shut out and considered it a breach of their intimacy."

"Wouldn't Stacey have known something about this since her family got a settlement too?"

"Her parents had never told her about Max being abused, or about the money. When Connor told her everything, she found the whole thing extremely disturbing and became very upset. I didn't feel it was my place to add anything to the situation, so I held my tongue."

"So when, exactly, did you decide to leave the Church?"

Toni sighed. "I didn't leave immediately. But things were never the same for me again. You know how it is when you fall out of love. It's impossible to get the stars back in your eyes after you've seen the blackness in someone's heart. As time went on, it became clear that Father Bellamy and I disagreed about the church's handling of priests who engaged in the sexual abuse of children. He wanted to keep things positive and not address the issue. I thought we should actively teach about it; I believe knowledge is power. I couldn't remain passive. Finally, I decided to do something, take my own small stand against the abuse and lies."

Antelope raised an eyebrow. "And what was that?"

"Catholic school enrollment was down all over the country, and it was no different here. I argued that actively addressing parents' concerns and raising awareness of abuse through sex education would retain students. But I needed the pastor's support to make it happen. Todd refused; he shut my movement down before it could get off the ground. That broke me. A year later, the diocese closed the school and I found the courage to leave." She snorted with disgust. "Finally."

"You did it. Don't beat yourself up for how long it took."

"Knowing how the Church enabled the sex crimes to protect the institution . . . there was nothing left for me to believe in. And it's not just at the lower levels. It goes all the way up to the Vatican."

"I get why you left the convent."

"I don't talk about it often. It makes me too sad, and when I get sad I drink too much."

"And what's your take on him?"

"Who?"

"Father Bellamy."

"I think we wandered a bit off track. My thoughts about Todd Bellamy aren't relevant to the case you're investigating."

"You're an insightful woman," Antelope pressed. "I'd like to hear your thoughts on the priest."

"Do you recall the definitions I gave you of the narcissist and sociopath and the thin line between the two?"

"Yes."

"Father Todd Bellamy rides that thin line."

CHAPTER 21

Jack woke up in a motel in Utah, his heart pounding in a pitch-black room. He reached for the edge of the bedspread and pulled the heavy fabric over his head. The loud window air conditioner worked like a freezer. On the bedside table, the digital clock radio read 12:10 a.m.

One day gone.

Only one person knew where he was. When he made the quick pit stop to ditch the van and pick up his truck, he'd told Val what happened on Cedar Street and how he planned to leave town for a while. It was Val's idea for him to hole up in the apartment at the Spring Grove Motel where he ran his Utah business.

He'd switched the license plate on his Dodge Ram, packed a bag, and gotten on the interstate heading west before anyone even knew to come looking for him.

The Spring Grove Motel was a dump near the train and bus stations, a place for transients and hookers. The three-story, red brick, L-shaped structure with wrought iron railings in need of a fresh coat of paint was located on the western edge of the city. Behind the front office, a chain link fence enclosed an empty, faded swimming pool, surrounded by a parking lot. Val liked the low overhead. He claimed his customers would feel exposed in a fancier place, a decent hotel, possibly run into people they knew.

A deep weariness had come over Jack when he closed the motel door, his legs cramped after hours behind the wheel without a break. He'd bolted and chain-locked the door, closed the thick, dusty drapes, and fallen into bed fully clothed. He'd felt safe in the battered, musty room, his familiar home away from home.

But now, awake in the middle of the night, his mind was racing. In the morning, there would be time to deal with her phone. First thing on the agenda: delete any texts or voicemails from him to Stacey. Then he'd tackle the tracking app. He couldn't wait to see what it had picked up. With any luck, he would find something to raise suspicion about Connor. His goal was to get himself off the sheriff's radar.

On the ride down from Rock Springs, he'd thought long and hard about how to get the phone into the hands of law enforcement. No way would he stick his neck out and deliver it personally. Connor Collins wanted him tried and convicted.

He took the two Big Macs and a bag of fries he'd bought on the way into town out of their greasy paper bag and warmed them in the microwave. At the window, he opened the drapes an inch, enough for a surveillance view. He propped his stocking feet on the dusty window ledge and settled in for his watch while he ate his fast-food dinner. From this vantage point, he could keep an eye on the locked garage where he'd parked his truck and spot any signs of police who might come nosing around.

He thought about how he'd woken up in the previous morning without any idea how things would turn out—how his life had just been turned upside down because of one decision.

He thought about Stacey and got an erection. Would it make him a creep if he pictured her when he masturbated? What he wouldn't give for one more time with her.

The rain came down hard again, the sound like bullets on the window air conditioner. The idea hit him like a bolt of lightning and he wondered why he didn't of it before: if he could find out who Collins was with, find solid evidence to show him in a bad light, it might help get him off the sheriff's short list of suspects.

Val could access the motel's records. His uncle had taught him everything he knew about women: how to get them, how to handle them, how to let them go when they got to be too much trouble. He'd want to help him now.

His body was stiff from the long drive and the tension his muscles had held for so many hours. A hot shower would help, but he didn't want to move. He closed his eyes and saw her again: blood in her hair, fear in her eyes.

He thought about the day Stacey Hart came into his life.

■ ■ ■

He was driving down Broadway toward home after finishing early at the job. She ran in front of the truck and he slammed on the brakes. A bright blue scarf flew like a kite in the wind; she went after it, moving like a colt, long legs in black tights and boots. She jumped, snatched the scarf out of the air, and wrapped it around her neck.

Traffic stopped at the light and he watched her make her way against the wind, her golden hair a mass of curls rippling behind her like a mane. She tried to hold it down, but it escaped, a wild thing, betraying what he thought must be her true nature.

In those first moments after seeing her on the windy street on a March afternoon, he began making up stories about her. One look at her and he wanted her, had to have her. She entered a café with a green and white awning, a fancy place he'd never been to, never wanted to go to, where he'd be out of place in his work boots and denim jacket.

A minute later, he squeezed his truck into a tight spot, smoothed his hair in the mirror, and followed her quickly toward the café, taking note of everything, knowing he'd want to recall it later.

The wind tore down the narrow street with a force that took his breath away. It was bitter cold, and he shoved his hands into the pockets of his denim jacket. He regretted leaving his black watch cap in the truck; he'd ditched it so he'd look less like a common worker.

He entered the café and found her seated at a table by the window. A wood stove warmed the small room and candles flickered in glass lamps on the tables.

When his eyes adjusted to the dim light, he saw that they were the only two customers in the place. She looked at him and he went to her, sat at the table as if he belonged there, as if she'd invited him.

She watched him without surprise, as if men did this all the time—walked into her life without introduction or permission. Blue eyes, the color of her scarf.

"Hello."

He waited for more, some protest or question, but nothing came. "I followed you," he said.

He sounded like a psycho stalker. *Great pickup line, dude—way to give the girl a reason to scream for the cops.* But she didn't. She gave him a long look and smiled, and he smiled back.

When she tossed her hair over her shoulder, long silver earrings caught the sun and reflected rainbow prisms on the ceiling. Around her neck a silver cross, set with turquoise, floated on a delicate chain. Up close he could see how thin she was, how prominent the bones of her shoulders and chest were.

"I'm Stacey."

"Jack," he said and held out his hand.

Her fingers were cool and lingered on his. "Did you really follow me, Jack?"

"You ran in front of my truck. I liked what I saw."

She looked thoughtful. "What did you like?"

"Your hair. It looks like that painting by Dante, *Helen of Troy.*"

With both hands she patted the curls that fell over her shoulder. "You couldn't resist me."

■ ■ ■

With Stacey it was love at first sight, the first time it had ever happened for him. It was easy between them, no effort at all.

Val had tried to brainwash him, warn him off women and love. None of it had stuck.

No one would believe it, but he didn't care. He'd never planned to share what he felt with anyone. Somehow, Val had found out about Stacey anyway.

Was that the moment when everything started to go wrong?

He fell asleep to the sound of trains coming and going—long, sad whistles, a melancholy song in the night.

CHAPTER 22

"Someone will end up dead if I don't fix my head," Max Hart told me when we'd met for his first therapy session a year earlier.

A few days before, he'd heard about the arrest of a Catholic priest in Greybull, Wyoming, on charges of sexual abuse of minors. The news had triggered flashbacks and nightmares of his own abuse as an altar boy. Those memories, along with everything else he'd experienced before age eighteen, had been lost when he suffered a head injury, and now they were coming flooding back.

The look in his eyes told me he meant what he said. I told him he'd made the right decision in seeking treatment, and we began therapy twice a week to "fix his head."

Now, a week after his sister's death, my patient again had murder on his mind.

We were in my office early. Outside, a brisk morning wind shook the western windows. Sunlight flickered as a band of high, thin clouds trailed erratic shadows across the desert floor. Max sat on the leather sofa across from me in full hyper-alert mode, blinking rapidly and scanning the room.

"Detective Antelope said he talked to you and you agreed to let me speak with him about our sessions."

Max nodded. "If you tell him I'm not crazy, he might believe it."

"I have the release here, if you want to sign it." I held up the paper.

He beckoned for me to give it to him. I handed it over with a pen; he signed it quickly and passed it back to me.

"So how does it work? You tell him everything, word for word?"

"It's more like I provide a general impression. Most likely he will have some questions and I will answer them based on my clinical impression and the work we have done together."

"Will he lock me up if I tell you I intend to kill whoever did this to her with my bare hands?"

Every muscle in his body was taut and ready to fight. His wild eyes and clenched jaw were the most obvious signs of his controlled violence.

I didn't doubt his capacity, psychological or physical, to take a life. He'd lived for years with suppressed rage, a volcanic force waiting for a reason to erupt. Could Stacey's murder provide that reason?

"I understand you want revenge in this moment," I said carefully. "But you may change your mind. So the answer is no. No one's going to lock you up."

"Even if I tell you I'm looking forward to it? It keeps me going, the thought of crushing the life out of him. She didn't deserve to die but someone took her life. Old Testament justice, right?" Max opened and closed his hands, stretched his fingers and popped his knuckles, made a white-knuckled fist he knew could do real damage.

"When and if you find out who killed Stacey and you still want to kill him and you make a plan," I said calmly, "I will have to act to try and stop you from killing a human being. My actions are prescribed by the ethics of my profession. The decision would be out of my hands. I would notify the Sheriff's Department and your intended victim." I studied Max's face. I wanted him to understand that I took him and his feelings seriously. "I'm telling you all this because I understand you're not making an exaggerated threat. I know what you've experienced and how it affected you. I know what you're capable of."

Max looked up, giving me his full attention now.

I shivered in the cold office and got up to adjust the air conditioner, set too low for the early-morning temperature. A sudden chill shook my body. Max's treatment, always intense, might descend into dangerous depths with this new development.

Time to return to the moment, I thought, *it's our only hope of dealing with this tragic situation.*

"I'd like to help you process what's happened," I said. "How did you feel when you heard about Stacey's murder?"

"I'm ready to commit murder myself. What do you think?"

"I think you're avoiding your feelings again."

He dipped his head. "That's accurate."

After his head injury and six months in a coma, Max endured a long recovery. As he got stronger through physical rehabilitation, he decided to make personal training his life's work.

Yet the man in front of me looked ready for a hospital— eyes bloodshot, skin slack and pale, sweatpants baggy and T-shirt tattered.

"How have you been managing?"

"Booze and risky sex, my usual. I'm entitled. Some bastard killed my sister."

"To lose someone you love in a sudden and violent way is one of the worst things in life."

"I can't sleep until I pass out drunk, I can't keep food down . . . my body's rebelling against being alive when Stacey is dead."

"Have you cried?"

"My mother cries enough for both of us." Max scowled. "What good will it do? Tears won't bring her back. Last night all I could think about was her funeral and the idea of her in the ground tore me apart. I got shit-faced and passed out and woke up with just enough time to shower and change clothes before coming here."

"This is a big deal. Did you see the relapse coming?"

"Hell yes! When he told me she was dead, I saw a bottle of Jameson's in my future."

"You're making light of something serious. You've been sober five years."

"Alcohol's reliable as fuck to shut things down. You know how crazy I can get. This is not the time to get arrested for fighting. The Liquor Depot delivers."

"Tell me about the risky sex."

"Not in the usual sense—no strangers this time, no diseases. Someone from my past hit me up. What can I say? I'm easy. It worked and I'm grateful, even though I know it will come back to bite me in the ass. So yeah, emotionally risky, mess-with-my head risky. I'm not at my best here, Doc."

"You won't be able to keep this up," I warned gently.

"Hey, if this session is a bust, at least I showered and left my room."

I didn't laugh. "I'm here when you're ready."

Max stretched his legs out and sank back into the cushions of the leather sofa, letting his guard down. "The night before she died, Stacey asked me to meet her at Johnny's Tavern for a drink after work. I've never seen her so uptight. Planning the wedding stressed her out. Connor is useless, or so she said. But on Friday she didn't talk about the wedding. Something else was winding her up."

"Are you going to tell me what it was?"

Max ran his hands over his face and shook his head. "Okay, here goes: she asked if I thought Connor was gay."

"He's a close friend. Did you have any idea he might be gay?"

"Never. But here's something interesting. I dreamed Connor was beside me, watching while the old priest jacked off. None of the flashbacks and memories, none of the nightmares, included Connor before. So did Stacey's question plant the idea in my mind, or did the same thing happen to Connor? Did the abuse turn him toward guys?"

"There's one way to know."

"How?"

"Ask him."

"Whoa!" Max shook his head. "Hold on, that is not gonna happen."

"Why not?"

"And admit the abuse? No way. I'm not ready for anything close to self-disclosure."

"I understand. How did Stacey react to your answer?"

"She ordered another glass of wine, very out of character for her. She's a lightweight."

"Were you worried about her?"

"You haven't figured out after a year that I'm not exactly Mr. Sensitivity? I didn't take it too seriously at the time. It's only now, looking back, that I'm putting things together."

"Why did she question his sexuality?"

"It seems Connor hasn't been very frisky lately. I told her to give the guy a break. With his new job, he carries a shitload of responsibility and the spotlight is on all the time. He sends people to prison—people we went to school with. Women think men are always ready to do it, and when we're not it's because we don't find them attractive or we're gay. Talk about performance anxiety. Women expect sex on demand."

"So your friend's lack of interest didn't raise any red flags for you?"

"Not at the time. Stacey and Connor have been together since college. When you only have one sexual partner, there's nothing to compare it to. Did she expect fireworks forever?"

"Neither one of them had other sexual partners?"

"That's the image they portrayed. What do I know? Connor never talked about sex, not like other guys. Even before he got with Stacey, he kept his sex life to himself."

I waited while Max stared off into space, lost in his thoughts—a lull in his process. Outside, the day grew dark as heavy cloud cover moved in from the west. The light inside the office dimmed.

"What are you thinking?" I finally asked.

"Looking back, I think she was considering breaking up with Connor. About a month ago, she told me she found some financial statements indicating assets and hidden accounts he'd never told her about. It shook her up. She started to question if she could trust him. I didn't know what to tell her. He's my friend. I never thought of him as the kind of guy who would keep secrets about important things like big money. I told her she should talk to him, get him to open up."

"Do you know if she took your advice?"

"She didn't mention it again and I didn't ask. We weren't seeing each other often because she was busy with the house and wedding stuff. Friday night all she talked about was him being gay. The money didn't come up. Then Connor got there and the conversation ended."

"How did they seem to get along on Friday night?"

"Everything was cool. I didn't hang around long."

Max got quiet again. I waited for him to process his thoughts. Often, it took a while for him to find the words.

"I hate what I'm thinking right now."

"Why don't you tell me? It's better to get it out."

"Looking back, it seems like things were coming apart. If she tried to call off the wedding, I don't know how Connor would handle it. His image is important to him, super important. How would it look if she called off the wedding?"

"Do you think he could be violent if she threatened to leave him?"

Max shrugged. "I've never seen the guy lose it—never seen him throw a punch or even hit a wall. Connor keeps his cool."

"Our time is almost up," I said, glancing at the clock. "Next time, let's come back to you using alcohol to cope. I'm concerned that if you keep drinking, you won't be able to continue your work in therapy."

"You know I like coming here, but no matter what I do in my life, I keep getting fucked over," Max said. "Can talking about the past really make my life better?"

■ ■ ■

As soon as Max left the office, storm clouds released a battering rain. Bouncing hail stones drowned out the sound of his truck driving away.

I considered Antelope's question. Max struggled with major issues, psychological and cognitive. He suffered permanent damage from a traumatic brain injury, volatile mood swings, and problems controlling his sexual and aggressive impulses. Add in the primitive rage he felt as the result of years of sexual abuse, and it was easy to see him as a potential killer.

CHAPTER 23

After the appointment with Max, my schedule was open until 1:00.

Antelope picked up on the first ring. "You got it?"

"Hot off the press."

"When can we talk?"

"My morning's open. Give me a time and I'll work around it."

"Nothing better than having a shrink on demand; I'm getting in the car now."

"I have an appointment at the county office at one and I need to review the file first. I'll come to you."

"That works."

. . .

It was a ten-minute drive from the Hilltop Medical Building to Antelope's office in the county building on C Street. I drove down College Drive and took a left onto Dewar, passing red rock cliffs so majestically gorgeous they belonged in a national park.

The Sweetwater County Building was a three-story yellow brick building. Inside, the air was cool. I headed straight up to the Sheriff's Department on the third floor.

When I came to his door, Antelope smiled and stood up. The office was small and contained only a desk, two chairs, and a horizontal file cabinet, on top of which he kept his Starbucks espresso maker. He placed two small, steaming cups on the desk between us and started drumming his fingers on the steel desktop.

"This is me being patient," he said.

"How do you want to do this? Shall I tell you about Max and his treatment more generally, or do you have specific questions for me?"

"I've got one burning question, but I'll hold it. Tell me about Max Hart."

"You met him, so you know he comes across as intense, confrontational, and combative at times. He can be impulsive and has difficulty regulating his mood—as in, he gets angry quickly. I've been treating him for a year. He presented with flashbacks and panic attacks. The week before he came in for the first time, a Catholic priest in Greybull, Wyoming, had been arrested on charges of sexual abuse. Max was driving home from work when he heard the news on the radio. A flashback of himself as a boy being touched by a man came out of nowhere and he pulled over, unable to drive, frightened out of his mind. Each day the following week he spent alone in his apartment; he called out sick from his job at the gym, slept, and self-medicated with alcohol."

"What about his accident?" Antelope prompted.

"He was eighteen when it happened. He fell eighty feet in a climbing accident, spent three months in a coma. When he woke up he couldn't remember anything from before the fall. The recovery was slow. He was in a rehabilitation center in Salt Lake for almost a year. His memories of people eventually came back."

"But he didn't remember being molested?"

"That's not unusual. Many people abused as kids manage to lock the traumatizing experiences away because the mind can't make sense of them. It's only later, when they're older and get triggered by something in their environment—"

"Like a radio story."

"Exactly. That news report released his memories—some of them, anyway. His flashbacks are impressionistic and sensual. He remembers the black cassock, the scent of incense, and church bells chiming. He spent a lot of time at church. He was an altar boy."

"I've heard that story before," Antelope said grimly.

"We work on processing the memories and managing his

feelings about the abuse," I explained. "In a general way, it connects to the other issues he'll deal with for the rest of his life, the chronic compromise in his ability to regulate and tolerate feelings. I'm trying to get him to a point where he can maintain more control over his behavior and choices."

Antelope shook his head. "He's a ticking time bomb."

"Except an explosion is not inevitable. It's more like many small land mines below the surface, not one huge one."

"Could he have killed Stacey?"

"If we look objectively at the cognitive and regulative functions of his brain, I would say yes, it is possible," I said cautiously. "If you asked me if Max has the personality characteristics and ego structure of a person capable of murder, I would answer no."

"So two parts of the same person, the brain and the mind, give different answers?"

"You've got it. The brain is a physical organ and the way it functions is a critical factor in human experience at every level. The mind is separate from the brain, though it does develop in accordance with the brain's parameters and limitations."

"I think I follow you."

"In Max's case, the injury changed his ability to manage his emotions and behavior. He can be volatile and impulsive. But his personality structure is essentially healthy, and that compensates for the cognitive deficits."

"Bottom line, could he kill?"

"Brain-wise it's possible, historical risk factors increase the risk, while interpersonal relationship capacity mitigates the risk. So bottom line, yes. But did he kill Stacey? My best guess is no."

"Last night I talked to Stacey's roommate, a former nun named Toni Atwell. She educated me about the way the Church handled the sex abuse cases here. She said the Bishop transferred the priest to another church, where he would have had access to a new parish of vulnerable children."

"That's how I got experience working with sexual abuse victims," I said. "In 2002, when the *Boston Globe* broke the story of rampant sexual abuse among Catholic clergy, I was a graduate student interning at a community mental health center in Boston. When the Spotlight team exposed the extent of the abuse, it opened the door for hundreds of other victims to come forward and seek help. My entire experience there was counseling clients, children, adolescents, and adults who'd been sexually abused by their parish priest. After my experience there, I decided to do my doctoral dissertation on the psychological profiles of clergy who engage in sexual abuse."

"Educate me."

"First of all, they appear completely normal, but they have characteristics of both narcissistic and dependent personality disorders. They see themselves as unique and lack empathy for the young people they prey on. They tend to be socially immature. They break down kids' resistance to sexual abuse by creating a special relationship—providing privileges and gifts and attention to kids who they see as vulnerable and in need."

"A power trip." Antelope's face darkened. "All their education and spiritual training and they don't get how what they're doing is screwing these kids up for life?"

"Fifty percent of abusing priests were abused themselves. It's not an excuse," I said quickly. "Behavior is always a choice. But many of them do identify with the kids they groom into sex."

"I'm due at the church in fifteen minutes to meet with Father Bellamy." Antelope pushed his chair back and stood up. "I plan to get his take on Stacey. She was very involved in the church. Care to join me? I'd like *your* take on *him.*"

CHAPTER 24

Our Lady of Sorrows Church was a stately gray stone structure with heavy wooden doors painted bright red.

We entered through the front doors of the church and walked past a corkboard on the wall filled with announcements about upcoming trips and activities. With its strong emphasis on youth and lively social calendar, the parish still managed to retain a large membership while so many other churches were floundering.

We found Father Bellamy outside his office behind the church vestry. When he heard our footsteps on the gravel path, he stubbed out a cigarette.

"You caught me red-handed—a nasty habit for a priest," he said affably. "Don't tell anyone, please; a priest and his image are one and the same."

He led us inside to his private office quarters, an architectural extension of the church. It was a masculine room, dark and cool, with ornate stained glass windows above mahogany walls. A flickering, mottled light played across a red-and-gold-patterned oriental carpet.

"This is Dr. Hunt, Father," Antelope said as we settled into the chairs the priest waved us toward. "She's a clinical psychologist who works for the county and helps out with some of our investigations."

When I worked my first case as a police psychologist, Antelope and I discussed the best way to introduce me when we did interviews together. We came up with this dumbed-down version, vague enough that it didn't create suspicion or invite questions.

"Pleased to meet you, Dr. Hunt," Father Bellamy said, seating himself in a chair facing the two we were occupying. "Detective, welcome. You have good timing; it's time for a break from my reading for next Sunday's sermon. I assume you're here about Stacey Hart. I don't envy your line of work. Like my own, it brings you in contact with the sorrows of the world. At least I also have the opportunity to celebrate the joyful times. How is the investigation going?"

"This early in the case we don't have any solid leads," Antelope said casually. "We're talking to everyone who knew the victim. The more we know about Stacey, the better chance we have of finding her killer."

"How well can anyone know a woman? They're mysterious creatures. Men are from Mars and women are from Venus, right? And in my opinion, Stacey was more elusive than others. I'm not sure I ever knew the real Stacey. That being said, I found her to be a delightful person, friendly and truly caring. I can't imagine anyone would have reason to hurt her."

"How long did you know Stacey?" Antelope asked.

"Since my first year at Our Lady of Sorrows—that would be fifteen years, since I arrived here in 2003. I came fresh out of seminary up in Spokane, wonderful country up there. Such great fortune to get a church of my own as a young priest. Stacey participated in my first Confirmation class. I got to know her quite well—as well as she allowed, that is. She was studious and devout."

"Can you think of anyone who would want to hurt her?"

"I'm going to give you the standard answer I hear on the police shows: she didn't have an enemy in the world until she was murdered."

"Have you given any thought to who might have killed her?"

"I assume it was random. The world is changing, and Rock Springs is changing right along with it. Right across the street we have an adult club drawing patrons from all over the West. It's only my opinion, but the kind of men who travel here for the purpose of seeing naked women may not be the highest-caliber creatures.

If the wrong person walked by late at night and saw Stacey in a house alone, all the lights on, he could be tempted."

"Would she have come to you if she'd been experiencing a problem with someone, if she felt in danger?"

"Now there's a question I can answer. Yes. I've been her confessor since she was a child."

"So it's safe to say she trusted you?"

"I hope so. I believe she trusted me completely as her pastor and confessor."

"But would Stacey really be likely to come to you with a personal problem, Father? You say she was elusive."

"My personal mission is to be the kind of priest my parishioners come to in times of distress. The Church is changing, and a parish priest needs to be accessible to his people. Ask anyone who worships at Our Lady of Sorrows: my door is always open."

"What about Max Hart and Connor Collins?"

"I knew all the altar boys. Max and Connor started serving when they were eight years old, after first communion, and continued right through the summer when they all graduated. Of course, I only came on the scene a few years before that, when they were already teenagers. But all the teens, the entire youth group, took to me. And those young men in particular—Max, Connor, and their friend Tim—took advantage of everything I offered. I thought highly of them—just the best, all of them stars, what a crew! Nothing short of tragic what happened to them." He bowed his head. "I'm sure you know by now about the accident in which Tim lost his life and Stacey's brother sustained brain damage. It was a truly sorrowful time, a very bleak time, for the young people of this church. My relationship with the youth group solidified around the tragedy."

"What about more recently?" Antelope asked. "Did you ever notice anything of concern in Stacey's life?"

The priest pursed his lips, as if thinking, then shook his head. "I know it sounds strange to you. I can tell by the look on your face. But Stacey seemed to lead a charmed existence. She derived strength from her spiritual life. She lived her faith. She was a special person, mature beyond her years—a perfect fiancée for Connor.

The two of them stood out among their generation. No one can say a bad word against either of them. I think you'll find that to be true as you question those who knew Stacey."

I looked at Antelope. His face was impassive; he was giving nothing away.

"Can you tell us about her relationship with her brother?" he asked.

"Close, but rocky. There was a lot of love there despite Max's volatility, his constant moods due to his brain injury. Stacey reacted to all the changes admirably, handled the relationship well, in my opinion."

"How about recently? How rocky would you say things were?"

"I noticed some tension in her. His name came up when we met last week to plan the wedding rehearsal. Stacey made an off-hand comment about how she hoped the two of them would be talking to each other again by the day of the wedding. She wanted him to walk her down the aisle. I didn't get the impression she was seriously worried about it, though."

"I understand Connor Collins went on the camping trip to Flaming Gorge?"

"Perhaps Connor has suffered the most, being the only true survivor of the incident." The priest's forehead creased. "He required countless hours of spiritual counsel for his overwhelming guilt. With the Lord's help, he got through it and became the fine human being we all know him to be. And now this has happened." He expelled a heavy sigh. "Connor knows he has my support. Hopefully, he will take advantage of it and the healing power of the sacraments. He has a long life ahead of him—a very bright future. If only he can remember that through the dark hours of the next days and months and not let his grief take over."

"Your parishioners are fortunate to have you, Father Bellamy," Antelope said.

"When we share our troubles with another, they are made more bearable, as you know, Doctor"—he turned his gaze on me now—"from your own work. When it's paired with spiritual guidance, it's an unstoppable combination. Are you a Catholic, Dr. Hunt?"

"I was baptized in the Church," I said. "My life experience has led me to a spiritual place that doesn't include organized religion."

"One is always saddened to encounter the loss of faith." Father Bellamy pressed his hands together. "But faith is an individual matter, and not something to be coerced. I'm sure you know the Church waits with open arms for the lost. You are always welcome here at Our Lady of Sorrows." He looked at Antelope. "And you, Detective, may I ask your religious affiliation?"

"I don't have one. But like Dr. Hunt, I was baptized in the Catholic Church."

"Interesting, don't you think, that both of you chose work that takes you into the heart of human suffering? Which is another way of saying you witness Satan's power on a daily basis. Two lapsed Catholics doing God's work without God . . . or so you think."

"I understood your question to be about the Church, not about God, Father," I said.

"And that is your mistake, Dr. Hunt, to think it is possible to separate the two."

I smiled slightly. "That's a discussion for another day."

"Thank you for your time, Father," Antelope said, standing. "By the way, I noticed Father Leo Emery from the reservation preached here last month. Will he be coming down again?"

"Yes, he's here the first Sunday of every month. He fills in and frees me to do my missionary work at the prison in Provo, Utah."

"I'll make a point to stop over and say hello. It's been a long time. In the meantime, I'll be back if I think of anything else I want to ask you."

"Agreed, Detective, your important work awaits. A killer walks among us."

CHAPTER 25

It was standard procedure in homicide cases for detectives to attend the victim's funeral. Aside from showing sympathy to the family, it was a time-honored portion of the investigation. Antelope didn't know of any studies that documented how often a killer showed his face at the funeral, but he didn't need science to confirm what his gut told him: Stacey Hart's murderer would be among those who came to pay their final respects.

Funeral parlors all look alike no matter how hard they try to be something else. Chase Brothers Family Funeral Home was built on a concrete-buttressed hillside near the I-80 overpass; it looked like Dracula's castle.

Chase's parking lot was full, so Antelope rode past, surveying the vehicles on the street as he went. He looked for a white van and wondered where Swailes had gone off to.

It was an open-casket funeral. When Antelope approached to pay his respects, he supposed it was Fern Hart who chose to have Stacey buried in her wedding dress.

When he read Charles Dickens's *Great Expectations* in high school, he'd found the story of a woman living a life obsessed with a man who'd deserted her at the altar pathetic and frightening. The idea that love could derail a whole life made him wary of feeling anything for a female. For a long time he'd been haunted by the image of Miss Havisham, the fictional character who wore her gown to tatters.

The high lace collar covered the evidence of the lethal assault—he'd give Mrs. Hart that much. The official copy of the Medical Examiner's report had arrived in his email just before he left the office. "Death by asphyxiation due to manual strangulation" was listed as the cause of death.

Though seeing Stacey in her wedding gown unsettled him, it also focused him on the job of finding her murderer. He made his way back to the entrance of the room and watched a line of mourners pay their respects to Fern and Max Hart, looking at every face, searching for signs of guilt or regret at the sight of the corpse in the coffin.

The job set him apart from the rest of the world at those times when others were part of a community, but he was no stranger to this kind of loneliness. Except for a few loyal people who would never let him go, he'd lost his own community when he left the reservation. The deal was sealed when he signed on with the Sheriff's Department. It's one thing to be a reservation cop, another to join forces with the legal institutions of the white man's world.

By six o'clock, the rush of people coming to pay their respects to the Hart family had slowed down. Father Bellamy arrived at six-thirty and announced that the evening hours would conclude with a prayer service and the holy rosary.

Antelope stepped outside. On the porch, a group of smokers congregated near a large outdoor incinerator decorated with angels. They talked and smoked and laughed like a group of coworkers on break. The night had turned chilly. Above the Green River Cliffs, the sky was a bold rainbow of layered colors that stood in stark contrast to the dark gray sky looming in the east.

He spotted Kelly Ryan in her Volkswagen, parked at the far end of the lot. She exited the car with her cell phone pressed to her ear, and moved slowly toward the parlor, seemingly in no hurry to get inside. She looked up and saw him and he held her gaze as she came toward him; as she passed by him she nodded her head but gave no indication that they were acquainted.

■ ■ ■

Antelope was listening to Mozart's "Don Giovanni" on his cell phone and watching the comings and goings at the entrance of the funeral home when Kelly came out twenty minutes later. At the far end of the porch, she leaned against the filigreed wooden post and lit a cigarette. Blue smoke swirled in the dim light of the dusk. She pulled a black lace shawl tight around her bare shoulders.

A minute later, Max Hart joined her. He stood beside her, their shoulders touching, both of them looking straight ahead into the shadowed woods of Expedition Island. She handed him her cigarette and lit another for herself, then turned and touched his cheek—a tender, intimate gesture, even from a distance. Max bent to kiss her and she let him, only their mouths touching, the red tips of their cigarettes burning in their hands, held at their sides. It lasted a long time; eventually, though, Max broke away and walked back inside.

Kelly finished her cigarette, adjusted her shawl, and scanned the parking lot and the street. She lit another cigarette.

At eight o'clock, the door opened and people started to file out. Kelly joined the group, hurried to her car, and drove off.

The kiss he'd witnessed hadn't been casual. No one he'd spoken to had mentioned Kelly Ryan and Max Hart being in a romantic relationship, now or in the past. He wondered about the need for secrecy, especially among a group of people who'd been openly known to be friends for decades.

And if they didn't want anyone to know about it, they'd taken a huge risk kissing out in the open like that, where they could be easily discovered.

CHAPTER 26

When Kelly left the wake, she didn't feel like going home. She felt afraid to be alone. It was early, and for some strange reason seeing her friend lying dead like that made her want to do something crazy. She wondered if Max would be interested in hooking up. She should be ashamed of herself for thinking about it. In the morning, they would bury his sister.

The strange, long, unexpected kiss they'd shared on the porch had taken her breath away. God, it made her want him. The sex on Saturday night had been so different from any of their other times together—both of them hungry and raw, two lost animals coming together out of need.

The other times they'd hooked up had come about for other reasons; one or the other of them would be lonely or bored to death and would text the other to meet up, have sex, and share a smoke. Afterward, they went right back to what they were doing before. No one got hurt. It worked for both of them. But it didn't feel right to try to go there tonight, though the loneliness felt like a pressure on her heart. This terrible, crushing pain she might have to live with.

As she drove away from the funeral home, her hands shook on the wheel, every nerve in her body switched on. Grief, a physical thing, like an injury, was taking hold of her body. Her sorrow over Tim had come back, piling on top of what she felt for Stacey.

The sight of her friend, so still and white in her wedding gown, had made her feel light-headed and cold. She'd forced herself to stop and give her condolences to Fern and Max, and then she'd hurried out to get some air. After that, she couldn't go back in.

The thought of being alone in her empty house started a queasy feeling in her stomach.

At the entrance to the interstate, she headed east, toward Rock Springs, without a plan, just a need to be away from Green River. She wondered if Max would stay at his place or with his mother.

At the first Rock Springs exit, she followed Dewar Drive and turned up White Mountain Road. After a half mile the paved portion ended and she was on the twisting dirt road that hugged the side of the mountain.

As she rounded the last turn to the summit, headlights flashed in her rearview mirror. A truck came fast around the hairpin turn and rode her tail.

She sped up and he followed. She maneuvered to the right, as far as she could, to let the idiot pass.

But the truck didn't pass; instead, it slid to the right and matched its speed to hers, inches behind her. Her heart beat faster and she made a quick decision to get out of there. There were sixteen miles of backcountry road ahead of her before the intersection with Highway 191.

She hit the gas and her little Volkswagen jumped and spun ahead. She planned to make a quick U-turn at the summit and gun it back down the mountain road.

Behind her, the truck picked up speed too.

She made it to the summit. The moment she had room, she turned her wheel hard to the left. Her tires squealed and she almost lost control of the wheel, but she completed the turn. She started to gun her way out of there—then saw the truck sideways in front of her, blocking the road.

She slammed on her brakes and her engine stalled. Her headlights lit up the side of the truck; the rest of the night was pitch black around her.

Trapped, she restarted the car, put it in reverse—and slammed into a boulder.

She opened the door to run. The passenger door opened as

she started to get out and a rough hand grabbed her arm, pulling her back inside. He caught her wrists in both his hands. Then he laughed and let go.

"What the hell, Jack, you scared the shit out of me!" She broke free and punched his chest with both fists. "What's wrong with you? My friend got murdered! Are you crazy?"

He grabbed her hard by her shoulders, his fingers digging into her bare arms. "Stop it. Relax. Just a little excitement."

"You're hurting me. Let go." She struggled to get free of him.

He held on tight, gave her a shake, and dropped her arms. "Calm down."

She rubbed the places where his fingers had touched her skin. "I'll have bruises tomorrow. You're an animal, Jack. Why do you have to be so rough?"

"You love it."

"There's a time and a place."

"I don't play by the rules, remember?" He cupped her chin in his hand—a familiar gesture, sweet and sincere. "Look at me." He smiled. "Let's start this night over again. Hello, Kelly."

She didn't return his smile. "Why'd you take off? The cops think you did it."

"There's your answer. I saw it going that way and decided not to stick around and land my ass in a jail cell until they figured out they had the wrong guy."

"So why come back?"

"I missed you. You missed me too—twelve missed calls from you."

"The detective wants to know what hotel you saw Connor at in Salt Lake."

"Oh yeah? What else does he know?"

"He's talking to everybody; everything's bound to come out. He said you're a person of interest. If you help him, he'll help you."

"You believe his bullshit?"

"If Connor cheated on Stacey and she found out, maybe they fought and he ended up killing her. He wants to follow up on the thing at the motel. There's no other evidence."

"Val will have my ass." Jack stared out the windshield into the night.

"Why?"

"He owns the place. But, damn, I have to look out for myself first. He taught me that. I saw them at the Spring Grove Motel, but leave out the fact that Val owns it."

"Okay."

"My turn. I kind of need your help. You're the only one I can trust."

"I wish I could say the same about you."

"Do we have to do this again? She's dead. Gone. No threat to you. Stop with the jealousy. People might think you killed her."

"You're crazy. No one would think I killed her. She was my best friend."

"Crime of passion, baby, happens every day. She did you wrong, you lost control, it happens to the best of us."

"She said things had gotten serious for the two of you. How do you think I felt, Jack, hearing that from her?"

"Call me Mr. Right Now. She planned to marry Mr. Right next month. End of story for me."

"What if she broke it off? Would you be with her?"

His eyes hardened. "Why are you doing this? It's over."

"She was my friend and you went after her!"

Jack ran his hands over his face. "I told you, I didn't know about you and her being friends."

"Would it have made a difference?"

He took a deep breath and shook his head. "I'm losing my patience here."

"Would it, though? I need to know you wouldn't knowingly betray me with my best friend."

"You and me, we never made any promises. Be honest. I saw you tonight, out there on the porch with that guy. Don't pull this holier-than-thou bullshit with me. I don't buy the double standard thing."

"A kiss is not the same as sex."

"My mistake." He reached for the door handle.

"You're going?"

"What happened with Stacey doesn't change anything for me. If it does for you, I'll deal with it. I am done with this conversation. You understand me? Done." He lifted her chin again and made her look at him. "Come here." He pulled her to him.

"I've been worried about you," she said, relenting. "I didn't know where you went off to."

"I'm here now." He kissed her.

"What do you need my help with?"

"That's my girl. That's more like it."

He took the phone from his pocket and placed it in her hand.

"What's this?"

"Her phone."

"Stacey's phone? Where did you get it?"

"I found it on the floor."

"I felt so bad when I heard you found her."

"Not your everyday kind of experience."

"Why did you take it?"

"I don't know. I panicked and I took it."

She stared at the phone in her hand. "It's a crime to take evidence."

"Are you on my side or what?"

"Of course I'm on your side."

"I deleted some stuff, nothing important."

Kelly didn't tell him the Sheriff's Department could get Stacey's phone records. She didn't want to set him off. She knew all about Jack's temper, and Detective Antelope had warned her to be careful. The way he'd just ambushed her had made her afraid of him for the first time.

"Give it to the detective," he said. "This is me cooperating."

CHAPTER 27

Father Todd Bellamy drove home to Rock Springs alone. The evening's service had gone well. He'd said a few words about Stacey and her wonderful family and fiancé and led the rosary and closing prayers, everything that was expected of him.

The hardest part of these things for him was being with people when they cried. The sound of sobbing grated on him the way nails on a chalkboard got to other people. And Fern Hart had cried with abandon, clutching at Max and Connor like they could save her from falling into the abyss of grief.

It got so bad, her moans had gotten so loud, that he'd gone to her and whispered that she might want to leave and compose herself. At that, the waterworks had turned off.

He'd wanted a minute with Connor but hadn't managed to make it happen. Stacey's mother and brother had pulled him close and wouldn't let him go, or let anyone else in. To be expected. Still, it irked him, because of his importance in Stacey and Connor's life. He'd hoped his special connection with the couple would be acknowledged by the family tonight.

In the center console, he found his cigarette case and lighter. He inhaled the first drag of an American Spirit, and his irritation faded. He most enjoyed smoking in the car and in the bath, where he could indulge at leisure in his guilty habit. Only occasionally did he allow himself the pleasure in other places.

It annoyed him that the detective and psychologist had

discovered his weakness. It would be important in the coming days to maintain control over his image and credibility. He knew how these investigations went. A small seed of doubt in a lawman's head, and a person could be under the microscope for months.

The life of a priest was inherently lonely. Everyone else in that mournful place tonight had gone home with someone to share the sadness with and find comfort in the sharing. Not Todd.

And now Connor knew aloneness. He worried about him. Stacey had always been the stronger of the two, and now she was gone. His unique role as the couple's spiritual counselor had allowed him to watch their relationship evolve. Over time, Connor had become increasingly dependent, insecure, and controlling. Stacey had confided in him about the burden many times.

Unfortunately, his best advice, to step down and let Connor take the lead, had created some balance in their partnership—which did not sit well with Stacey. Looking back, it was clear that their relationship had been on a collision course for some time.

In the end, her strength had ruined everything. Nothing he did or said could have changed the course of events. Stacey, stubborn and determined; Connor, uncertain and hesitant. Could it have ended any other way?

They were his parishioners, his spiritual children, and also his friends. He'd tried to do right by them, and he'd failed.

All his life, he'd found it hard to make friends. His mother had always said others envied him and all the gifts God had bestowed on him—his looks, his intellect, his superior athletic ability. She said someday he would find friends of his caliber: quality people, people worthy of him.

After he was ordained, he found a way to be comfortable with others. The young people of the parish had needed guidance and attention, and they'd looked up to him.

A depressed young teen when he met her, Stacey Hart had welcomed his interest. As her priest, he'd offered spiritual guidance and comfort—and, when she grew older, friendship. The grief he felt over her death he would now manage on his own, with only prayer to sustain him.

He'd chosen this life, though, and he'd never once regretted it, even on the hardest days. The particular difficulties of life in the priesthood suited him better than the life of a layperson. He smiled, pleased with himself, relishing the comfort of self-awareness.

Still, a sense of unease lingered; he hadn't seen this terrible thing coming—a life taken, a life story ended. What else waited ahead, out of sight, out of his control?

CHAPTER 28

The funeral procession left Our Lady of Sorrows Church on Broadway and traveled up the South Side Belt Route to the back entrance of the Rock Springs Municipal Cemetery. The route bypassed Cedar Street and the house where Stacey Hart was murdered.

The historic cemetery was lush and serene, planted with flowering trees and ornamental bushes—the greenest spot in an arid, high desert town. I parked under a sprawling cottonwood tree and stepped out of my car. It was twelve noon and heat rose in waves off the black asphalt lanes.

I'd never met Stacey. Max had asked me to come. Even after a year in treatment, it had taken a lot for him to ask.

I joined the others at the gravesite. Detective Antelope stood at a distance from the circle of mourners. I knew he wanted a vantage point from which to watch all who came to say goodbye to Stacey—hard to do if he was right in the middle of things. He'd called earlier to set up plans to meet for lunch at the Village Inn after the funeral.

Father Todd Bellamy said the final prayers. Max held a basket of long-stemmed white roses, which Fern distributed to the assembled guests. After the mourners tossed the flowers on the bronze casket and the service was over, Max led his mother to the limousine. He nodded to me as he walked by. Tomorrow morning, the process of working through his grief and anger would continue.

One by one, the vehicles rolled away. Only a couple of people stayed to watch as they lowered Stacey Hart into the ground. The afternoon wind came up right on schedule, carrying the sweet smell of the funeral flowers into the air.

I walked to my car before the gravediggers finished the hard work of burying Stacey Hart. A gentle wind rustled through the trees, making a muted sound like the lazy shuffle of playing cards. Antelope was still standing and watching them as I drove away.

CHAPTER 29

Antelope hadn't spotted any new faces at the church. A smaller group had made it to the cemetery. Scruggs was there as the official representative of the Sweetwater County Sheriff's Department.

Antelope watched from the shade of a cottonwood tree, studying each face closely. If the killer was going to pay final respects to Stacey, this graveside service would be the last chance.

The women from the Our Lady of Sorrows Convent were all in attendance in formal habits, heavy black robes, and white surplice collars. Standing close together, they looked like one single unit rather than individual women. It reminded him a field of birch trees that shared the same DNA: if one of the trees was cut down, there would be no need to plant a seed; it would sprout back from another tree on its own.

Father Bellamy officiated, of course. Toni Atwell was there, but she stood apart from the rest of the mourners, keeping a distance between her and the sisters and the sheriff, too. She might have been mistaken for a security guard in her navy blue pantsuit and dark glasses.

Kelly Ryan arrived alone and joined the prayer circle. She wore the same long black dress and black lace scarf she'd donned for the visiting hours at the funeral parlor. Her polished toes gleamed red in the green grass.

When the prayers began, she pulled the scarf up to cover her head and exposed a bruise on her right shoulder that Antelope hadn't noticed the night before. She turned her face away as the casket was lowered into the ground. She spoke to nobody and no one spoke to her as the prayers ended and the crowd dispersed under the weak morning sun.

Besides the gravediggers, he was now alone in the cemetery. White flower arrangements, cross and heart shapes, surrounded the open grave.

He was about to leave his post, leave Stacey in her grave, when a truck pulled up and parked.

It slowed and stopped; the door opened. A male stepped out, hand on the open door. He took one step toward the gravesite, did a quick scan of the surroundings. Jeans and a black sweatshirt—hood up—and sunglasses. He must have felt someone watching. He stepped back inside, slammed the door, and sped away.

Antelope raced down the hill and got a look at the license plate before the truck squealed around the corner and disappeared from sight. He radioed Sweetwater County dispatch, read off the numbers, and ordered an all points interstate bulletin put out on the Dodge Ram, white, with Utah plates. He was sure it was Jack Swailes.

As he walked to his car, a yellow Volkswagen sped toward him. It stopped, bucked, and stalled out when Kelly yanked the emergency brake.

"Got something for you, Detective," she said when he leaned toward the open window. She handed him a brown paper bag.

He spotted a bruise on her left shoulder—an exact match for the one he'd spotted earlier on her right. He lifted the bag. "What is it?"

"Jack wants you to know he's cooperating with the investigation. It's Stacey's phone."

"Did he do that? I warned you not to see him." He pointed to her arm. "Are you okay? I'm sorry I put you in this situation."

"I kind of didn't have a choice. He came to me." She shrugged. "Remember I told you about the tracking app? She downloaded it."

"Good work. We've been looking for this."

"He deleted some things. Probably love messages between him and Stacey. But you guys can get those records, right?"

"I already put in a request for the voicemail transcript."

"Don't you want to ask me something?" She twirled a section of hair around her finger.

"You got the name of the motel?"

"It's the Spring Grove Motel. And oh, here's a little something extra—Val Campion owns the place."

He thanked her and she drove away.

There was no point hanging around the cemetery. He'd like to go after the Dodge, but he didn't have a clue which direction it had gone in, and he'd lost time talking to Kelly. The road to the cemetery came out on a highway that bypassed Rock Springs's business district. The interstate highway exits were less than a quarter of a mile away.

He cruised around for a while. No white Dodge Rams on the road. He checked some parking lots in the area; no luck. He was gone.

He gave up and drove over to the Village Inn to meet with Pepper Hunt.

CHAPTER 30

I was sitting at the corner table Antelope and I both favored—the one with the view of White Mountain—when he arrived.

"Sorry I'm late," he said, sliding into the booth. "I almost got run over by a yellow Volkswagen."

"Who was it?"

"Kelly Ryan—Stacey's best friend, or so she says. She cut out of the funeral early, then came back to give me something."

"And you're going to tell me what, after pausing for dramatic effect?"

"It's Stacey Hart's phone."

"Why did Kelly have it?"

"She claims Jack Swailes paid her a surprise visit last night and gave it to her."

"I thought he left town."

"He came back. But he's gone again."

"What's her connection to Jack Swailes?"

"Kelly has a secret life. She met Swailes at the Astro Lounge, she's a dancer there. His uncle owns the place. She said what happened between them was a hookup, but I'm getting a different vibe."

My mind went into overdrive. "She wanted Jack for herself? She killed Stacey because she was jealous?"

"I wouldn't rule it out at this point. I've just upgraded her to 'person of interest.'"

"You don't think she's credible?"

"She didn't tell me she worked at the Astro or knew Swailes. She didn't let on to Stacey about her and Swailes. And she never indicated any romantic connection with Max Hart, past or present. I saw the two of them together last night, and from the way they kissed I'm sure it wasn't the first time."

Max and Kelly? This was news to me. "So you're wondering what else she isn't saying."

"She's a master at deception. I didn't get it at first. I usually pick up on that kind of thing."

"You don't like being wrong. Neither do I. As a therapist, I get to hear all the secrets—at least, that's the delusion I operate under. But Max has never said a word about anything romantic with Kelly. He's only talked about her as a friend from the past."

"Different situation, though. He holds back on you, and he stays a sick puppy. She holds back on me, a murderer goes free."

"Possibly."

"I'm being dramatic?"

"Possibly."

"And self-important."

"Yes. But your work is important. And hard. You don't need someone intentionally misleading you, whatever reason she might have to do so."

"I have to trust Kelly enough to follow up on some information she gave me. According to her, Swailes spotted Connor going into a no-tell motel with another man. He passed the info on to Stacey. I have no corroboration for this, haven't even questioned Mr. Collins about it. He's due at my office in an hour. But I might hold off on that line of questioning for now. I've got bigger fish to fry with him."

I leaned forward, intrigued. "Can you tell me?"

"I went back to Cedar Street the night of the murder. It was dumb luck, but I found Stacey's engagement ring on the ground. Like she took it off and tossed it."

"He hasn't said anything that would indicate she was in that frame of mind?"

"He admits they argued about Swailes and he asked her to fire him, and she wasn't happy about it. Otherwise, he's sticking to the lovebirds in paradise theme."

"You have your work cut out for you."

"I'll follow up on the Salt Lake angle when I have some facts. I have the name of the motel. I don't want to tip Connor off and give him time to get the hotel and destroy any records they might have. For the time being, he can relax and think he's in the clear about his activities there."

I raised my eyebrows. "That was fast. How did you narrow down the motel?"

"Kelly Ryan got it out of Swailes last night."

"He's being so helpful. What's his motivation?"

"He could be our killer, looking for Connor to take the fall."

"He left town; why not just keep going?"

"Probably figures it's only a matter of time until he makes a mistake and someone spots him and calls it in. I put out an all-points bulletin for surrounding states the day of the murder."

"You have the name of the motel; what will you do now?"

"A year ago I'd have taken a drive down there and asked to see the register and security footage. By law they have to keep ninety days of records. But there's a recent change in the law that makes it more difficult. Not impossible. But I do need a warrant showing reasonable cause. It's on my to-do list. Here's the interesting thing, though: the Spring Grove Motel is owned by Val Campion."

"His name keeps coming up."

"He's a shady guy with fingers in a lot of dirty business. It would be an honor to take him down, but right now I'm not seeing a way he connects to Stacey other than through Kelly and Swailes."

"Do you think Swailes could be holed up at the Spring Grove?" I asked. "Probably not, he'd be stupid to give up the name."

He looked at me and picked up his phone. Within minutes, he was on the line with the sheriff's department in Salt Lake. They agreed to send someone undercover to the Spring Grove Motel to see if there was any sign of Swailes. If not, they'd set up a watch for the next forty-eight hours. If he showed, they'd take him into custody. If not, they'd reevaluate the situation.

Antelope was shaking his head when he got off the phone. "I'm going to spend some time figuring out how I missed that, Doc."

"It's Kelly Ryan," I said, shooting him a wicked smile. "She gets you off track. You said it yourself: sexual chemistry short circuits the brain."

CHAPTER 31

Back at the county building, Antelope stopped in to see Scruggs before his meeting with Connor Collins. The sheriff was at his desk with a bowl of taco salad and a sweet tea in front of him.

"I hate funerals, and this one didn't do anything to change my mind," he said. "Pull up a chair and fill me in on the latest."

"I've got the Connor Collins interview in five minutes."

"Somehow this got routed to me by mistake," Scruggs said, rummaging through a stack of papers.

"You're still the man in charge."

"I don't need to be bogged down in details. Where is the damn thing now?" Scruggs slapped the desk. "Ahh, I can't find it. It's a note from Forensics saying they'll have the DNA back on the cigarette butts from Cedar Street soon. Not exactly earth-shaking. Why don't they stop wasting time documenting stuff they're going to do and do it? Might get us what we need to do our jobs."

"I can't disagree."

"But you're not gonna get worked up about it, either. Probably why my heart needed some new hardware. I sweat the small stuff too much. Did Toni offer anything useful?"

"She said Max Hart, Connor Collins, and Timothy Ryan were all sexually abused as altar boys by Father Gerard Kroll. He's the guy Bellamy replaced. Whether that has any bearing on current circumstances, I don't know. Toni says he knew about it, and he kept it secret from the nuns who taught at the school and from the parishioners. I don't know enough about church policies on these matters. Is it suspicious, or is it standard operating procedure? He was chosen to create a new culture and heal the wounds with the affected families. He seems to have fulfilled the expectations."

"These churchgoers are real sheep, aren't they?" Scruggs wrinkled his forehead. "How'd they keep the families quiet?"

"Financial settlement, with the condition they don't speak about the incidents."

"As if money can fix perversions. I know how I'd react." Scruggs's voice was growing louder by the second. "I'd tell the perverts where they could stick their cash and be on every talk radio and television station that would have me. The church be damned. What good is a church that allows this kind of evil to go on?"

"Like I said," Antelope said calmly, "I'm not seeing the connection, but the fact that the sister of one of the victims was murdered makes me want to look a little deeper. It's too much coincidence for someone who doesn't believe in coincidence."

Scruggs nodded. "Find out how much the payout was—and what they did with the money."

CHAPTER 32

Connor parked under a cottonwood tree in the lot beside the Sweet-water County Building. He hated getting into a hot car. The yellow brick building, adjacent to the county cemetery, looked haunted, like something out of a horror movie.

Behind the building, the headstones of the cemetery, rows and rows of white granite, stretched as far as he could see. Stacey was in the ground at the far corner, unthinkable. Earlier, in the back of the grotesque hearse, the thought had struck him that as her fiancé, it was wrong to leave her.

Always weak when it counts. He couldn't face the truth of her death.

Nor would he visit the grave—no point, and his thoughts would go to a bad place.

Exhaustion fell over him like a sudden onset of the flu; his limbs were heavy and aching. Sleep eluded him, though he'd tried with every trick he knew to knock himself out for the last couple of nights. His face in the mirror showed the strain of grief and sleep deprivation: dark circles under his eyes and a lifeless, blank stare. He finished off the water bottle he was holding. Hydration might help. One thought brought relief: After today, there would be no one watching, and he could do it his way. With the funeral and the public grieving over, he planned to drink himself into oblivion tonight.

Too many bad associations to the cemetery caused him to avoid going there—his parents, Tim. He couldn't forget what had happened; the memory followed him like a shadow.

He sat for a minute in the cool of the air-conditioned car, not wanting to face the next hour or however long the detective would keep him, haranguing him with the same questions. He knew the drill, could practically write the script. For the first time, he wondered if he'd made the wrong decision choosing law as a profession. The last few days had showed him another view of the legal system. His position as assistant prosecutor offered no protection. His boss had called as soon as he heard about the murder and said all the right things. But as far as he could tell, the Sheriff's Department was treating him like any other significant other—boyfriend, fiancé, or husband—of a murder victim. The crime statistics pointed law enforcement in the direction of the one closest to the victim.

He got out of the car and immediately felt like he'd stepped into an oven. He worked up a sweat on the short walk from the parking lot. Before walking through the front door, he wiped his face and neck with a monogrammed handkerchief—a Christmas gift from Stacey.

When he entered the old building, he immediately wanted to flee. An insane idea, bordering on cruel, Detective Antelope's push for a meeting the same day as Stacey's funeral. But he had agreed to it—reluctantly, and only to show cooperation and avoid a pissing contest with an overzealous homicide detective.

The first floor housed the county jail and a security checkpoint to get to the Sheriff's Department offices on the third floor. He set off the security alarm before being cleared to enter. The guard instructed him to remove his watch and ring for the security screening. Connor argued—unsuccessfully—that as a member of the court, he shouldn't have to remove the items. He recognized the futility of the request, but his protest gave him a chance to let off some steam with the guards and defuse whatever attitude he might bring into the interview upstairs, where keeping his cool mattered.

He took the elevator to the third floor and presented himself to the Sheriff's Department secretary. Before he turned away to sit down, Detective Antelope appeared and nodded for him to follow. They went to a small office: a desk, two chairs, and a filing cabinet.

The one window faced west and looked out at the front lawn of the building, which was still in shadow.

The detective motioned for him to take the only available chair. "Good morning, Mr. Collins. I appreciate you coming in. It can't be easy after the shock of the last few days. But I'm sure you know from your training and practice as an attorney, the sooner we pick up the trail, the more likely it is we'll solve this. You must want that as much as we do. That being said, I'll be making a video and audio recording of our conversation this afternoon."

"With all due respect, your request to meet today, especially here, surprised me," Connor said. "I thought our meeting at my home on Saturday indicated my strong motivation to work with you. The formality of the setting is off-putting, to say the least. But, of course, whatever you need to do to move forward with the investigation, you can count on my continued cooperation with the process."

"Glad to hear you understand. It's a matter of documenting progress in the case. Have a seat and we can get started."

The detective turned on the recording devices and entered the identifying information. "In an interview on Saturday, June 21, you stated you believe Jack Swailes, the contractor hired to renovate your home, murdered your fiancée, Stacey Hart. Please state for the record the reasons behind your conclusion."

"Motive and opportunity," Connor said firmly. "He worked at the house every day and met with Stacey every day to review the progress of his work. As I expressed to you on Saturday, I observed his manner of conversation, which I described as flirtatious. After discussion with me, Stacey planned to terminate his work on the house. It's my opinion that the termination resulted in feelings of rejection and in that state of mind, Swailes became angry and aggressive and attacked her. As I'm sure you are now aware, he has a history of violence. I have access to the same criminal database as the Sheriff's Department; his record shows two prior domestic assault charges."

"You own the house on Cedar Street?"

"Yes, I inherited it from my parents. I rented through the years and the income paid for my living expenses in college and law school. When Stacey and I got engaged at Christmas, she indicated that she wanted to live there. I had planned to sell it, but once she brought it up, it started to seem like a sound financial idea. After six years of tenants, it needed a lot of work. Stacey took on the job of getting estimates for the work. It took about a month, and we hired Swailes at the end of January. I only learned after the fact that she hadn't made the decision in the most thorough way. Other than that one lapse in judgment, we were a team. I had all the funds and she did all the work on the project."

"Did Stacey supervise the work or did the two of you do it together?"

"It was all Stacey, and she was great at it. Most women would be intimidated supervising the work of men, especially the kind of men who work in construction."

"You didn't have any concerns about Stacey spending a lot of time alone with a man in an empty house?"

"Not at first, but as I said, I started to pick up something not right about Swailes—the way he looked at her, talked to her, set up these private jokes between them."

"When did you notice it?"

"A few months ago, I can't give you an exact date. It's been going on for a while. At first I hoped it would stop. Some balls on him; the cocky bastard did it right in front of me, like an animal acting on instinct, some inborn primate thing, trying to attract the female though she belonged to someone else. Stacey didn't see it the same way. We argued about it, and like I said, on Friday I put my foot down and told her he had to go."

"Stacey didn't see his behavior in the same way you did?"

"Clueless." Connor threw up his hands. "She loved his work, how they worked together, his dependability. True, as far as it went, he did quality work. No way would I have kept paying him otherwise. The guy showed up when he said and I get it, most of the time it doesn't work like that. She felt she could count on him. After a while, though, I began to put it together. Of course he's there doing everything he can to make her happy. He wanted her—all part of the plan."

"But you let it go on for months?"

"I trusted Stacey after all our years together. You didn't know her, but she happened to be a gorgeous woman; everywhere we went, men looked at her. I'd dealt with the situation for years. I felt confident if Swailes made a move on her, Stacey would have no problem putting him in his place and ending the whole thing, job and all, immediately. I never micromanaged her relationship with me, ever."

"You told her to fire Swailes. You thought it was best she handle it? Why not meet with the man and do it yourself?"

"Not so easy to do with my fiancée. Any hint of me taking control away from her got to be a problem. She lived with a control freak for a mother her whole life. I understood that, she helped me see control could be a big issue for her. But we argued on Friday. I was adamant I wanted him gone, out of our house and our life. In the end, Stacey respected my feelings and accepted the decision. She wanted to do it herself. Now I see the problem with the plan. I wish I had thought to check his criminal history before. I'm kicking myself for not doing it."

"Did you know she planned to meet him at the Cedar Street house on Saturday?"

"Just as I didn't micromanage her relationships, I also did not micromanage her schedule. We didn't talk about it. So no, I didn't know about her plans to meet him Saturday morning. Why do you ask?"

"I'm trying to understand how things worked in your relationship with Stacey. Other than the issue with Swailes, was there anything else you argued about?"

"No, nothing. We had a perfect relationship with excellent communication, apart from the problem with him."

"I have a message here from the property room. They received a request from Chase's Funeral Home; they called on your behalf requesting the release of Stacey's engagement ring."

"It's an expensive ring. I followed the recommendations in these matters and spent two months' salary on it, only the best for Stacey. I'm sure you can understand why I didn't want it buried with her. But Chase never received it, and they told me to follow up here. When can you release it to me?"

Antelope opened the top drawer of his desk, removed a photo, and slid it toward Connor.

Connor leaned forward to see. It was a shot of Stacey's left hand, clearly taken at the crime scene.

Antelope pointed to the ring finger. "As you can see in this photograph, taken at the crime scene on Saturday morning, there is no engagement ring."

"The motherfucker stole her ring? What are you doing to find him?"

"It's possible, I suppose. But why would he throw away a valuable ring?"

Antelope opened the drawer again and removed another item. He placed a plastic envelope on the desk and pointed to the time and date stamp. "Can you identify this as the engagement ring you purchased and gave to Stacey Hart?"

Connor wanted to grab the bag out of his hand. Six thousand dollars, a perfect two-carat diamond, caked with dried mud. "Yes," he croaked. "That's Stacey's ring."

"This ring was found in the front garden of the Cedar Street house on Saturday evening, and was officially entered into evidence on June 21," Antelope said. "Perhaps Swailes put it there. Another possibility is Stacey took it off and threw it there herself. It's the kind of thing a woman does in extreme anger. I asked about other things the two of you fought about. What would make her mad enough to break off your engagement?"

Connor wondered how much he could disclose and still maintain control of the situation. The detective would interview other people who might say things that would put him in a bad light. He took a deep breath and decided to go for it. Nobody could prove anything.

"Let me preface this by saying this is not easy for me to talk about. Both Stacey and I were intensely private about our relationship. I don't know why, but she thought I'd cheated on her. She claimed someone told her I had hooked up with someone else. I vote for Swailes here—guessing he was trying to make himself look good. I guess it's possible she took off her ring, but I swear to you, she didn't break off the engagement. If she was still alive, this ring would be on her finger."

CHAPTER 33

Todd returned to the rectory after the funeral service, where he removed his clerical collar and the black shirt and pants, heavy garments for a summer day. Exhaustion, emotional rather than physical, had sapped his energy, and he knew the remedy.

Ten minutes later, in khakis and sneakers, his swim trunks and goggles in a gym bag, he headed to the pool at the Preserve for a swim. Typically, the upscale complex didn't give out guest passes, but Connor had used his influence and powers of persuasion and gotten one for him. Of course, his status as a member of the clergy had undoubtedly worked to his advantage as well.

When he first moved to Rock Springs as a young priest, he'd been wary about showing his true self to the conservative community. Comfortable in his body, he enjoyed challenging himself physically every day. Most of the other seminarians he trained with lived in their minds; they were cerebral and intellectual types, some of them nerds, all of them naturally book smart, while he had to push himself to get the grades that came so easily his friends. In the end, though, he got those grades. He wasn't an intellectual and he wasn't going to feel bad about it.

He changed into his swimsuit, slicked back his hair, and slid on his bathing cap. When he looked at his body in the mirror, he liked what he saw. At forty-two years old, he was in the best shape of his life, if he did say so himself.

But he didn't have to rely on his own assessment. He saw the way women and men looked at him at the pool when he worked out. It pleased him to think he could have anyone he wanted, though he would never act on it. According to the church, a prideful act, his enjoyment of others' attraction to him, but he gave in to the guilty pleasure. In a world full of evil, his minor sin counted for small change, not worthy of his concern.

CHAPTER 34

Antelope left the station and drove to Our Lady of Sorrows Church. The housekeeper, Sister Julia, answered the front door of the rectory.

"Good afternoon, Detective. Are you here to speak with Father Bellamy?"

"I have more questions, if he can spare a few minutes of his time."

"I'm afraid he's not here. He's worn out from the funeral service."

"Where might I find him?"

"He's gone for a swim."

"Where does he swim, at White Mountain or downtown?"

"Usually he'll go to the Recreation Center, but in summer he prefers to swim outside. He's got a guest pass over at the Preserve."

"That's the apartment complex where Connor Collins lives, isn't it? I didn't realize they had guest memberships there."

"I don't believe they do. Connor set it up special for Father because he likes being outdoors so much. And he needs all the relaxation he can get after what he's been through with Stacey and Connor." She shook her head. "Frankly, I don't know how he does it."

"Thank you, I won't take up any more of your time today."

He drove straight to the Preserve and parked where he could observe the activity at the pool. Father Bellamy walked out of the locker room a few minutes later. When he spotted Antelope, he waved and held up a hand, indicating that he should wait. He disappeared into the office and a few minutes later came out with the manager of the pool.

"Good afternoon, Detective. I wasn't expecting to see you. It's been a stressful, exhausting time for all of us. But I guess the policeman's work is never done. I arranged with Jeffrey here to find us a small conference room to meet in and he obliged us, thank you very much, Jeffrey."

"No problem, Father," the manager said brightly. "Follow me, it's right down here. Will Mr. Collins be joining you also?"

"No, not today, it will be the two of us, thank you. Oh and some ice water would be very welcome, Jeffrey."

The pool manager gave a salute and went off to get the water.

"To what do I owe this honor, Detective?" Father Bellamy asked, turning his smile on Antelope. "I thought you got what you needed the last time we met?"

"A few more questions, Father. Thank you for your time. I know it's been a long day for you."

"A sad day, most certainly. Stacey's been laid to rest. Now the real grieving can begin for her poor family."

"I'm sure the family appreciated you going down there to officiate."

"I didn't realize you were there. I spotted the sheriff, expected to see you. I don't know how I missed you in such a small group."

"I made it my business to stay out of sight."

"Thinking the killer might show his face, were you?"

Antelope shrugged. "It happens."

"Did he?"

"I'd be down at the station questioning him right now if he had."

Bellamy sighed. "No luck for you today. Let's hear those questions."

Jeffrey knocked on the door before entering. Bellamy waved him in; he placed a pitcher and two glasses on the table, and then left them alone.

Antelope waited until the door closed before he began. "Did you know Father Kroll?"

Bellamy's eyes widened slightly. "What's he got to do with your investigation?"

"Before I leave here today, the reason for my questions will become clear. Right now, though, I need you to answer them for me."

"All right, you've made your point. Father Kroll celebrated forty years in this parish and moved to a smaller church. I replaced him as pastor. We never served together. There was no overlap. So the answer is simple and clear: I don't know Father Kroll at all."

"This will be a difficult question perhaps. Are you aware of any allegations of sexual misconduct against Father Kroll?"

"It's not a difficult question, Detective. It's an absurd question. It doesn't deserve an answer but I'll give you one. I am not aware of any allegations of sexual misconduct against Father Kroll. And further, if I had heard any such allegations, I wouldn't believe them. Father Kroll is above such egregious behavior."

"How can you be so sure when you stated you don't know the man? This kind of behavior remains an ongoing problem within the Catholic priesthood, as I'm sure you know."

"I'm aware of this scourge upon the clergy." Bellamy's face was growing red. "It's a sadness and an utter disgrace. Is this where you tell me the reason for you coming here today?"

"We received some information indicating that Father's Kroll's transfer wasn't voluntary—that it was hastened by reports of sexual behavior with minor children. Are you saying you were not made aware of these allegations at the time you took over from him?"

"I was never informed of anything of the kind. Who made the allegation, if I may ask? And what does it have to do with Stacey being murdered? We're talking about fifteen years ago."

"I'm not at liberty to say," Antelope said mildly. "Presumably, though, the victims remained in the parish. Has anyone ever told you they were molested by Father Kroll?"

"Never. I can assure you, I would have followed the guidelines set up by the Church in regard to these unsavory matters. We are all educated and aware today, as we were not in the past, about the proper way to respond."

"Does the Church tell you not to discuss these cases?"

"What do you mean?"

"I have it on good authority that three altar boys were molested by Father Kroll and that's why he was transferred out of Our Lady of Sorrows. The Church subsequently made financial settlements with the families of the three victims. This happened right before you became pastor. You must have known. You said you have a knack for connecting with the young people in the church. Did any of them talk to you about being sexually abused?"

"I pride myself on my ability to read people. I can honestly say, in all the years I've been working with the children and adolescents in this parish, I have never thought any one of them had ever experienced such a traumatic betrayal."

"Sounds like I'm at a dead end here. Thank you for your time, Father."

"You've put me in a foul mood I'm afraid," Bellamy said, pushing back his chair. "This whole sexual abuse thing turns my stomach. If you haven't got any more questions for me, you'll excuse me while I indulge in my swim. I need it even more now."

"I didn't realize the Preserve offered memberships to the community."

"They don't. Connor worked his magic and secured a seasonal pass for me. I'm forever indebted to him."

"The two of you are pretty close, it seems."

"When I first came to this parish, Connor was a lost soul. It would be tough for any child to be orphaned at five. Connor was a sensitive boy; I sensed he wouldn't make it without some guidance. I saw it as my pastoral duty to take him under my wing. He remains grateful and repays the support every chance he gets."

■ ■ ■

Antelope stopped at the Burger Bar on his way back to the office and picked up two cheeseburgers and a vanilla shake for dinner. As always, when he worked a murder case, his meals consisted mostly of fast food.

The route took him past the church, the Astro Lounge, and

the house on Cedar Street—the small radius in which the story of the crime was playing out.

He ate at his desk quickly, eager to spend some time with Stacey Hart's phone and cull any secrets the electronic device held. When he finished, he opened the file containing the printed pages downloaded from the tracking app. It didn't look like much, just two pages detailing Connor Collins's travel in the BMW for six weeks, beginning May 13 and ending June 21.

He wondered how Stacey felt when she did it—the whole process, from the point of decision to the execution. A combination of sadness and a secret thrill, the truth about the man she loved revealed? Did she want to know the truth? Confirmation of his deception and betrayal would have meant the end of her future with him.

He opened the folder and went through the information line by line. Stacey had acted fast on Kelly's suggestion. She'd begun tracking Connor's whereabouts the day after meeting with Kelly.

On Tuesday, May 13, recordings of the location of the BMW began.

Antelope read each date entry methodically.

Weekday mornings he traveled from the Preserve to his office in the Sweetwater County Building on US Highway 191.

Weekday mornings he traveled to and from the office to the county courthouse in Green River.

Weekday afternoons he traveled to and from his office or the District Court to local restaurants.

He made three trips each week to Our Lady of Sorrows Church, including on Sunday, presumably for Mass.

Every Saturday, he traveled to the Cedar Street house, with the exception of Saturday, June 7.

On Friday, June 6, he traveled to Evanston, Wyoming, and returned on Sunday, June 8.

There were no trips to Salt Lake City.

Antelope flipped to Friday, June 20. Connor told him he'd met Stacey at Johnny Mac's Good Time Tavern, and that he'd gone straight home after they argued.

The tracking device showed him leaving the tavern at 9:10 p.m. He arrived at 2276 Reagan Avenue at 9:27 p.m.

At 10:30 p.m., he left 2276 Reagan Avenue and drove to Our Lady of Sorrows Church.

Collins had intentionally and willfully provided false information when he said he went home after leaving Johnny Mac's Tavern the night Stacey was murdered.

From the first day of the case, he'd had a bad feeling about Connor, but he'd kept it in check in the absence of any real reason to distrust the man. Now his instincts were beginning to seem more credible.

As an attorney, an assistant prosecutor for the county, Connor would have understood the problem he was creating for himself in providing false information during the investigation of a homicide. Whatever reason he had for concealing his visit to the church, it must be very important.

Antelope spent another hour reading the text messages Stacey Hart had sent and received in the week before her death, as well as scrolling through her call log.

As he expected based on what Kelly had said about Swailes deleting messages, he found no evidence of communication between Stacey Hart and Jack Swailes.

The phone log confirmed what Collins had told him: Stacey's last phone call was to her fiancé at 1:17 a.m.

The only other activity in the call log was an incoming call at 10:05 p.m. from a number he recognized as belonging to Max Hart.

Max never mentioned placing a call to his sister on the last night of her life.

CHAPTER 35

It was late afternoon, long after my last patient left the office, the last light of day soft at the western windows, when Fern Hart called. I debated whether to let the call go to voicemail. Given the recent circumstances, however—her daughter murdered, her son falling apart—I decided to go with the personal touch and answer.

Professional ethics and HIPAA laws are designed for maximum protection of patient confidentiality. Max Hart had never given me permission to communicate about his treatment with his mother. Quite often, though, patients' families have information important to the safety of the patient. The laws and standards have evolved to allow psychotherapists to listen to what a family member says, as long as we don't give any information in return.

"This is Dr. Hunt," I answered.

"Hello, Dr. Hunt, this is Fern Hart, I'm calling about my son Max. I know you can't tell me he's your patient, but I know he is. I didn't know if I would get you directly or if I'd have to leave a message. Is it okay if I go on? I mean, do you have time now, or should I call back and leave a message?"

"Now is fine," I said. "I have a little time. What is it you want to tell me?"

"I wouldn't bother you except I'm very concerned about Max. I've never felt the need to call before. But he's not been himself since my daughter was killed. I suppose you need me to be specific.

He's been sleeping a lot. I know this because he tells me he was sleeping whenever he manages to pick up the phone. He isn't meeting with any of his training clients."

"He's taking some time off from work?"

"You make it sound so normal. Of course he needs time. It's not even a week since Stacey died . . . I don't know, maybe I'm being dramatic to be concerned."

"Is there something else?"

"He's very shut down, very inward focused. And he can get lost inside himself. This kind of slip into isolation never ends well for him. The way he gets out of it is always through some forceful acting out."

"I'm not sure I understand."

"Of course not, I'm being vague and unhelpful. Maybe a few examples will help. Maybe he told you about his record—three separate assault charges, hundreds of dollars in fines, anger management classes twice. Those incidents happened after a period of depression, like what he's going through now."

"Tell me more."

"He starts drinking and ends up attacking someone in a rage. Twice it's been a man, and the last time it was a woman. People at the party told police the girl provoked him; he tried to walk away but she got in front of him and threw a pitcher of beer in his face. But still, there's no excuse for what he did."

"What did he do?"

"He grabbed her by the arms and pushed her away from him; she fell and hit her head pretty bad on the floor."

"And what happened with the two males he assaulted?"

"Same kind of circumstance—he was drunk, someone said the wrong thing, and he started swinging. With one of the men, there was a bottle involved; Max broke it over his head."

"You're worried he's going to hurt someone."

"Yes."

At the time Max entered treatment, in the process of taking his history I'd gotten all the details about the events Fern Hart was relaying to me now, so none of this was coming as a surprise. In part because of his tendency toward violence when intoxicated, Max had voluntarily quit drinking and entered recovery with Alcoholics Anonymous. Before Stacey's death the previous week, he'd had five years of sobriety. To my knowledge, his anger had never escalated to include violent behavior when he was sober.

"Is there anything else you want to share, Mrs. Hart?"

"I don't know if you noticed, because you only see him once a week, but when Max is drinking, there's trouble. And he started drinking again a few weeks before Stacey died."

I kept my surprise at this revelation to myself. "And what are you thinking?"

"This is such an awful thing for a mother to think."

"I'm not here to judge, Mrs. Hart."

"It's just . . . I'm so worried for him. And the two of them were arguing, Max and Stacey. They drank together that night. Max doesn't handle alcohol well. He can go a long time without drinking, but when he starts he can't stop."

"I see."

"And so it makes me wonder, as horrible as it is to think it, God forgive me for saying it, I wonder if Max lost control and killed Stacey."

I kept my silence.

"And there's another thing: Max and Stacey argued the last time the three of us were together. I should have told the detective the day he came to the house, but in front of Max I didn't feel comfortable going into it."

"Mrs. Hart. I know you're calling to give me information to help with Max. But what you just said takes our conversation into another arena. I think this is something Detective Antelope needs to hear directly from you."

"Of course. I'm just so worn out from everything. And I'm not sure it makes one bit of difference, this little thing between them. Can I tell you about it, and I promise I will call Detective Antelope tomorrow? I don't think I can go through it twice today."

"I understand. Why don't you tell me the gist of it so I can follow up with Max."

"I'll never forget her words because of the way she said it, so different from her usual way, the way I want to remember her. It's like the words are burned into my brain, when all I want is to forget she ever said these things."

"What did she say, Mrs. Hart?"

"She said, and I'm going to quote her, 'I'm getting sick and tired of having to be the one to carry the torch of the perfect life. I am damn sick of having the perfect life or trying to make it seem like I have the perfect life. Let somebody else try doing it for a while and see how either of you like it.'" Fern stifled a sob. "I can't remember what set off the tirade. I remember apologizing and saying I didn't mean to upset her. It didn't help. In fact, it upset her more."

"What did she say?"

"The worst thing ever. She said, 'I hate my life.'"

"And I shouldn't have said what I did, but I wanted to point out to her how fortunate she was, so I reminded her of her wonderful career, her vintage home and all the money to make it a showcase for her taste, and, most important, her engagement to the love of her life. And you know what she said? She referred to all her blessings as golden handcuffs. She said she felt trapped."

I was taking notes now. "Had she ever suggested this before?"

"Never. She's been planning this wedding, looking forward to it for years, we all have. I called it wedding jitters, cold feet, said every bride feels nervous at some point. The wedding was so close . . . her feelings were breaking out right on schedule."

"Did Max take part in this conversation?"

"Oh, he was right there, listening and taking it all in. But you know Max. Sometimes he uses his head injury as an excuse not to get involved."

"I never noticed."

"Whenever things get uncomfortable, he checks out or leaves. He's told me it's his way of not getting overstimulated and losing control."

"That makes sense, given what you said occurs when he loses control."

"I suppose. Sometimes, though, it would be nice to feel there's an ally, someone on my side. No chance with Max. He takes care of himself and leaves me to deal with whatever."

"So he sat quietly as you and Stacey talked? But they argued at some point?"

"I'm getting there. He did say something later, and it sent Stacey over the edge."

"What did he say?"

"He said it was her life and she should do what she wanted. He said if she didn't like her life with Connor, she should call off the wedding. Sometimes he's too blunt and it never helps. Because Stacey got mad. She said she would never call off the wedding— that unlike Max, she didn't suffer from impulsivity and volatility. Max started laughing, as if there was anything to laugh about. So I tried to smooth things over by telling her he didn't mean it. Max said I was acting codependent and got up and left. And I know they didn't talk after that for a long time, no matter what Max says."

CHAPTER 36

At nine o'clock, a fading sunset outlined the rocky ridges of White Mountain. On the lawn outside Antelope's window, a row of cottonwoods cast thick violet shadows.

Often, in the long twilight hours, a familiar, lingering melancholy came over him. He wanted to be outside, fishing and cooking supper on a camp stove, falling asleep on the ground, a bowl of star-filled night sky overhead.

Instead, he was alone in the office after hours, long past the time when the sheriff and second-shift detectives left for the day.

At quiet moments, it came to him how much his life had changed when he joined the Sheriff's Department. The things he encountered each day in his work were a constant reminder of the dark side of humanity.

Every part of him went into his mission to fight crime—heart, mind, and soul. If he kept up his usual pace, he would be depleted long before his time, like the old men in town who had spent their lives working the mines and whose bodies were now bent shells, collapsed and useless, after giving everything to hard physical labor for years. Would his mind suffer the same depletion if he continued to push it to the boundaries of his capabilities?

A question he couldn't answer: why did it take a brilliant detective to catch a dumb criminal?

Even if he changed careers at this point, the knowledge of what his fellow man was capable of filled his head; he was forever branded with the true nature of the world.

Only in sleep did he get a respite from his warrior stance. On those nights when his dreams took him to places and memories of his childhood, the time before his work made its mark, he landed briefly in a place of innocence. On those nights, he savored the sweetness, the gift-wrapped beauty of the delusion.

If he didn't watch out, he'd put himself to sleep with this fairy tale . . . and he still had work to do. Important, hands-on police work. The best and most necessary kind of detecting, the sheriff had taught him.

He stood and stretched.

Earlier that day, the district court judge had granted the motion to search the Spring Grove Motel's guest records for the previous ninety days. Antelope had faxed the paperwork, and two hours later hundreds of pages had come through the fax to the Sheriff's Department.

On his desk, the documents waited: the guest register from the Spring Grove Motel for the previous ninety days, as well as the printout from the tracking app on Stacey's phone.

Outside, the night sky was black and starless; restless clouds rolled and tossed in the wind. He turned on the brass reading lamp on his desk and started on the guest register.

■ ■ ■

One hundred eighty pages and one hour later, Antelope had found no evidence of Connor Collins as a guest at the Spring Grove Motel.

One name stood out from the others, however. He wondered what business had brought Father Todd Bellamy to Salt Lake City three times in the last three months.

Easy enough to find out, he thought and dialed the priest's cell number, but it went straight to his voicemail, which was full. Only 9:00 p.m., but not everyone kept late hours.

He dialed the rectory landline, intending to leave a message. On the first ring, Sister Julia answered.

"Good evening, Our Lady of Sorrows Church, Sister Julia speaking, how may we help?"

"Good evening, Sister Julia, I'm sorry to call so late. I wanted to leave a message for Father Bellamy. I tried his cell phone first but the voicemail is full."

"He's very bad about clearing it." She chuckled. "You're not the first one to have that problem. I can write him a note that you called."

"Thank you, and while I have you on the phone, maybe you can answer something for me."

"I will do my very best to help, Detective. Is it about the murder case?"

"Just a small thing I'm curious about. When Father Bellamy makes his monthly trip to the prison in Provo, where does he stay?"

"He stays in Salt Lake to take advantage of the city's cultural offerings."

"Thank you, that's very helpful. Please have Father Bellamy call me as soon as he can."

"I certainly will, Detective, he's very anxious to do everything he can to help find Stacey's killer."

In every case, as bits of information, seemingly unrelated, moved toward each other like magnets, a tingling feeling came over Antelope—a pleasant, electrified buzzing. He didn't know what it all meant yet, but there were plenty of questions to ask.

CHAPTER 37

Wednesday morning, I arrived at the office early for another session with Max. An eerie gray light, created by the low-hanging fog, illuminated the building.

After the night I found my husband murdered in our office, I said I'd never enter a dark office alone again, ever. And here I was with my key in the door. A sign of stupidity, or progress? I wasn't sure.

The one-story office building was deserted. Tall pine trees rose up behind it in a black and impenetrable wall.

Behind me a door slammed, and I jumped. When I turned around, Max was right behind me. I hadn't heard him drive in; I hadn't heard his boots on the pavement.

"Good morning, Doc, I didn't mean to scare you. Sorry I came up on you like that, I thought you saw me."

"I didn't. It's okay. Come in and have a seat. Give me a minute to open things up."

"Take your time, I'm early."

I needed the time to settle my nerves, slow my breathing, and quiet the story that had started up in my head the minute my autonomic nervous system registered danger—which happened when I turned and saw Max right behind me.

It happened less and less as time went by, this post-traumatic stress response. With every passing day my nervous system calmed a down a little more. Still, when I encountered the right combination, the perfect storm of sensory stimulation, my primitive brain transported me right back to the murder scene.

When I opened the door again, Max was there with his back to me. He must still be wound up from yesterday. His heightened state required a daily session for the time being, the short-term goal being to provide a safe therapeutic environment, moderate the intensity of his emotions, and steer him away from impulsive acting out.

When we sat down, his first words matched my thoughts.

"Thanks for fitting me in, Doctor. I don't think I could have made it without seeing you. I didn't drink last night, and I didn't sleep much either. When I finally knocked out, I had a nightmare and woke up freaked out. I need to get the poison out of my head."

"Tell me about the nightmare."

"It felt so real. How does that happen?"

"The dream state is another layer of your mental processing. When our dreams approximate reality, the experience is hard to shake off."

"Do they approximate reality, or *are* they are reality?"

"Let's hear the dream and maybe we can find out."

"I was with Tim. It was our senior year of high school, and we walked to the church after track practice. I can't remember why, maybe something to do with services for graduation. We were laughing and everything felt alive, the way it can on a warm day after a long winter.

Ordinarily, Connor would be with us; the Three Musketeers. But Connor wasn't with us today. We were going to meet him at the church."

Max stopped and held up his hand. He appeared to be hyperventilating. His chest rose and fell rapidly.

"It's okay, Max. Take deep breaths, try to slow your breathing down."

"This is where it gets twisted."

"Take your time."

"I opened the door and stopped in my tracks. I couldn't believe it. I must be a sick fuck if this is what's in my subconscious mind."

"What did you see?"

"The priest was sitting in his big chair near the fireplace. He had his black shirt with the white collar on over it, so he still looked all priest like. But his belt was unbuckled and his pants were open. And Connor was on his knees on the floor in front of him, his face right down there, the priest with his hand on Connor's head. They were going at it."

"You were shocked?"

Max covered his face with his hands. "It was sick and wrong, just like with Kroll."

"What happened next?"

"I woke up."

"No wonder it was hard to shake," I said gently. "You woke up with a disturbing, graphic scene in your head."

Max swung his head from side to side. "Am I crazy? Am I making this up?"

"You've been recovering memories since you first came into therapy, and also in dreams and flashbacks. I think we have to wait and see what happens with this new material about Connor."

"I can't ask Connor, not now . . . he has enough to deal with."

"I understand. The most important thing is to be patient and see what else comes up for you. The goal is to recall as much of your experience as possible, and then process those memories so they no longer rule your life choices."

"I've been spending time with Kelly." Max brightened a little as he said her name. "We go way back. She was Stacey's best friend, so she's a mess herself, and she's Tim's sister. I'm working up the courage to talk to her about this shit."

"Where does courage come in?"

"The thing is, you never know with Kelly. She's brave and strong, but she spooks easy. She's like those wild mustangs up on the butte. You want to get out of her way if she's running free."

"I see." I looked him in the eye. "Your mother called me last night."

"What the fuck? She can't do that, can she?"

"Without your permission, I can't disclose anything about your treatment to her. But as a family member—and this would be true for anyone, a friend or significant other—if she wants to share information she considers important to your treatment, it is perfectly ethical for me to listen and take it into account so I can talk with you about it."

"That doesn't seem right." Max's jaw clenched. "I put a lot of work into keeping her out of my life, and now she sneaks into my therapy sessions? Fuck me!"

"If you tell me not to communicate with her—not to take her calls, or listen to voicemails, or read any email messages she might send—I will respect that, and all contact will stop from that point on."

"Let's do that, then. I don't want her talking to you, poisoning you against me. This is my treatment and *I* get to tell the story."

"Fair enough. I understand. Do you want to know what she said?"

"Might as well. You heard it; give me a chance to defend myself. I know she didn't call to tell you something good. My mother has a knack for putting a negative spin on everything."

"She told me she's been concerned about you for about a month. She thinks you've started to withdraw and isolate, which makes her think you've started to slip into a depression."

"Newsflash! We both know I'm depressed. What am I supposed to feel when every hour of my life, day and night, it's in my face—memories and flashbacks of the twisted things that sick fuck did to me? Sorry, Mom, I'm not a happy camper, deal with it. I do!" He turned his face away from me and bit his lip, trying to hold it together. He slammed his right fist down on the leather sofa cushion repeatedly.

When he finally stopped he rubbed his hand, grimaced, and flexed red, swollen fingers.

"Sorry about that. I might have to get you a new couch if I stay in therapy long enough."

"There's more when you're ready."

"Go on. I have another hand."

"She said you started drinking again, weeks before Stacey died."

He didn't punch the cushion, and he didn't say anything for a long time.

Finally, I said, "Is it true?"

Another few minutes of silence, head down, the fingers of his bruised hand tapping on the cushion. Then he looked at me and said, "Busted."

"You didn't talk about it here," I said—no judgment in my voice, wanting to keep the way clear for him to feel safe enough to talk now.

"I have a lot to talk about. Forty-five minutes goes by fast."

"I don't think time is the issue, and you're wasting it right now."

"Not gonna cut me any slack, are you?"

"Do you think I should?"

"That would be out of character."

"Alcohol caused you big problems in the past. You got sober because you didn't want to live like that anymore. After five years of sobriety, a relapse is a big deal, Max. You led me to believe you drank for the first time last weekend."

"It's the shame that gets to me. A drink takes the edge off. I thought I could control it."

"You're working really hard in here. Trust me, it gets better, your life will get better, but not if you use alcohol. You'll get stuck in a cycle of pain and drinking to self-medicate. You have to deal with your feelings; there's no other way out of the past."

"I'm sorry. I screwed up. That's why I didn't tell you."

"Are you still drinking?"

"I've slowed down. I know I have to stop, but if you want me to be honest with you, I don't think I can give it up completely right now."

"Let's keep talking about it and make a plan to get you back on track soon."

"Yeah, the idea of a track I can get back on . . . that just seems impossible to me right now."

"I understand that's how it feels to you right now. We can pick up there at our next session."

Max stood up and strode to the door. Before he walked out, he turned around. "Something I didn't tell you because I didn't want to put her in a bad light: My mother's a functioning alcoholic. She keeps it together during the day, but at night she hits it hard and all hells breaks loose. She's been that way as long as I can remember."

CHAPTER 38

In the car, before heading to the office, Antelope checked his messages. Toni Atwell had left a voicemail asking him to come to her office. Fern Hart wanted him to call her, something important about Max. He tried her number but got no answer.

After his morning stop at Starbucks, he drove around the corner to Foothill Boulevard and the office of the domestic violence program at the Sweetwater County YMCA.

As the assistant director of the program, Stacey had facilitated the processing of victims of domestic violence into the local safe house and prepared them for negotiating the legal system. He wondered about her recent cases. Was there someone angry enough to take her life?

He found Toni in her tiny, crowded office. Her battered steel desk took up most of the floor space; the rest was taken up by gigantic plants blooming in the southwest windows. He knocked on the wall and she looked up from a file she was reading.

"Good morning, you found me. There's a chair under there somewhere. Throw everything on the floor."

He lifted a three-foot stack of catalogues from a metal folding chair and pushed them into the corner.

"So the director gets the big office, right?"

She laughed. "Don't be snarky. I bet I've got more square footage than you do."

"You're right. What have you got for me?"

"I was going through Stacey's files to decide who to assign them to when I came across something I thought you should be aware of. I'm not sure if it has any bearing on the case, but I'll leave it to you to determine. Last month Stacey did an intake and arranged temporary housing in the safe house for a young woman. There was nothing out of the ordinary about the case: the client was living with an older, controlling male. Initially it was jealousy and control; that was followed by emotional and verbal abuse. Eventually, the physical abuse started. When the violence escalated, she left him in the middle of the night and walked crosstown alone. She was on the back door steps when we opened up in the morning. She had nowhere else to go—no support system, no family here, and he controlled her money."

"Rough stuff," Antelope said.

Toni shrugged. "Par for the course. At first she was reluctant to identify the perpetrator of the violence. That's pretty common. Many of our clients have a hard time taking the step to press charges. She stayed at the safe house for a while, where she received support and counseling. Last week, she finally divulged the name of her abuser. Stacey planned to accompany her to make a police report on Friday. But when Stacey went to the safe house on Friday morning, she learned that the client had reneged on her statement. Turns out she left the program the next day. We don't know for certain, but we suspect she went back to her abuser, which is what happens with these women who aren't emotionally prepared to make the break. On Saturday, Stacey Hart was dead."

"It sounds like it would be worth my time to talk with this client, as well as the person she identified as her abuser."

"Stacey never told me. But she listed her place of residence as belonging to Val Campion."

Toni handed the file to Antelope. He read the report, which gave the details of the domestic violence case. At the bottom of the page, he found the signature and printed name of the woman reporting the abuse: Sharnelle Brightwood, age nineteen, aka Star Bright.

. . .

Val Campion owned a small apartment building off Bridger Avenue hidden in the hollows of the dusty hills at the edge of town.

Antelope hoped to find Sharnelle alone in the apartment she shared with Campion. He hadn't invited Pepper Hunt to come along for this interview. It wasn't because he didn't want the benefit of her insights; what had kept him from asking for her assistance this time was personal, not professional.

The Doc had been right on when she'd said sexual chemistry could make it harder to keep focused on the job at hand. He didn't want her witnessing anything that might pass between him and Sharnelle.

He stepped onto the sagging wooden porch and knocked on the door after noticing the cut wires on the doorbell. A growling dog slammed against the inside of the door. Behind the blinds of the window to the right of the door, its front paws clawed and scratched.

A high-pitched whistle silenced the pit bull, and he heard a door slam in the house.

A minute later, Sharnelle unlocked the door and opened it an inch, keeping the safety chain on. "He's not here. Try at the club."

He held out his ID card for her.

She looked at it and a smile came and went like a cloud over her face. "I see you there sometimes."

"I have some questions on a case I'm investigating. Can I come in?"

"Wait. I'll come out."

She closed the door and locked it again. He waited on the porch and listened as the dog went on barking and scratching behind a closed door somewhere in the house. If he lived in this place, he'd feel trapped by the ugly neglect.

A few minutes later, she came out. It was a hot day but she wore jeans and a black hoodie—the uniform of the abused female, every inch of skin covered up, the bruises hidden.

Her eyes darted back and forth between him and the door to the club across the alley. At any moment Campion could walk out the door, and it was clear the idea made her nervous.

"I'm not here about your domestic violence case. I won't cause you any trouble."

"There's no case."

"No. Unless you press charges."

She nodded at him and her breathing eased a little. Her skin was fine and thin and the pulse in her neck throbbed too fast for a woman standing out in the sun. He wanted to reassure her, but there was nothing true he could say. His presence here could mean trouble for her later. But that couldn't be avoided.

"Okay," she said. "I don't know anything, but ask me what you came here to ask."

"I understand you returned home on Friday. Did you sleep here Friday night?"

"I came home, like you just said. Where else would I sleep?"

"You live with Val Campion."

"I live in his building."

"Do you stay in the same apartment?"

"Yes."

"What time did he come home Friday night?"

"At two the club closes and he comes here."

"And last Friday night, could you say for certain he was here?"

"No. I was sleeping in my own bed."

"So you can't provide an alibi during the hours when the murder took place?"

"Why would he kill her?"

"She's the one who got you into the safe house. She's the one who advocated for you to go to court and file charges."

"You said you didn't come to talk about my domestic."

"I'm talking about the murder of a woman who tried to help you."

"She gets paid for it. I won't go to court. What's the point?"

"To stop Val Campion from abusing you."

"You got your story wrong. It wasn't Val."

Antelope tried to hide his surprise. Toni had said she listed her place of residence as belonging to Val Campion. She'd never filled in the name of the perpetrator. They'd just both made the assumption it was Campion.

Sharnelle looked frightened.

"Who hurt you bad enough you went to the safe house?"

"If Val thinks I named him, I'll be on the street with nothing."

"He won't stop, you know."

"Val never hurt me," she insisted. "It was the young one, Jack. When I saw on the news that he'd left, I came home."

CHAPTER 39

Max left his therapy session with Dr. Hunt relieved she knew the truth about his drinking. Besides Kelly, she was the only person he felt he could trust, and he knew that had to go both ways or the relationship would eventually crash and burn. If a quasi-normal life was in the cards for him, therapy would get him there.

The emotional work drained him just as much as his physical workouts at the gym. He'd been awake for two days, and was feeling an exhaustion that threatened to tank him. At the Dewar Drive stoplight he nodded off and only woke up when some asshole hit the horn behind him.

As he approached the gym parking lot, the turn signal ticked hypnotically and he dozed off again—but snapped awake almost immediately, the sun too bright in his eyes, the sight of the shopping center, his gym included, just a pile of worn, shabby real estate.

A sour taste in his throat, a claw in his gut—he opened the door, bent over and spewed vomit onto the curb. Eyes closed, he sat in his truck, wiped the sweat from his face, and waited for his wrecked body to tell him what to do next.

He could skip the gym; there was no reason to open up, he'd cancelled all personal training sessions for the week and the sign on the door, CLOSED DUE TO DEATH IN THE FAMILY, said it all.

He'd worked out so hard the day before; he could do some real damage if he worked out again so soon. Of course, the option of exercising different muscles existed—but that wasn't his style. Nothing less than 100 percent effort for him, all day, every day. Except when he relapsed and lied to his therapist about it. Maybe he didn't have to destroy his life in order to bring balance into his world. He decided to take it one small step at a time and see what happened when he let himself get close to the place where it all happened.

He parked a ways down from Our Lady of Sorrows. For some reason he could not explain to himself, he did not want anyone to drive by and see his truck in front of the church.

He opened the heavy wooden door and entered the church. The Mass was in progress, Father Todd Bellamy on his knees on the altar for the opening prayers.

Max slipped into a pew at the back on the right side of the church, in the shadows behind a pillar. He wanted to watch the man do his thing, unsuspecting, until the end of the Mass; only then would he stand and show his face, let the priest know he was being watched.

■ ■ ■

As soon as Max opened the church door, he spotted the Sheriff's Department Dodge Ram parked in front of his truck. He thought about heading off in the other direction, leaving the truck and walking home. Screw him for hunting him down in church. Old, self-righteous feelings instilled by years of religious education sprang up, surprising him. So vivid and intense, these things he once believed.

He came back to reality fast—him being in church had nothing to do with anything good.

At a break in the traffic, the Dodge door opened and the detective stepped into the street.

He'd hesitated too long. Might as well get it over with; whatever the man wanted to talk to him about, he wouldn't quit. Their eyes met and the two of them began walking toward each other.

"I didn't know you were a churchgoer," Antelope said.

"I'm not usually. Grief does strange things."

"I saw your truck, decided to wait out here rather than try to track you down. Your place is closed."

Max nodded. "Did you get a break in the case?"

It didn't occur to him before he spoke the words that the detective might be there to report on the progress of the investigation. Instead, his only thoughts were of his own guilt, of others' suspicions and mistrust of him because of his damaged mind.

"That's not why I'm here."

"You didn't answer my question."

"It's an active investigation. Unfortunately, nothing I can talk to you about. You made a statement on Saturday, and I since learned it's not accurate."

"Saturday was a rough day. I'm not surprised if I didn't perform perfectly as a witness. I guess you get that a lot, especially after you tell people their loved one's been murdered."

"Your mother said you and your sister had some kind of falling out and didn't see each other for a while. You denied that at the time. Do you want to stand by that statement?"

"She called you too?" He snorted. "Mother's been busy. The problem is, she has a hard time remembering what's true from one day to the next. Since she doesn't seem to have a problem throwing me under the bus, I guess I'm free to do the same. Can I ask, was she drunk when you talked to her? After five o'clock, you can't believe anything she says."

"I spoke with her an hour ago."

"Good to know; even sober she's out to get me."

"Where did you go when you left Stacey and Connor at Johnny Mac's Tavern Friday night?"

"I stopped at the Liquor Mart for a bottle and went home and drank it. While some evil bastard was busy strangling my sister, I was blacked out on my kitchen floor. The only bright side of that tragic story is that she didn't call me for help."

"She didn't call you, but you called her. Why?"

"I don't remember."

"Bullshit."

"I told you, I blacked out. I don't remember anything from that night."

"Is that your alibi? You don't remember driving to Cedar Street and strangling your sister?"

A black rage like toxic smoke filled Max's body. He wanted to let it loose right there in front of the Church, ignite the hallowed ground with his righteous anger. If he had alcohol on board, the detective would already be bleeding on the ground. But he hadn't had a drink that morning, even though he'd wanted one badly.

He walked to his Jeep and drove away. In the rearview mirror, he saw the detective still standing on the sidewalk, watching him leave.

CHAPTER 40

The DJ blasted "Cat Scratch Fever" as frenzied blue and pink strobe lights flashed in front of her eyes. Fans called out to her, "Here, Kitty, Kitty." Some of them purred, some meowed, and others barked. The house was full and hot; she felt trapped in a furnace, stoked by the heat of the men below her.

It was her favorite routine but her heart wasn't in it. She didn't want to work, didn't want to do anything except escape into oblivion.

That was a lie. She wanted Max again. He'd made love to her the night Stacey died, and it had torn her heart open. Every day since, she'd been a bleeding, hot mess of feeling.

She hated the sweating, leering, lecherous men who watched her as she moved on the stage. At what point would one of them lose control? It was a chance she took every time she got on stage. Impossible to trust that the same men who surrendered to their sexual and voyeuristic impulses would control other, more dangerous impulses.

The shoulder strap of her silver top cut into her shoulder. She wanted to take it off and be naked in bed with Max, who was no part of this life.

Legs around the pole, her body moved in sync with the bass. The lights blinded her to anything beyond the stage and she pretended she danced for someone who loved her, not the gross strangers who paid for the pleasure of seeing her body.

The music stopped, the strobe shut down, and the stage lights dimmed. She bowed and raised her arms to her audience.

When she looked up, she saw Max.

He stood in the doorway, arms crossed, laser-focused eyes dark with fury.

She left the stage and headed toward the bar, where her job was to get men to buy her a drink and maybe inquire about something more.

The pressure of a hand on her back; she turned around and smiled. "Well, hello there, this is a nice surprise."

The fake flirtatious voice came automatically: she was still in performance mode. But it didn't play well with Max, who glared at her and grabbed her by the arm.

"Knock it off, Kelly."

"What are you doing here?"

"I came for you," he said. Cold fingers pressed deep into her flesh.

"Take your hand off me, Max, or you'll be on your ass. They're watching."

He let go and thrust his hands in the pockets of his leather jacket. As he did, she saw the Smith & Wesson holstered there. "Walk out with me. You're done here for tonight."

She walked alongside him toward the exit, but turned toward the dressing room before they got there.

"Hold up, where you going?" Max demanded. "I said we're out of here."

"I want my things—"

"Let's go. Now." He grabbed her by the arm again and pushed her toward the door. Two security guards broke loose from the crowd and made their way toward them from across the room.

Max propelled her over to his truck, yanked the door open, and pushed her roughly inside. They took off just as the security guards came out of the club.

"How'd you know to find me here?"

"I didn't. I came in to get my mind off things."

"You said you came for me?"

"I called and texted, went to your house. I called Connor thinking you might be with him."

"What's wrong? What's the emergency?"

"Let's go to my place. I have to calm down."

She thought of Campion and shuddered. "You probably got me fired."

"You shouldn't be there. You don't belong there. You have a son at home."

"Who are you to remind me of my parental duties? And for the record, he's with my parents on vacation."

He took off his jacket and threw it across the seat at her. "Here, cover yourself up."

"What the hell's wrong with you? You're acting like a prude! You of all people, who are you to judge?"

"What do you mean?"

"You know what I mean. Your perversions, your deviant sexual acts, and the things you need."

"You were the prude. What happened to you? How did Miss Vanilla Sex end up in a brothel?"

"It's not a brothel; it's an adult night club."

"With strippers and prostitutes."

"Exotic dancers. You didn't see me take my clothes off on stage."

They were at his trailer now. He parked the truck and gave her a long look. "I know you, Kelly, and I didn't like seeing you there."

"Let's be honest. It's been a long time since either of us has been able to say we know each other."

"I'm still pissed off. You can't tell me not to be. It's been a hell of a week and this, seeing you undressed up there in front of those creeps, it put me over the edge."

"I'm not undressed."

"Barely."

She dropped her eyes. "I'm sorry."

"Are you hungry?" he asked, his voice softer now.

"I thought you'd never ask."

"Come on, I'll make us dinner."

When they got inside, he went into his bedroom, came out with a T-shirt and a pair of socks, and handed them to her. "Here, put these on."

She slipped them on over her dance clothes.

While he put the spaghetti on to boil and sliced garlic cloves into oil, she chose a playlist from his CD collection. Max felt his mood lift as John Coltrane's "A Love Supreme" filled the air, a soulful soundtrack for his life. Kelly sat cross-legged on his futon, her hands resting in her lap, her head back, and her eyes closed.

They ate dinner in silence, surrendering to the music and the mood it created.

She helped him clean up and when they were done, she took him by the hand and led him to the futon. He bent to kiss her but she stopped him.

"Not yet. Sit down and close your eyes."

She put on another of his favorite artists, Sam Smith, singing "Stay with Me." When she told him to open his eyes, the room was dark except for the candles she'd lit. The T-shirt and socks were on the floor. She stood before him in her silver dance clothes.

"This dance is for you, only you," she said. When the song ended, she crawled onto his lap. "You can kiss me now."

They made love twice, and the second time she told him he could do whatever he wanted to her. She wasn't afraid anymore.

Before she could fall asleep, he lit a joint and they smoked together. For the first time since his sister died, he felt like it was going to be possible to live.

"Is that why you needed to see me so bad?" she said.

"For sex? No. I didn't plan on sex."

"Why were you looking for me?"

"What is it with women? You always want to talk after. Way to ruin a mood."

"Don't play with me, Max. Something's bothering you and you couldn't stop until you found me. What is it? Don't shut down like you always do."

He sat up and turned on a light. The rain came down all at

once and made a hard sound above them, drilling into the old roof, running in fast, fat coils down the rattling windowpane.

"I've been seeing my therapist every day. Partly because of Stacey, partly because for whatever reason my mind is deciding now is the time to spew out everything. It's kind of overwhelming. Today's session was intense."

"You want to tell me about it?"

"It stays between us until I decide what I'm going to do, all right?"

"Sure. Of course I won't tell anyone."

"Because I don't know if I'll ever do anything with it or if it means anything. I'm still figuring it out. But the way it's making me feel, it must be important. I mean more than the actual fact of it. Like it's bad enough as it is, but it's only the tip of the iceberg, a fucking big iceberg. You know what I mean?"

"I think so." Kelly nodded slowly. "Why don't you tell me what you remember?"

He took a deep breath and blew it out. "All right. Here goes. The basics, though. I don't want to trigger myself talking about the details."

"What do you mean?"

"Like, set off a panic attack or some other bad reaction."

"Okay. I'm here. I'm listening." She reached for his hand.

"This could be upsetting for you. But maybe you know about it and I was the only one who didn't know. I mean, I *knew* . . . but I forgot."

"I am so confused now."

"Tim and Connor and I were all molested by Father Kroll. Did you know about it?"

She exhaled. "I did."

"Stacey didn't know until I told her. It upset her and she didn't want to talk about it or see me after I let her know. I couldn't figure out why. You never told her about Tim?"

"No. It was a long time ago when Tim told me. He talked to me about everything. My parents were furious and forbade me to ever say anything to anyone. Stacey didn't bring it up and honestly, it wasn't something I wanted to think about after he died. There are so many good memories of him I wanted to focus on. It made me sad to think of him going through something so weird and sick."

Max nodded. "I get it."

"Is that what you wanted to tell me?"

"Part of it."

"What else?"

The next thing he said would move them into dangerous territory. In the background, Sam Smith still sang his heart out, and Max felt his own heart lit on fire by his voice and songs. The music rolled out a ribbon of possibility.

The joint had gone out. "So today something new came up." He reached for his lighter but his hands were trembling so much he couldn't do it.

"Give it to me," she said.

He handed it over, and she lit up what was left of the joint.

"Tell me, Max. It can't be so bad."

"Are you sure about that?"

"I don't know anything until you tell me. Please tell me."

"I had a dream about Connor and Father Bellamy hooking up. Not like when it was the three of us kids and we hated it but felt trapped in it. This was different. Connor was full-on into it."

The CD finished and the room went quiet except for the incessant, lonely sound of the rain.

"That's crazy." Kelly shook her head. "It was just a dream, though? Maybe your subconscious is mixing things up."

"That's what I figured you'd say. Maybe you're right. It would be good if you were right. But here's the thing, Kelly. It was a dream, but it feels like it really happened."

CHAPTER 41

Max held the weights and watched his deltoid muscles twitch as he grimaced in the mirror. It was more than he'd ever pumped before, and he felt the pain shoot through his body like hot metal. He wanted it, needed the pain—now and days after, when the lactic acid grilled his overused tissues. As an experienced body builder, he knew his limits. A few more minutes and he could do real damage.

Enough. He didn't want to land himself in a hospital.

At 4:00 a.m. he was alone in the gym, and he liked it that way. In the high-ceilinged room, every sound registered loud and sharp in the empty space. The barbell rolled from his hands into the metal holder, clean and distinct, an ice cube in a glass. No other sound could rouse him from inertia. In the old days, the sound of ice in a glass had started him looking for a drink.

It used to be his default remedy: down the booze, lose the pain. Tequila magic. But five years ago, on an ordinary day, for no reason he could explain, he'd decided he was done with weakness. He'd quit drinking.

Then, a month ago, for a reason he didn't understand, he'd started back up again. That's the reason Stacey hadn't wanted to see him. Even his mother didn't know the truth.

Weakness caused all his problems. He would squash his weakness, his reliance on drinking to deal with his pain. There were other ways. He knew now.

It started when he had to rebuild his body. Those hours of workouts, getting his body back in shape. In the process, he'd made himself strong—able to defend himself, capable of tearing someone apart. Let someone try something. See what happens. He clenched his fists and could feel the flesh and bone of a face shattering on impact.

He'd be ready when the time came. Pride rose up like a big bass jumping from a lake. It was a new feeling. Before therapy, he could only feel pain. The talking had diluted the toxic poison from his mind and body, emptied him out and left a space for other feelings. The human part of him had moved in and he'd found small moments of pleasure and joy. At first these feelings had crushed him with their beauty; more than once, he'd broken down crying from the joy of being alive.

He told Dr. Hunt a lot. He never told her what he wanted to do, what his body ached for, the release he would feel if he let himself do this one thing. He walked a thin line. He spilled his guts but held back his plan to make things right.

She'd explained to him early in his treatment that he could tell her anything, express any feeling; no matter how bad, she would hear it and help him work through it. But if he told her about a plan to do serious harm to a specific person, she would have to break the confidentiality.

When she explained that, therapy stopped being a safe place to talk. In cases where a patient intended to murder someone, her professional ethics required her to alert the police and also the individual intended victim. So he kept his mouth shut and rode a thin line.

Six months into treatment, the flashbacks ended. He could remember what had happened to him, feel the appropriate and necessary anger and sadness, without being debilitated or flattened.

He'd been more honest with her than he had with anyone else in his life.

■　■　■

In the shower after his workout, he ran the water scalding hot, punishing his body. He turned it off and stepped out of the stall.

The room was opaque, filled with steam, like he'd stepped into heaven and was blinded and protected from the ugly, earthy image before him.

He wasn't the only one who deserved to be punished.

Time to settle the score; it wasn't over yet. At least he was strong enough now; he could count on himself now. He would figure out what needed to be done next, and do it.

CHAPTER 42

Though I felt like a stalker, I logged on to my computer to do some research on Max's climbing accident. In my capacity as a consultant to the Sheriff's Department, I had access to a law enforcement database I didn't have as a private psychologist.

Without too much trouble, I retrieved the *Green River Star* article about the accident. The reporter gave a standard, who, what, when, and where version of the incident.

It was the most common type of climbing accident. The ropes and knots were not properly adjusted. But that wasn't the only thing I learned from the article.

I heard the door to my outer office open and close. I wasn't expecting anyone. There was a knock; I opened my office door.

Antelope stood there with two cups of Starbucks espresso. "Do you have time for a coffee break, Doc?"

"Your timing is perfect." I smiled. "I'm about to take a break."

"What are you working on?"

"Did you know Bellamy supervised the Flaming Gorge rock climbing trip?"

He shook his head. "It hasn't come up."

"I wanted to know more about the accident, so I googled it. The article in the *Green River Star* mentioned him as one of the members of the climbing party."

"I'm surprised no one mentioned it."

I shrugged. "They might have assumed you knew. It was big news. What brings you here today?"

"I've been doing some research myself and have a few questions for the prosecutor. I'm headed to Green River now. I'd like you to come along, if you've got the time. I have the feeling he'll be a little more receptive with you along. He's getting pretty tired of me and my questions."

"What are we talking to Connor about today?" I asked, already retrieving my bag from behind my desk.

"The tracking app didn't record any trips to the Spring Grove Motel in Salt Lake City. But there are two things I want to ask him about. June 6 through 8 he was in Evanston, possibly a different rendezvous venue. And he lied when he said he went straight home from Johnny Mac's on Friday night. The records show he stopped at the church before going home."

"He was upset and wanted to speak to his priest?"

"Possible. It's curious, though, why he wouldn't mention it if that's the case."

"Let's ask him."

"I'm thinking a surprise visit. Let's go."

■ ■ ■

Connor was in his office in Green River. Antelope stopped the department secretary when she picked up the phone to announce that we were there. We walked down the hallway and found Connor at his desk, suit jacket off, sleeves rolled up, and tie loosened. He was lost in thought, staring out the window, and didn't turn when we stopped in his doorway.

"Mr. Collins?" Antelope said.

He didn't startle or flinch as I expected. He simply turned toward the sound. It took a while for him to register our presence.

When he figured it out, he stood abruptly, pulled his shirtsleeves down, and got his jacket on in seconds.

"Detective, hello, you caught me unawares," he said. "First day back, but not really back if you know what I mean. Have a seat."

"I've brought Dr. Hunt along; she's a psychologist who consults with the Sheriff's Department on some of our more difficult cases."

"Very impressive," Connor said. "Please, come in. Would you mind closing the door? My life is an open book at this point, but I'd like to preserve as much privacy as possible. Has something happened?"

"Just following up on a few loose ends."

We all sat down and Connor leaned forward on his desk, arms outstretched and hands folded like the perfect Catholic schoolboy in class.

"Okay. Something I can clear up for you?"

"Did you make a trip to Our Lady of Sorrows on the night of the murder?" Antelope asked.

Connor's face gave nothing away. "Why do you ask?"

"You have a habit of responding to my questions with questions of your own."

"Sorry, it's a law school thing."

"This isn't school, Mr. Collins, it's real life and death. I asked you a question. You can assume I think it's relevant and provide me with an accurate answer about your whereabouts on the night your fiancée was killed."

Connor stared at Antelope and said nothing for a while, then raised his eyebrows and blew out a breath. "Okay . . . I did go to the church."

"My notes reflect your statement to the contrary. My notes indicate you said, 'I came straight home and passed out.' Our Lady of Sorrows is located exactly 2.3 miles from Johnny Mac's Tavern. To travel to the church you have to veer from the route to your residence. How do you explain the discrepancy between your statement on Saturday and your statement today?"

"Shock," Connor said immediately. "Hyper-focus on a traumatic event can make anyone leave out nonessential details."

"What was the reason for your visit to the church?"

"I went to there to pray. I find it comforting to be in the church. I feel closer to God there."

"You left Stacey at Johnny Mac's Tavern and drove to Our Lady of Sorrows to pray before going home for the night. Is this your revised statement?"

"Correct."

"One more question. What were you doing in Evanston June 6th through the 8th?"

Connor looked surprised. He smiled, looked out the window, and shook his head. "You upgraded me to a suspect in the case?"

"You've always been a suspect. Does that surprise you?"

"You're right to do that, of course, I'm the significant other."

"And you're doing a good job of putting your neck in the noose. What aren't you telling me? What's the story with the Evanston trip?"

"I had a job interview with a private firm there Friday afternoon. They asked me to stay on for the weekend and meet all the partners in a social setting."

"Why didn't you mention this before?"

"Why would I? It has nothing to do with Stacey's death."

"Are you sure? I thought I made it clear the more I know about the circumstances surrounding the victim, the more likely I am to find her killer. No one in her life said anything about a job change or a move. Did she know you were looking to change jobs? Did she approve, or was it another thing you argued about and tried to hide?"

"She was all for it—in fact, it was her idea. In the last year, she started feeling stuck here and the only thing that seemed to cheer her up was fixing up the old house. But even that was starting to lose its excitement. She was getting restless. I was afraid I was going to lose her. And there was Swailes, ready to step into my place. So I told her we could move, we could do anything she wanted. She wanted to go; I applied for jobs. Us moving was going to cause a shitload of problems with her mother, so we decided not to tell anyone until I accepted a job offer and it was a done deal."

"You didn't think any of this was relevant?"

"When you arrest the person who murdered her, I'll be interested to hear how your knowledge of my career plans led you to him."

CHAPTER 43

The Saddle Lite was packed when Antelope arrived at ten o'clock. Ladies' Night brought in the crowds: women got in free and the men didn't mind the cover charge when they were assured a full house of females. He gave the guy at the door five dollars and went straight to the bar.

His cousin Diego was behind the bar. He caught his eye and Diego poured two fingers of Honey Jack and started a tab Antelope knew he wouldn't let him pay later. The cover band played Brad Paisley's "American Saturday Night."

Loud music and cheap whiskey and a room packed wall-to-wall with women looking for a good time. Many nights he left the Saddle Lite in the company of a new friend. Tonight would be different, though.

He finished off the whiskey and Diego brought another before he could ask for it. Glass in hand, he found an empty table in the back and took his time with the second one while he waited for the others. A few minutes later, Pepper Hunt walked in with Scruggs and Toni Atwood.

He finished off the Honey Jack before they reached the bar. He wasn't much of a dancer, and he'd agreed to meet Pepper for the free Western dance lessons.

■ ■ ■

"I think we all needed this," Pepper said, loud enough for the three of them to hear over the music.

"Just what the doctor ordered," Toni said.

"We see too much of the dark side of life in our work," Pepper said. "We need a break and some fun for a change."

"It's been a long time since I've been out like this," Scruggs said. "I almost bailed at the last minute," the sheriff said.

Toni nudged him with her elbow. "I'm glad you didn't."

"This case, though," he said. "Where are we at with it?"

"No shop talk." Toni gave him a light punch on the arm.

Scruggs shrugged. "The job is my life. Get used to it."

"You want to try that again?" Toni said.

"The job is my life, sweetheart, and the only other thing as important as you."

"Prosecutor denies he was cheating and we can't prove it," Antelope said. "If he was and if it had anything to do with the murder, it won't stay buried. It might take a long time, but nothing happens without a trail. Not in this day and age. Of course, it's possible the contractor, Swailes, lied to the victim for his own purposes and in the process wasted a lot of county resources."

"Any sign of him?"

"Not yet. Salt Lake deputies are still keeping an eye out at the Spring Grove Motel."

The band went silent and the square dance caller stepped up on stage and called everyone onto the dance floor. Time to start learning those beginner's steps.

Antelope grimaced and downed his drink.

■ ■ ■

The place emptied out after the dance lessons were over, and the band switched to ballads.

When the sheriff and Toni left, Antelope expected Pepper to go with them, but she stayed behind.

"You can buy me a drink now," she said.

He went to the bar and came back with a Coors and a Yellowtail Chardonnay. It was the first time he'd been out with Pepper in a social situation with other people. She was more relaxed than he'd ever seen her.

Suddenly, he was filled with a lightness he didn't attribute to alcohol. It was everything in the room—the sweet love songs, the laughter, normal life and pleasure happening around him. All week the case had sat heavy on his heart. He savored this moment, this reminder that murder wasn't everything.

"I hope the talk about the case didn't ruin things," he said as he handed the wine glass to Pepper.

"Not at all. What did the sheriff say? I am the job? Same is true for me." She arched an eyebrow. "I'm surprised you didn't mention my patient as a possible suspect when the sheriff asked how the case was going."

"He was trying to impress Toni."

"You know him well."

"Three years working together, it's hard not to."

"Zeke and I were married and in practice together for three years. But I didn't know him at all."

"Because of how things went down at the end?"

Pepper took a long sip of wine. "He was cheating on me with my best friend and colleague, and I didn't have a clue."

"He didn't want you to know."

"What does that say about me? I'm a psychologist! I'm trained to be observant and aware of the unspoken dynamics of relationships. Yet I was clueless."

"Maybe you wanted to be."

"What do you mean?"

"You loved him; it wasn't in your best interest to know he was cheating. You were blind to the signs."

"You're making my point. Three years together and I didn't know him. So how do you know the sheriff so well?"

Antelope stared out at the room. "At first, he could do no wrong. I needed a mentor and he was there. I was blind to his faults. Things changed and I got to see the real man when the truth came out about his involvement with Kimi and the woman in Lander."

"You lost respect for him."

"I did. But that weakness and dishonesty is part of the man, part of what makes him who he is. I had to accept I chose a mentor who wasn't perfect. It was tough. I only wanted to be associated with someone who everyone looked up to. I needed that because I didn't have enough confidence in myself and my ability to make it in the job. I've figured it out now, though: I'm the only one who can do it."

"By the time I learned about Zeke's faults, he was dead."

"No chance to find out if you would have loved the whole man."

"It's been easy to hate him."

"Suppose he'd lived to tell the tale? Suppose he'd come to you and told you about the other woman, begged your forgiveness, and wanted to save the marriage?"

"I'll never know."

"Why did he cheat?"

"You mean besides the fact that he was a handsome, charming narcissist who could have any woman he wanted?"

"Yeah."

"I have thought about that."

"You don't need to tell me."

"This case has been good for me. It's helping me see some things I hadn't thought about before. Interesting thing: Zeke was sexually molested by a priest when he was in boarding school. It went on for a few years. He never told anyone until way later, but it's the reason he sought therapy in college. He said he became a psychiatrist because therapy saved his life. A nice, neat ending. Now I'm not so sure. Maybe his problems with intimacy stemmed from the abuse—maybe that's why he went outside the marriage."

"It's guaranteed to mess with people's relationships, right?"

"It's impossible to get away without some kind of scar. There are so many different ways it can show up in people's lives. It's the same for any interpersonal trauma: each individual responds in their own way."

"What about our guys, Tim, Max, and Connor?"

"Tim died so young, so we don't know how it would have affected him long term. And Max's head injury changed him dramatically. It's hard to know if any of the changes can be attributed to his abuse experience."

"And Connor? How did the sexual abuse affect him?"

"A few possibilities: first, he's into some kinky sexual things—erotic asphyxiation we know about, there may be more; second, he's sexually jealous and insecure, avoidant of sexual intimacy, and possibly unfaithful; and third, he might have murdered his fiancée."

She looked so serious counting off the reasons on her fingers. But her hair had come loose from its topknot, and the low light and music made him forget for a minute all the reasons he shouldn't touch her.

He leaned over and brushed her hair off her face.

She went still as a hunted animal sensing the hunter. Then she smiled at him, and he saw the barrier was gone.

"I never saw us doing this, Doc—drinking and talking about sex in a bar." He took a long sip of his Coors and gave her a wicked smile.

She returned the grin. "Do you want to take a drive with me down to Flaming Gorge? I want to see where the accident happened."

"How's tomorrow morning work for you?"

"I head out to ride as the sun's coming up, and then I have some work to do in the morning."

"Give me a call when you're done. I'll come and we can check it out."

CHAPTER 44

Up before the sun, restless and excited for the trip to Flaming Gorge, I drove out to the ranch where I board my horse, Soldier, a light gray, formerly wild mustang.

It was a fine morning for riding, the air still cool from the cover of night and sweet with the perfume of dew-moist desert flowers, and both Soldier and I needed the workout. With all the extra hours I'd been devoting to the murder investigation, I wanted to grab these morning hours for a trail ride.

Two years earlier, I'd fallen in love with Soldier at the Rock Springs Wild Horse Holding Facility. The small ranch, located north of town, was a ten-minute drive from my house, which made it easy to ride a couple of times a week. After months of work with a Native horse trainer, I got on Soldier for the first time.

I saddled him and we headed out through the back acre and onto free range. The sun, a small white ball of energy on the eastern horizon, chased the falling moon across the indigo sky.

An hour later, as we came up to the rail fence at the border of the ranch, a warm wind stirred the grasses.

Back in the barn, I went through the usual post-ride routine.

"I'll be back soon," I told Soldier before giving him one last pat and heading for home.

■ ■ ■

Antelope and I made plans to head out to Flaming Gorge at noon. He offered to buy dinner if I agreed to drive. He suggested the White Mountain Mining Company, where we could visit with Diego, who'd recently started a second job there as a waiter.

One of my jobs for the county is facilitating a community aftercare group for sex offenders returning from prison. It's not easy creating a respectable life with a good job with a sex offender label. Diego had participated in that group for the length of his parole, so I'd gotten to know him fairly well.

I fixed a quick breakfast of coffee and oatmeal and sat down to tackle the custody evaluation that had languished at the bottom of my priority list all week. I finished the report by eleven, leaving me time for a long shower.

Next, a small challenge: choosing clothes appropriate for the various activities of the day, which included hiking a deadly rock climbing route and dinner at a fancy steakhouse.

After giving it way too much thought, I chose my black tank top and black jeans, silver medallion necklace, red leather sandals, and new red Mexican shawl for the afternoon chill. I brought my boots along for the trail.

It bothered me a little that I'd taken so much time putting together an outfit because I wanted to look good for Antelope.

■ ■ ■

By 12:10 p.m., we were heading south on Highway 191. A four-wheel drive vehicle wasn't required—the loop road around the lake was paved—but my Jeep would give us more flexibility to explore the dirt roads around the campground and bouldering sites.

"Have you been down this way before?" Antelope asked.

"I haven't." I glanced out at the sparkling water. "It's amazing. I miss the ocean. I'll have to come back and swim here sometime."

Most of the drive on Highway 191 resembled the terrain between Rock Springs and Green River. It only turned mountainous on the Utah side of the Ashley National Forest.

Pagan Cave, the spot where the accident had happened, was a slanted rock face of black, white, and pink granite. The grove of trees surrounding it gave it the appearance of being in a tunnel.

A pristine spot in an almost untouched area, the inverted slant of the rock face represented a thrill for an experienced climber, a challenge and opportunity to test skills.

"Impressive," I said. "I can't imagine trying to scale it. But it's not my thing. And this is not my country. Am I overreacting, or is this a beautiful deathtrap?"

"The thing with this sport—it's real easy to die," Antelope said. "Sometimes the more experienced you are the more likely it is you'll die doing the thing you love, because skill is only one factor. There's the rock itself and its unique challenges; the mindset and attitude of the individual climber and of the group; and the weather—which, I'm sure you've noticed by now, is a moody thing here in Wyoming. Other than forgetting to tie a knot in a line, the weather is the most aggressive factor in climbing deaths."

"Those boys were inexperienced climbers. How could he have taken them here?"

Antelope shrugged. "Testosterone is a powerful drug. I guess the clergy is not immune to its effects on competition."

"And they wanted to impress him. I keep wondering about Connor returning home alone after this special graduation trip. The three boys went out together excited, the whole summer stretching out in front of them, their whole lives ahead of them after that. But only one of them comes home intact. This horrible tragedy wipes out Tim's future completely and changes Max's future so profoundly, and Connor is left to go on without his friends."

"Not sure someone can ever really recover from that kind of thing," Antelope said.

I nodded. "I believe Father Bellamy when he says Connor's suffering was great. Survivor guilt, the feeling that somehow you got lucky when the others didn't, makes it hard to be happy after that kind of experience."

Antelope grew thoughtful. "I wonder if he ever came back here."

It didn't seem likely to me. "It's a gorgeous spot, but for Connor I imagine it would be like visiting a grave."

"One of my favorite places is just down the way a bit, a short dirt road out of the Firefighters Memorial Campground. It's three miles out and back, but we can drive most of it, and it will give you a sense of the scale of this place. I can show it to you if you have the time and the footwear?" He looked down at my sandals.

"My boots are in the Jeep."

■ ■ ■

I let Antelope drive, since he knew the area. At the campground, he made a sharp turn onto a nearly invisible entrance to a dirt road. We bounced through heavy pine forests until the trees gave way to a grassy plateau. When we reached a bank above a high, fast-moving river, he stopped and threw the car into park.

Without a word, he hopped out of the car, jumped down off the bank, and started walking along the water's edge. I followed, happy to be out of the car, to have the soft resistance of the riverbed under my feet. The sun beat down and I heard the rhythmic murmur of river water moving over rocks.

We came to a wide boulder with a flat top and a view of the lake. I sat down and let my legs hang over the edge, leaned back, and raised my face to the sun. Antelope sat beside me on the warm, rough surface and looked out over the expanse of water in front of us.

"This is my place," he said. "Bear Canyon Overlook. It's where I come when it all gets to be too much."

"We all have those times. We all have our places."

We sat for a while in companionable silence.

"It looks good now," he finally said, "but the best time is either sunrise or sunset."

"It must be outstanding in the right light."

He smiled slightly. "We'll come back another time."

■ ■ ■

In no time we were back on I-80 keeping time with eighteen-wheelers, dwarfed by their long shadows, the wind blowing my hair across my face. We didn't speak. Antelope seemed lost in his own thoughts, and he was still driving; I wanted his full attention on the road as he maneuvered in and out of the spaces between the speeding trucks.

The noise from the wind and the trucks would have made talking impossible anyway.

The roar of the highway dimmed as he downshifted and slowed his speed to manage the turns coming into Green River.

"Tell me more about what you know about priests molesting kids," he said. "I keep thinking what happened to those boys is somehow related to Stacey's murder. I could be wrong, but I've learned to listen to my gut on these things."

"Perverted priests molesting altar boys happens so often it's almost a cliché," I said, shaking my head. "The Church's response to disciplining the offenders is notable for its utter disregard for the impact the abuse has on the innocent child victims. It's all about protecting the perpetrator, protecting the church's image in the community. Clergy at every level are in denial. And that's not just an historical fact; the same thing continues today, all the way up to the Vatican."

"That's what Toni said." Antelope's fingers drummed the steering wheel. "It's why she left the convent. She didn't want to be associated with a organization that functioned that way."

"She's just one of legions who had to give up a dream about the Church's righteousness."

"She didn't like Father Bellamy's approach, either. She felt really let down when he fell on the side of the deniers. She said he's either a narcissist or sociopath. What's your sense of him?"

I thought about our meeting with him. "I need more time with him alone to give you a clinical impression. I can see her point. He's superficially charming, but underneath I sense he's a cold fish. But let's be clear, not every narcissist, not even every sociopath, is a child molester."

"You think he's got what it takes to be an abuser?"

"It would be taking a big risk. He seems to have a good thing going, and from everything we hear, from him and others, he's loved by all. Widespread popularity is not typical of the priests who abuse; isolation and dark corners is more their thing."

"But like you said, the church is an old boys' network, and the response is just a slap on the wrist, a transfer to a parish in the boondocks. For someone depraved enough to molest kids, that seems like a small price to pay."

"Antelope, this may come as a surprise to you as a Wyoming native, but Rock Springs *is* the boondocks. And now there are protocols that prohibit transfer as a way of dealing with an offending priest."

"So if he got caught he would be looking at bigger consequences?"

"Most likely. It could mean the Church being done with him, or legal consequences; or maybe financial consequences, such as losing his pension. Trapped in a situation like that a person could become desperate, even dangerous."

"And what would a dangerous priest do?"

■ ■ ■

We arrived at the White Mountain Mining Company with the first of the early bird diners.

"I hope you don't mind the early hour," Antelope said. "I wanted a chance to talk to Diego before the place filled up."

"It's hard to ruin a steak for me—I'll take medium rare any time, any day."

"The county's buying, so order the best, Doc. It was Diego's idea for me to bring you here."

"Is that right?"

"I think he wants you to see him being successful."

We stepped out into a summer evening made for romance. We were at one of the best restaurants in the county, and likely the only two people there who wanted to talk murder.

From the outside, the building resembled an airplane hangar. The location, behind a chain link fence on an acre of dry desert surrounded by a gravel parking lot devoid of vegetation, didn't help the curb appeal.

Inside it was an Old West log cabin with white tablecloths and antique oil lamps.

"You look great, Doc," Antelope said. "Too sophisticated for any other place around here."

I smiled. "I like it when you call me, Doc, Detective."

Diego came over to meet us with an armful of oversize menus and led us to a corner table beside a west-facing window. A first glimmer of sunset, a wide crayon streak of bold orange, outlined the curving spine of White Mountain. When viewed from this vantage point, the two mounds of limestone rock resembled a woman reclining. Behind the restaurant, the desert stretched up to Pilot Butte, where a herd of wild horses roamed free on miles of open land. The wilderness, mysterious and menacing always, tonight felt taut with a frenzied energy

Across the table, Antelope studied the menu in the golden light; the strong flame cast quick, dancing shadows over the fine planes of his kind face.

Diego came to the table to take our order, handsome in a white shirt and black tie. He'd called it—I enjoyed seeing him here, working a job he could be proud of, looking respectable and pleased with himself.

"How's the case going?" he asked. "I'm thinking that's why I get to see the two of you out two nights in a row?"

"We're coming up short," Antelope said. "All we hear is there's no reason this woman got herself murdered."

"How do you do it?" A shadow crossed Diego's face. "Just hearing about it brings Kimi's murder back for me"

"It hasn't been so long," I said. "Just six months."

"People say it gets easier. You can't tell by me."

"If you want a place to talk about it, you know where to find me," I said.

"I been thinking about it, yeah—I'll call and we can do that soon," Diego said.

A few minutes later he returned with the wine and glasses. When he finished pouring, he gave a small bow and said, "Time to enjoy. No more talk of murder."

We followed his advice. Over the next hour and a half, Antelope told me about his time breaking horses in Riverton. I asked him if he could recommend a riding instructor—I felt like I'd hit a plateau in my skills—and he rattled off three Native names and promised to text their phone numbers later.

When Diego brought the check over he looked serious, and I immediately wondered if he'd done something to get himself in trouble. In all the time he'd spent in treatment, he never lost the need to challenge everyone and everything. But it wasn't a run-in with authority that had caused his change in mood.

"I felt Kimi close by me all night," he said. "She wants us to remember curiosity is a good trait, even though she met death while searching for the truth. What about this woman? Was she curious?"

CHAPTER 45

Max sat in the dark bedroom with the window open. The smoke from the joint floated out into the night. His mother hated it when he smoked in the house—hated the smell of weed. It was easy to appease her in this way. Things went better between them when he didn't give her anything to nag him about.

Most of the time he controlled his temper, but lately it had been getting harder to maintain, no matter how much he smoked. The funny thing was, she couldn't tell when he was high. Even when he sat zombie-like for hours without uttering a word, she left him alone. It must say something about his non-high personality. Or maybe she just didn't pay much attention to him.

He wrapped up the weed and put his things away in his backpack. In his sock feet he made his way through the house with careful footsteps. In the dark hallway, he counted his steps to the sewing room, opened the door, and slipped inside.

He went straight to the closet and reached behind the hanging plastic bags of off-season clothes to the built-in shelf where she kept the tin file box. He retrieved the box, snapped open the lid, and removed the file containing the documents related to the settlement. He located the pages containing the bank account numbers and mutual fund and stock certificates where the payout money was invested, slipped them into his backpack, put the tin box back in its hiding place, arranged the clothes, and shut the closet door.

He stopped in his tracks. The snoring had stopped. He heard his mother's door open, her feet on the floorboards. He ducked into the closet. If she went looking for him in his room and didn't find him there . . .

From the closet, he listened for more sounds. She was in the bathroom. He heard the toilet flush, water running in the basin, her footsteps on the floorboards, and her door close shut.

He knew her sleep patterns—knew it could be awhile before she began snoring again. It was late, though, and he couldn't wait any longer. He didn't know what the night would bring, and wanted his things in order. Before he met up with Connor, he'd stop at his place and put these documents with his will and the personal note he'd attached so there would be no confusion when the time came to execute his intentions.

He raised the window and stepped out onto the roof of the sunporch. He closed the window behind him and, using the drainpipe, lowered himself to the ground.

On both sides of the wet highway, shallow pools of rainwater reflected silver moonlight like pearls in the desert. Despite everything, his heart filled with joy. The simple gifts of the senses brought him to his knees with wonder and gratitude

Kelly came to mind—his true love and truest friend. He'd missed her the last three days, but he couldn't be with her. Her energy and her physicality would have kept him tethered to the present when what he needed to be doing was time-traveling.

Just the thought of her woke every cell in his body and got his blood moving. She was a magnet, his true north.

At the light on Dewar Drive, he scrolled through his phone for her number and called her.

CHAPTER 46

Gray shadows drifted in through the vinyl blinds when Kelly woke late in the day. When the rain had started at noon, she'd taken it as a sign to go back to bed. With no reason to get up, nowhere she had to go, she rolled over onto her stomach and fell back asleep again.

Throughout the afternoon, a steady rain fell while she slept a troubled sleep, waking often. Each time she stirred, the summer storm lulled her back down into a dreamless peace.

Since the funeral, she'd had a hard time staying awake.

She finally rousted herself sometime late in the evening. She turned on one light and sat in the small circle of illumination. She didn't like being alone in the big, empty house; this presented a perfect time to work on her fear of being alone. She felt naked, spinning and freezing in black empty space, her open hands reaching out and finding nothing. It would be another week before her parents and Timmy got home.

She decided to play video games, a distraction from her feelings. Later, when she got bored, she might text Max and see what he was up to. He'd want to get high, and she would join him.

She checked her phone again. Jack still hadn't called. She might never see him again. His stupid thing with Stacey had ruined everything. She'd always known he was a liar and a cheater. So why did it bother her so much?

Because he chose Stacey.

The phone vibrated in her hand. Max.

"Hello stranger," she said.

"Sorry I haven't called. I've been going through some stuff."

"Me too."

"What's wrong with your voice?"

"It's been days since I talked to anyone; I've just been sleeping over here all by my lonesome."

"Are you sick?"

"Sick in the heart, sick in the soul."

"I know the feeling. Life sucks sometimes."

"Like now."

"I need to see you. Can I come over?"

"Sure. I'm a mess, though. Give me an hour. I need to clean up and shower."

"I might be later than that. I'm meeting up with Connor. We have a few things to talk about. I'm not sure how it will go."

"How's he doing? I haven't talked to him."

"I'll tell you when I see you. Remember what I said the other night? I'm 100 percent sure of it now. And Tim knew about it too."

"About Connor, you mean?"

"I don't know how he's going to take it. I can't say any more right now. I have to talk to him first. It's between me and Connor tonight, the way it always has been."

A knot formed in her stomach. "I'm getting a weird feeling. Should I be worried?"

"Everything's going to be all right now. I remember what happened the day Tim died and I busted my head open."

"Oh my God, Max! That's great!"

"It is and it isn't."

"It's what you wanted, though, right? Wasn't that the whole point of therapy?"

"Be careful what you wish for." Max's tone was dark. "I gotta go, he's waiting."

"Now you've said too much. I can't wait. You have to tell me."

"What happened on the rock was no accident."

"It was the weather, that freak storm."

"No, nothing was an accident. My busted head wasn't an accident. Tim dying wasn't an accident. You have to trust me. I'm not crazy and I'm not making this up. That's all I'm going to say right now."

CHAPTER 47

The rain came down hard and the old wipers made noisy, useless swipes across the window in an angry beat that suited him—pounding against a thing defeated. He was angry, and for once he felt in control of it. He wanted it at his service and knew he could keep it in check. Gone were the senseless times of letting loose on someone or something to take down the pressure and keep from exploding. He'd been blind and deaf and locked out of his own memory and experience.

But now he could see and hear every last detail of what had happened the day he fell eighty feet from a rocky ledge with an inverted drop. The memory had come forward, clear and true, with the same swift ease a correct password opens a website. He'd finally gotten into his own head, and now he was welcome to explore everything stored within.

Connor had sounded incredulous, unbelieving, when he'd told him the news.

"I can't believe it buddy, after all these years," he said. "That's amazing."

As he thought about it now, stalled at the light on Dewar Drive, the words were right but the tone was wrong. That's why he had to see Connor face to face. He'd been too long alone, isolated from himself and his friends, because he couldn't remember his own days.

He saw it again: the memory of one thing after another, so fast, inevitable from the start—the rope slipped, he twirled in space, a weightless crab mid-air, legs kicked, hands clawed for a hold, missed it, the rope slipped, there was a weightless stall mid-air, like a plane engine stalling before the drop, and then the crash, the dark. He saw it all, and he was home.

He pulled into Connor's parking lot and was about to turn off the truck when Connor jogged over and opened the door. "Let's take a ride," he said, already climbing in.

"Okay."

"This damn rain, I have cabin fever."

"It's starting to let up." Max started driving. "Where to?"

"Take the mountain road. I feel like I've been trapped in this town for too long."

"I wouldn't mind a cold one."

"Head over to the Liquor Mart, I'll grab us a six-pack for the road like old times."

When they got there, Max parked in the lot and started to get out, but Connor said, "Stay put, it's on me," and was out of the truck and into the store before Max could protest. He felt the excitement build. He couldn't wait to tell Connor what he remembered. For the first time in years he would show up as his real self, his remembered, known self. He could give Connor more of himself in friendship than he had since they were kids.

Connor got in and opened two bottles. "Try this, my friend, the latest craft beer out of Denver. Prepare to have your mind blown."

"Not what I'm in the mood for right now." Max chuckled. "I feel like I just got my mind *back*."

"So you said. Tell me all about it."

Max took a long pull on the beer. Connor was right. It was dark and went down smooth. He finished it off in one go. "How 'bout another?" he said, handing Connor the empty.

"Here you go. Watch yourself on the mountain, though, it's about to be slick up there after the rain."

Max took a sip and set the fresh bottle in the holder. He made a right turn onto Foothill Boulevard going north, back toward Connor's place and the entrance to White Mountain Road.

The road was wet but the truck held the course. They rode

in silence for a while. This was the first time they'd been together in a normal, social way since before Stacey died.

Max suddenly felt the loss, the wretched absence, of Stacey spread out between them like a yawning sinkhole.

Ever since she died he'd felt a small comfort when he spoke about her. That was part of why he kept going back to Kelly. He liked talking to her about Stacey. She got it, and he didn't need to pretend to be brave.

He looked to Connor for different reasons, for comfort and validation of another kind. He wanted that tonight, but now he didn't know how to start.

"It's like old times cruising, with no real destination in mind," Connor said. "You remember those days with you and me and Timmy, riding for hours because we could? No plans, with gas money and time to kill?"

"I don't remember everything," Max admitted. "But I'm hoping it will all come back. Right now it's stuff connected to trauma. Like, it's all linked together, so when one thing comes to the surface, the others follow along after it, tied together with invisible string."

"You freaked me out the other night, talking about Kroll and all the sick things he did to us. I put it behind me a long time ago. If you're smart, you'll do the same. No point thinking about it now. The guy's dead."

Max shook his head. "My head's been empty for years. It fucked me up not being able to remember my own life. I'm not going to stuff it down again."

"Suit yourself. But if you're looking to me to listen to you vent, I'm sorry, but the answer is no. I have enough to deal with right now. You're the last person I should have to say that to, man."

They reached the summit just as the last wisps of storm clouds dispersed, revealing a huge moon the color of lemons. Liquid light rippled over the rocky terrain.

Max parked the truck. "I can't talk and drive. The beer went down too quick."

Connor shifted in his seat. "Say what you got to say, man."

"I thought it'd be easy, but it's not," Max said. He picked up the beer bottle and took another sip.

"Just spill it. Rip the bandage off. Putting it off only makes it worse."

"I remember the accident. I can see the whole thing."

"Welcome to my world. I've lived with it for ten years now."

Max looked at Connor. "I have a question for you. Who tied the ropes?"

"What?" Connor stared out the windshield, unmoving.

"Who tied the ropes the day we climbed Pagan Cave?"

"That was ten long years ago, my friend, and the whole time all I've wanted to do is forget. You got lucky, losing your memories. I didn't have that luxury. I lost two friends on that rock. Tim died, and you—well, you said it yourself, you're not the same."

"We were novice climbers, inexperienced as fuck," Max said slowly. "He made us do the knots ourselves to learn, practicing over and over until we got it right, until our hands bled. But he still checked them over every time because he had to, he was legally responsible for our safety, was the only one who knew what the fuck he was doing. So how did the knots fail?"

"What's your point?" Connor looked at him now, hard.

"He messed with them. Can you think of another reason they didn't hold?"

"I don't know! Everything went wrong. We were fucking unlucky with that storm coming out of nowhere. It must have been the rain. It loosened things up. The rain messed with the gear."

"So my life was fucked in a freak accident caused by a freak storm that resulted in random freak equipment failure? There was no human factor—that's what you think?"

"That's what everyone thinks, because that's what happened. Don't you think they investigated back then? And they concluded exactly what you just said. But you think you know better than anyone else because you suddenly remember a few things from ten years ago." He sighed. "Anyway, what's the point? Nothing will bring Tim back."

"The truth is the point."

"You seriously think a priest would commit murder? Why, for God's sake?"

"Did you tell him about our plan?"

"What are you talking about?"

"Did you tell Bellamy Tim and I were going to bust his ass?"

"I think you're losing it, man. Stacey dying has us all messed up."

"We were going to do it after graduation. Drive over to Cheyenne to see the Bishop. We told you and you tried to stop us. Are you seriously saying you don't remember?"

"You need to put this behind you," Connor exploded. "It's water under the bridge, man, ancient history. I'm looking ahead now. Because when I look back all I see is Stacey and what I was supposed to have in life. I loved your sister with all my heart. Nothing that happened before or since her death means anything to me. Think about that before you open up something that could very possibly destroy me."

"I can't leave it like this. It's unfinished business."

"Do what you need to do. I won't be a part of it."

Max shook his head. "Ten years and you haven't changed."

"I'm done with this conversation," Connor said. "Take me home."

They drove back to the Preserve in silence. A mile out, Connor unbuckled his seat belt.

"Pull over," he said. "I'll walk from here." He opened the door and jumped down out of the truck, then leaned back inside. "Take my advice. Put this stuff back where it came from. No good can come from stirring things up. Good night, my friend."

Max looked at Connor, saw the sorrow in his eyes, and something else, too, there and gone in an instant—the acknowledgment of the truth they shared. He watched his friend walk away toward home, skirting the pockets of water in the potholes and depressions in the dirt road.

CHAPTER 48

In the Saddle Lite Saloon the cover band was playing Johnny Cash and a few couples had just started to dance when Antelope left the smoky bar for the cool air of the summer night. Under low-hanging clouds, the scent of rain-soaked sagebrush and diesel fumes filled the air.

A late-model red pickup was blocking his Cadillac. He considered going back in to find the driver, but traffic from the rodeo fairgrounds north of town would be all backed up on Elk Street right now anyway. He'd sit for an hour, at least. The moon was high and a cool breeze came off the desert. He would walk.

He jogged up the gradual slope of the ramp onto the overpass and turned left onto Pilot Butte Avenue. Traffic was gridlocked, as he'd expected. The lights changed three times while vehicles stayed in place. Horns started up, loud, raging, everyone done with being cooped up and stuck in traffic.

Three blocks ahead, Our Lady of Sorrows loomed dark and deserted. In five minutes, he'd be home and in bed. He crossed the road between two out-of-county SUVs and began running along the sidewalk through the blaring horns and chaos.

The clock struck midnight, and the church bells tolled a dozen lazy swells above the noisy street. They silenced the horns and echoed back from the mountain. A silent moment followed, a pillow of soft air, before a gunshot tore a hole in the night.

As soon as Antelope heard it, his feet moved fast under him, legs galloping toward the blast and the ringing aftermath. He knew for certain in his ruined lawman's heart that the shot meant trouble.

Doors opened and people jumped from vehicles, a herd on the run, headed toward danger. Sirens screamed and lights flashed as county and city cars bullied their way through the glut of vehicles in the streets.

At the front of the church, a crowd had already formed. The porous stone face of the Gothic structure was damp and smelled of moss and slime. Antelope entered the dark church as the county ambulance came to a stop and cleared the onlookers from the sidewalk.

He broke his stride and stopped short before the casualty that waited for him. His breath came sharp and fast, and too loud in the holy, silent space.

Trouble follows the guilty, he thought when he saw the dead man. It was one of his crazy Aunt Estella's sayings, and he couldn't figure out how it could be relevant to a body lying dead in a church.

Max Hart was on the floor near the confessional with a bullet in his heart and a gun in his hand.

The church was dark except for the red sanctuary light and the glow coming in through the stained glass windows from the security lights in the alley. The painted saints looked down, the only witnesses to the human drama that had just unfolded.

Antelope stood aside as the medics did a quick assessment and confirmed what was clear to him from the first look. They wouldn't be taking Max Hart to Sweetwater County Memorial Hospital. The EMTs packed their equipment and left. In a few minutes, they would be replaced by the crime scene technicians. For the moment, it was just him and the dead man.

He heard a rustling sound behind him and turned, startled. "Father Bellamy."

The priest looked down at Max.

"Where can we talk?" Antelope asked.

"In the vestry; come this way."

The deputies arrived to secure the crime scene and communicate with the forensic crew and coroner's office as Antelope followed

Bellamy down the aisle to a side door. They stepped through it to a narrow passageway, and then through another door that led into the priest's private quarters.

Father Bellamy poured two glasses of water from a crystal carafe and handed one to Antelope. "The first time in ten years Max Hart entered this church was for his sister's funeral. I had hopes he'd come home and find his faith again in the wake of the tragedy. It wouldn't be the first time it happened." He wiped sweat from his face with a starched white handkerchief.

"When you're ready, Father, I need you to tell me everything from the beginning."

Antelope recognized the signs. The priest was in shock, an experience shared by those who discovered a dead body. The memory would never leave him.

"I called right away from phone over there."

He gestured to the phone on the wall, an ancient rotary model that had to be one of the last working models of its kind. The movement caused him to spill water on himself; he dabbed at the wet spot on his chest with his handkerchief.

"I'm going to need something stronger than water. Care to join me in a whiskey?"

"I'll pass. And you will too until we're finished here, Father. I need you clear-headed."

Bellamy nodded. "Right." He sat down, and gestured for Antelope to do the same.

Antelope perched on the chair he indicated. "Tell me what happened."

"I was doing some preparatory reading for Sunday's sermon. Max called and asked if I would be willing to hear his confession. I said, of course, I could do it in the morning before the first Mass and he could receive communion. He said he couldn't wait. He sounded absolutely tortured. He asked if he could come this evening and I told him he could.

"Hours went by and he didn't come. I was getting ready to call it a night. I figured he'd had a change of heart. Then I heard the front door of the church slam shut. I took a minute to put on my vestments and prepared to hear his confession. When I entered the church he was kneeling in the last pew, his head in his hands. I put my hand on his shoulder and told him I was ready to hear his confession.

"Max looked at me with pure torment in his eyes, and I knew in that moment he was right: he couldn't wait any longer. We entered the confessional booth. I heard his confession and gave him absolution. I waited for a while in the booth after he left and then I made my way back to the vestry. Just as I opened the door, I heard the shot. I ran back and found him dead on the floor."

Antelope knew from growing up as a Catholic that Father Bellamy was prohibited from telling him what Max had confessed. Confession was a sacrament in which the priest served as the intermediary between the penitent and God. What was told in confession was told to God, and the priest could not reveal it to any living person without risking excommunication.

"I wouldn't be surprised if you were wondering if Max's confession bears any relation to your investigation, Detective," Bellamy volunteered.

"I would be very interested in anything you could share with me, Father."

"Unfortunately, my hands are tied, as I must maintain absolute secrecy and uphold the trust of the Sacrament of Penance."

"I understand, Father. How about you just tell me everything you know about Max Hart?"

"I knew Max as a boy. I don't know much about Max Hart the man, except what I told you the other day about his relationship with his sister. She attributed his mood swings to his head injury. Frankly, the only time she spoke of him was when he caused her stress."

"You said it's been ten years since he stopped coming to church?"

"It has to be that long. It was after the accident; up until then he was an active member of the church. He was in a rehab down in Salt Lake for a long time. When he was able to come home, I went to see him, but he had amnesia from the head injury and didn't remember me or his time as an altar boy in this church. I visited him a few times, but there was nothing to build on. It's a sad case. He never came back to church. And I stopped going to see him when it became clear he had no interest in what I had to offer."

"What was he like before the accident? I understand there were some personality changes."

"When I knew Max, he was a serious boy with a somber nature, dutiful and reliable. Not the life of the party, by any means, but a brilliant kid, destined for great things academically. I got the feeling he wasn't so popular at school—he was what we might call a nerd—so it was special to him, the place he found with Connor and Tim."

"All right, Father, I don't have any other questions for you right now." Antelope made for the door.

After leaving the priest, he walked back through the church. The deputies were finishing up their work; one of them came over to him.

"Detective, we're done out here. We're about to transport. Do you need any more time at the scene before we load up? Forensic wants in here, too."

"Hold it up for a minute," Antelope said. "I need five minutes alone with him. I'll be right out."

When the church was empty, he lit a candle in front of the statue of the Blessed Virgin. He didn't believe God had anything to do with this murder, but if he received help from beyond on this case, it wouldn't be the first time.

Spirit sounds behind him—soft rustling of fabric, whisper of breath released into the stillness. In the moving, shadowy light of the altar, shapeshifters darted and played. Behind him he heard the vacuum sigh of rushing air, the crack of heavy wood slamming into place.

He sprinted down the carpeted aisle and into the fresh night air. From the stone steps of the church, he scanned the avenue in both directions. Not a soul in sight. All the onlookers had gone home, and he was alone with his thoughts.

Max Hart had left the world and taken his memories with him. His secrets and sins were sealed forever behind the veil of confession.

CHAPTER 49

Keyed up, her eyes strained and her fingers numb from hours of *Grand Theft Auto*, Kelly felt bored and overstimulated at the same time. Where was Max?

With the later hour, the empty house felt even creepier. Every slasher movie she'd ever watched came back to her in the quiet, lonely rooms. The rain had finally let up, but now the damp and chill had settled in and she couldn't get warm. She turned on the gas fireplace and lay down in front of it.

When Max said her brother was murdered, a cold terror had unfolded inside her, like a thick snake unwinding and circling her spine.

In the shower, she alternated ice cold and steaming hot water, back and forth, switching fast between the extremes, blasts of contrasting pain. Better than dealing with the rotten swell of feeling in her gut that wasn't going to go away until Max came and told her everything.

After the shower, she scrubbed her red skin and applied soothing lotion, took a long time with a manicure and pedicure; the slow process was like a reverse meditation.

She thought about Max and what the night might bring and chose her white jeans and a black lace tank top.

The first night she'd slept at his place, she'd seen a gun and known without asking that he slept with it all the time. Even before

Stacey's murder he'd been kind of crazy, and maybe dangerous. But his strangeness drew her to him.

What the hell? She hated waiting. *where r u?* she texted, then threw the phone down.

She felt herself getting ready to release her own kind of crazy, texting him over and over, but she didn't want to show him that side of her, so she opted to distract herself. She went back to her video game but couldn't get into it. She checked her phone. In the kitchen, she stared into the well-stocked refrigerator; nothing appealed to her. She changed out of the jeans and tank into more comfortable clothes.

The stove clock read 11:30 p.m. In a half hour, Domino's would close. She ordered a Meat Lovers Supreme, buffalo chicken wings, and cinnamon sticks. As soon as she hung up, she hit redial and added bread sticks.

She texted Max again—*WAITING!*—and got no answer.

She felt cold again. She went to lie down by the fireplace again while she waited.

■ ■ ■

The phone rang. Kelly's heart jumped and fluttered in her chest, but it was just the food.

The pizza guy was a skinny teenager who looked her up and down in a lecherous, lingering way she recognized from the club. The look said he wanted to fuck her. Even in simple clothing, yoga pants and a white T-shirt, she turned men on.

She got those looks all the time and it reinforced her decision to get paid for being sexy. Every day men got free pleasure from women, but at the club they paid for the privilege.

She placed the stacked boxes in the oven and set the heat on low. Her stomach growled and she knew she could eat every bit of food she ordered. Better to wait for Max, though. If she ate anything the way she felt—hyped up and turned on—it wouldn't be pretty. Max could show up in the middle of her throwing it all up.

One more text and she was done.

WTF?

She sat cross-legged on the window seat and watched for his truck. Outside, the wind howled like a beast, the ruthless weather not yet finished. Another storm was coming, she could tell from the sinking fatigue of low pressure and being stuck in thick air.

A white moon, bright as a floodlight, exposed the details of the neighborhood; the houses and vehicles glowed in the cold fluorescence.

Where was he?

She needed a cigarette; she found her pack stuffed in the couch.

Pacing now, about to lose it, she grabbed the remote and turned on the late news. "BREAKING NEWS" scrolled across the bottom of the screen. Down on her knees, close to the television, she held her breath.

ROCK SPRINGS MAN DIES OF GUNSHOT WOUND.

No no no goddamn you, Max.

She called his phone. It rang and rang and rang.

Her heart beat on every ring. Ashes fell on her white shirt.

Pick up, Max! The ringing stopped. She held her breath and waited. *Thank God!*

"This is Detective Antelope on Max Hart's phone."

"Where's Max? Why are you answering his phone?"

"Are you at your house?"

"Yes! Watching the fucking breaking news! Is it Max? Is he dead?"

CHAPTER 50

Antelope called after midnight to tell me Max Hart had just died from what appeared to be a self-inflicted gunshot wound. He asked me to go with him to Green River to take a statement from Kelly Ryan. Apparently, Max had made plans to see her that night.

I dressed quickly and waited outside for Antelope pull into the circle.

"Sorry to be the one to tell you," he said. "It must be rough, losing a patient like this."

I shook my head in disbelief. "What happened? I saw him today. He gave no indication he planned to take his life. If he'd said anything about hurting himself, I would have put him in the hospital."

"Something changed his mind. He called Father Bellamy and said he had a confession to make, and immediately after confessing, he shot himself. Does that make any sense?"

"This is crazy. It sounds like you're talking about a different person. I can't believe it, any of it—that he went to church to ease his guilt. Max stopped going to church years ago. And with everything he'd been remembering about the abuse, he'd lost all respect for the Church. I don't understand. And, of course, the priest can't share anything that was spoken of in confession."

"That's a dead end."

"So we'll never know."

"No disrespect, Doc, but he was pretty messed up, right?"

"Yes, but this complete turnaround in hours . . . that isn't possible unless he had multiple personalities, which as his therapist I can say I never saw any signs of."

"But it's not impossible, right?" Antelope pressed. "Something could come out under pressure. There's a first time for everything."

"Of course, but I think there would have been some sign. If there was one, I didn't catch it . . ." I put my hand over my mouth. "Was it there and I missed it?"

Antelope put his hand over mine. "Don't try to sort it all out now. It's too much of a shock."

"Who's the shrink here, Antelope?"

"Sometimes the shrink needs some support."

"Thank you."

"Besides, I brought you along because I need your professional help with Miss Kelly Ryan. Can't have you falling apart now."

I managed a tiny smile. "Can we stop for a coffee at the travel plaza before we go?"

"You read my mind."

■ ■ ■

Kelly couldn't stop crying. Antelope and I sat on either side of her for twenty minutes while Antelope practically spoon-fed her coffee. As soon as she got it all down, she ran to the bathroom and threw it up.

She came back white-faced and quiet, clutching a wad of Kleenex.

"He called me, asked if he could come over. I waited for him for hours and he kills himself without even saying good-bye? I hate him!"

"How did he sound on the phone, Kelly?" I said.

"Not fucking suicidal!" She flopped back down on the couch.

"Can you remember what he said?"

"He was meeting up with Connor."

"That's all he said?"

"He'd just remembered a bunch of stuff about the day Tim died. He wanted to talk to Connor about it."

With every therapy session, Max had gotten closer to recalling the accident. But at our last session, just yesterday, the events of the day of the accident had remained out of reach. If he'd had a flashback after the session, it could have triggered a dissociative episode and possibly result in the unusual behavior of wanting to go to confession.

"Did he tell you what he remembered?" Antelope asked.

"It got me kind of upset. He said it wasn't an accident that Tim died. Why would he say that?" She turned her wide, questioning eyes on me.

"This is great, Kelly, you've been a big help," I said gently. "What can we do for you tonight? Are you going to be okay here by yourself?"

"What about Fern? Does she know yet?" Kelly blew her nose. "I'd like to be with her. We're kind of in the same place. She'll most likely be drunk, but I don't mind. I could use a drink myself."

"I sent two of our senior deputies to give her the news," Antelope said. "I'll swing by there and see what she thinks. Doc, how about you hang here with Kelly while I pay a visit to Mrs. Hart? One way or another, we'll get you two ladies together for the night."

"We'll be fine. Why don't you pack a bag, Kelly, so we can drive over as soon as Detective Antelope says it's okay?"

∎ ∎ ∎

An hour later, we left Kelly and Fern Hart crying together and headed back to Rock Springs to break the news to Connor, most likely the last person to see Max alive.

We no sooner got on the highway than the rain started coming down again, steady and hard. The windshield wipers couldn't keep up with the flood of water streaming down the window.

Antelope stopped under the cover of an overpass. "It's safer if we wait it out," he said.

"We don't have weather like this in the East. I'm always surprised by the violence of the storms out here."

"We'll see some flooding." He peered out the windshield at the downpour. "I don't like to drive blind, and there's zero visibility when it comes down like this."

My mind had already moved on from the weather. "What did you think of Kelly's response?"

"Eerily similar to yours, and she knows this guy well."

"It's not uncommon for people to react to the suicide of someone close with shock and disbelief. When a person is determined to end their life, they usually don't let others know what their plans are because they don't want to get talked out of it."

"It's not like he didn't have a reason—or a lot of reasons."

"I'm still not there yet, seeing Max as a suicide. I don't know if I'll ever make peace with that."

"Maybe, if he killed his sister and the guilt was too great . . ." Antelope shrugged. "He could be violent. You think it couldn't have happened with her?"

"The way he talked about her before and after she died convinced me he didn't do it; his grief was so uncomplicated, so pure. And why would he kill her?"

"That's a good question, and one I can't answer." He started the car. "The rain's letting up. Let's see what Connor can tell us about tonight."

■ ■ ■

After years of doing therapy and treating hundreds of people, I'd come to believe that the way people acted under stress revealed a lot about their essential personality and character. I was curious to see how Connor would react to the news.

"Does he know I'm coming?" I asked as we turned into the parking lot.

"No. I didn't tell him anything. This will be a surprise for the prosecutor."

"When you call him 'the prosecutor,' I get the feeling you don't like him much."

"I don't like him much when I call him Connor Collins, either."

"Why?"

"I've seen him in court a few times. My impression is he's arrogant and likes himself too much."

"Not your kind of guy."

"I'm trying to keep an open mind. It's bad for the case to go in with prejudice. It's how Scruggs lost his gig up in Lander. Snap decisions don't work in law enforcement." He pulled into an empty spot. "Here we are. Let's do this thing."

I stifled a laugh. "You've been watching cop shows, right?"

He raised his right eyebrow, a thing I'd noticed he did when he couldn't think of a smart response.

The parking lot at the Preserve resembled a lake, but I didn't have to walk on tiptoes in my new Aquatalia waterproof riding boots.

It was four in the morning now. It took three long presses on the buzzer to wake Connor. His voice on the intercom sounded like it belonged to something pulled from another dimension.

Disoriented from being pulled out bed, he scowled when he opened the door. The black hooded bathrobe he wore made him look like a boxer ready to enter the ring. He looked back and forth between me and Antelope—creatures out of a nightmare, there to torment him.

Finally, Antelope spoke. "Can we come in, please? I have some bad news. Something happened tonight."

"Come in, then." Connor took several lazy steps backward and we walked past him into the dark room. A sliver of light came through the half-open door to the master bedroom. His silence made me wonder if he'd taken a sleep aid and now he couldn't wake up.

He hit a panel on the wall with the palm of his hand, and mood lighting brought the living room into focus. Connor covered his eyes and dimmed the lights.

The place wasn't my style, more *GQ* metrosexual, but it was classy and clean—unusual for most heterosexual bachelors of this century.

At the kitchen island, he pulled three chrome stools out, hopped up on one of them, and swung his legs. The digital clock above the stove read 4:15 a.m. Connor stared at it and shook his head like a swimmer surfacing from a deep-water dive.

"How bad?" he finally asked. "What now?"

"Did you see Max Hart earlier tonight?" Antelope asked.

"You know the answer. What happened to Max?"

"We'll do my questions first; it works better that way."

Connor stood up and leaned toward me, so close I smelled the alcohol on his breath.

"Good evening, Dr. Hunt. May I inquire about the reason for your presence in my home tonight?"

Beside me, Antelope shifted in his seat, but he didn't say a word at first. I held my tongue, knowing that Connor was attempting to take control by bypassing Antelope's instructions.

After a beat, Antelope answered for me, signaling his alpha status, his determination to run the meeting. "Dr. Hunt is consulting on the investigation of Stacey's murder. What happened tonight may have bearing on that case. What time did you start and end your visit with Max last night?"

When Connor didn't answer, Antelope reached into his pocket and took out his phone. "I want a video and audio recording of this interview," he said and handed me his phone. He looked at Connor. "Five minutes, Collins; here or at headquarters, you choose. At this time I'm not charging you with any crime. Call an attorney if you want. I'm here to investigate an unattended death by gunshot, and you're getting in my way."

Connor's head went back and his eyes widened like he'd been hit in the head with a basketball; he looked stunned and hurt. "No way, you're bullshitting. He's dead? What happened?"

Antelope stood. "Get dressed. Play time's over."

"No, hold on, do it here, ask your questions."

"Start the recording," Antelope told me.

I pressed play.

"This is Detective Beauregard Antelope, Sweetwater County Sheriff's Office, with Dr. Pepper Hunt, consulting psychologist, interviewing Mr. Connor Collins at his residence—The Preserve, Unit 306, Rock Springs, Wyoming—in the matter of the unattended death of Max Hart on June 28." He focused on Connor. "Please state the time you met with Mr. Hart on June 28."

"Roughly 10:00 p.m.," Connor said. "I didn't make note of the specific time."

"Where did this meeting occur?"

"He picked me up here. We drove around town."

"Why did he pick you up?"

"He called me earlier in the evening and said he had something he wanted to talk to me about."

"Was he intoxicated?"

"Max could hold his liquor pretty well. He might have been. It's hard to tell with Max. He wanted a beer, so we went to Liquor Mart and I bought us a six-pack. He drank two craft beers."

"What did he want to talk to you about?"

"Old times; our friend Tim who died; honestly, I was in no mood. I can barely keep my head up these days. Max was in a bad place too. Both of us flat-out ruined about Stacey. We talked for a while, and then he dropped me off. He wanted more from me and he didn't get it. I had no idea he was ready to do something like this."

"Did he tell you he remembered the day he was injured?"

Connor laughed and looked away. He had the same faraway look I'd noticed that day when we'd visited him in his office—in another world, where he preferred to stay.

"Mr. Collins?" Antelope said.

"How is this relevant?"

"Did he tell you he didn't believe the injury was accidental?"

It was almost dawn. Pale light came through the cracks in the drapes. Connor looked like he hadn't slept in a week. Antelope, on the other hand, looked strong enough to take on a wild horse.

"No. We didn't discuss anything like that." Connor looked at the stove clock again. "I have to be up in a few hours for court. We're way past five minutes."

"One last question. Did Max give any indication he planned to take his own life?"

"Hell no, he never gave any indication he was suicidal. I never would have left him alone if he had."

∎ ∎ ∎

We walked out into a rosy dawn that felt at odds with the night's tragedy. As we drove back to my house, I thought about how it would take time for me to process Max's death, the loss of this person, my patient. Psychotherapy is intimate work. It takes place between two people in a small room where emotions, memories, sense of self, relationship to others, the patient's whole internal world, opens to the therapist like a gift wrapped up in many layers. Inside those four walls, the heart and soul, the mechanics and meaning of a life, are revealed for the purpose of analysis and understanding.

It wouldn't be easy saying good-bye to Max Hart.

"You once told me you don't require a lot of sleep," Antelope said as he pulled up in front of my house.

Halfway out of the car and half-asleep, I turned and looked back at him.

"Can you come with me to the morgue tomorrow morning? Fern Hart is scheduled to identify the body, and I anticipate she'll need some professional support."

"What time are you thinking?"

"We scheduled it for 9:00 a.m."

I did the mental calculation. "Time for two hours of sleep, a shower, and breakfast. I'm there."

CHAPTER 51

The morning was too achingly beautiful for the terrible task of escorting Max's mother to the morgue, with a bright sun and temperatures predicted to rise into the nineties by the afternoon. The weather forecast indicated a few days' reprieve from the recent rainy spell that had made the week since Stacey Hart's murder especially desolate.

The morgue was located in the county Detention Center south of town on Highway 191. When I signed the contract to be on the county payroll on an as-needed basis, I'd toured the multimillion-dollar complex. It was an impressive, technically sophisticated law enforcement center—funded exclusively, like every county building in Sweetwater County, by the proceeds the county received from the oil companies who mined in its rich land. Deputies were to bring Fern Hart there; I rode with Antelope.

On the way there, Antelope told me a search of Max's trailer house had yielded a handwritten will, stock certificates, and $20,000 in cash. Max had named me as executor of the will.

I was still processing this information as we entered the Detention Center. There were so many different departments in the building, each in a different spoke of the wheel fanning out from the central command control center. Although I'd had a tour of the morgue and the medical examiner's quarters when I first visited, I couldn't remember exactly where they were located. Antelope, however, seemed to know exactly where he was going.

We had just been buzzed in by the officer at the door of the morgue when the receptionist called to say Fern Hart had arrived.

"You stay here. I'll escort her in," the duty officer said.

We waited in the small cubicle between the door leading to the corridor circling the wheel spokes and the one that led to the morgue.

"You can wait outside for us," Antelope said. "No need for two of us to be in there with her, and I have to be. I just need you here for after she makes the ID."

I nodded. "It's bound to be difficult for her."

"Here they come now." Antelope looked past me through the glass window toward the main steel door to all the pods.

I heard the sound of their shoes hitting the squeaky-clean floors, a mild crunching sound, as they made their way to the morgue. The door opened and the four of us were temporarily trapped in the glass cubicle; I felt an immediate, claustrophobic crush in my chest. I looked at Fern Hart's face; she looked like a zombie, red-eyed and empty of strength. She said nothing.

Seconds later, the door opened, and they filed into the cool inner space housing the morgue.

I leaned back against the wall, my feet crossed at the ankles and my arms across my chest. I closed my eyes and tried to imagine I was somewhere other than a morgue. I didn't want to think of what Mrs. Hart and the two men were seeing on the other side of the door.

The only dead body I'd ever seen was not cleaned up and laid out on a slab in a morgue. It was covered with blood from two gunshot wounds, one to the head and one to the heart. I shook my head in a futile effort to dislodge the image I knew I would never be able to get out of my mind.

It was the last time I would see him. The damage from the bullets was extensive. I went along with his family's suggestion of cremation.

I knew someday I'd want to look at the photographs of him alive and handsome, so I put all the pictures from our life together in a safety deposit box. They were proof that I'd once had a normal life. Two years had passed since then, and I still wasn't ready to look at them. The picture I held in my mind, as ugly and disfigured as it was, was an accurate depiction of my deceased husband—liar, cheater, betrayer of trust. What I hadn't admitted to anyone was my belief that he'd gotten what he deserved.

When Antelope and Mrs. Hart were finished in the morgue, the three of us met in a conference room with a wall of windows overlooking the desert. There were sofas and chairs upholstered in pale green. It was a comforting space, and I felt grateful to be there instead of some windowless inner office.

I looked at Mrs. Hart. "Can you tell me what happened last night?"

"Max came to stay with me for a few days," she said. "I was having a hard time after the funeral. He left the house for a few hours to go to therapy and the gym. He came home early and went upstairs. Around six o'clock, our usual suppertime, I went up to check on him. He was asleep in his old room. He looked as peaceful as a baby, and I didn't have the heart to wake him. I came back down and picked on some of the casseroles people left. I watched a little television—the news and my shows, *Jeopardy* and *Wheel of Fortune*. A movie came on, some Lifetime thing, but it didn't catch my interest. So I went up to bed. I stopped to check in on Max first. He was still sleeping, so I headed off to bed myself."

"Tell me about the money. How is it Max had twenty thousand dollars in cash in his trailer?"

Her eyes widened. "I don't know. Where would he have gotten that kind of money?" She shook her head. "I don't know why I didn't put it together . . ."

"What didn't you put together, Mrs. Hart?" Antelope asked.

"He'd been falling apart for weeks. Max was depressed, Detective, don't think I didn't know. And I believe he had a significant substance abuse problem. He denied it, but are any of us the best judge of our own faults? The depression and the chronic marijuana use and alcohol on top of it—it all got the best of him. Remember, Doctor, I called you right after the funeral?"

"You thought Max killed Stacey."

"It's unbearable to be right about something like that. But if he went to make a confession, I guess it's true." She raised her eyes to the ceiling. "Dear God, what has happened to my family? I thought I knew my children, but it's obvious I didn't know them at all."

CHAPTER 52

Connor dressed in black jeans and his leather jacket, dark watch cap, leather gloves and sunglasses stashed in the pockets. The bulk of the Luger strapped to his ankle brought him comfort.

With Stacey gone, he lived in fear. He walked through his days like a hunted man with a feral animal darting in and out of his path, a predator advancing from the shadows. He needed to talk to Kelly. *What did Max tell her?* The more he thought about it, the more convinced he became that Max would have talked to the only living person who would care about this sad part of their shared history.

And what did she think? What would she do? These questions had cycled through his mind all day. He felt dizzy with fear and utterly unable to plan.

The two people he'd always talked to when he got in this state, Stacey and Max, were dead. He thought about talking to Father Bellamy, but whenever he talked to him it felt like having a magic wand waved over him: the worries disappeared but a low-level anxiety remained. Sometimes he thought the priest lived in a world of his own, with different rules and logic.

And he was too dependent on the man. The two of them had talked more than once about how it had developed—a natural need, seeking a father figure because of growing up without his own father. As a child and as a teenager, he'd craved the attention of adult men. Even now, as he considered becoming more independent, making decisions and living life on his own terms without seeking Bellamy's advice, he wondered if he could do it. Stacey had wanted him to lean on her.

He was exhausted and stressed from days of questioning, being asked the same questions over and over—first about Stacey and now about Max—all designed to trap him in a lie. The detective wanted to break him down.

He needed to talk to Kelly. He could make the twelve-mile drive to Green River in less than fifteen minutes if he pushed the BMW to the limit. He switched on his radar detector and flew past the big rigs driving over the speed limit on the interstate. In no time at all he could be at Sage Drive and the fancy house Kelly lived in with her parents and son.

Just after midnight he drove into the quiet neighborhood and cruised past the dark house to a low-rent apartment complex three blocks away, where he parked on the street next to the crowded lot. No one cared who came and went there, and no one would notice one more car parked on the suburban street late at night.

In less than ten minutes he was back at Kelly's place. He found a dark house and an empty driveway.

Idiot! He'd planned to surprise her, catch her off guard, even scare her, anything to make her open up and tell him the truth. After all, only the two of them remained—a situation he planned to use to his advantage. In his heightened state of anxiety, he hadn't thought about the possibility that she might not be home.

At the rear of the house, he found her room. Stacey had told him once that Kelly always slept with her window open. Her fear of closed spaces had started when she saw her brother in his coffin.

■　■　■

On a small hill behind the house, he found a spot hidden by the juniper shrubs with a view into the large bedroom. Moonlight poured in through the skylight onto an empty, queen-size, four-poster bed with a silk canopy.

When she texted the other day, she'd said to come by any time, that she missed him and wanted to see him. *Where did she go off to?*

He walked back around to the side of the house and hoisted himself up to the high windows of the attached garage, checking to see if her car was inside. Nothing.

An idea formed: he could slip in through her window, take a look around to see if Max wrote anything down, while he waited for her to come back.

As he contemplated doing this, full awareness of the illegality of that action lit up in another part of his brain. He worked on one side of the law; breaking in would put him clearly on the other side. But deciding to go into her room without permission gave him a sense of control, and for the first time in a week his heart pumped in a steady beat, not with the galloping pulse of fear. That was enough to propel him into action.

He slipped on the leather gloves before he touched the screen, which resisted and stuck in its track. After a few moments of pushing and pulling, just as he was about to give up, it released and slid up and out of his way.

As he stepped into Kelly's private space, an unexpected thrill—the same thing he'd felt as a kid shoplifting, the mark of a twisted soul—made it worthwhile. He lowered the screen and clicked it back into place.

Being in her room alone and unseen filled him with a sweet feeling of exhilaration. He searched her desk, a slow task using the light from his phone. It was stacked high with files and papers; the drawers were the same, stuffed full with no sense of order. It would take days to do a thorough search.

A new idea cracked open, and he felt a sudden, physical snap in his brain as his mind changed and the truth of his intrusion—the violation and deceit, the depravity of it—emerged.

He should not be there.

As he headed back to the window, headlights flared outside, flooding the space outside the window.

Not enough time to get out the back window and replace the screen. He ran into the kitchen.

A car door slammed outside and footsteps sounded on concrete.

He was through the door running. He heard a crashing sound in the kitchen.

He slipped on the wet grass and went down on his knees. Got up and started running again.

Security lights on the lawn. The shadow of a woman.

He made it up the bank, over the low wall, and away into the night.

CHAPTER 53

Funeral services for Max Hart were private and scheduled within two days of his death. Fern said she couldn't bear going through the ritual of calling hours and an open funeral mass for the second time in a week.

Midway through the short graveside ceremony, news vans arrived and set up cameras before the Sheriff's Department could dispatch enough personnel to persuade them to leave.

Kelly spent the evening after the services with Fern. She felt so bad for the woman. In one week she'd lost both of her children. She couldn't imagine surviving a double heartbreak like that. Though the truth was, she had virtually no one left in the world she felt close to, either. She wanted to feel close to her parents but didn't. There was Timmy, but she had to be there for him, not the other way around. She would never make the same mistake her mother had. He had a right to a childhood.

One day, she would tell Fern about Timmy. But she wanted that day to have the light and joy it deserved. For now, Fern was trapped in an airless swamp of grief, one that threatened to swallow her down into its noxious source.

It was obvious Fern was exhausted. Kelly made her a cup of tea. She drank it down and covered herself with an afghan. A few minutes later, she fell into a sound sleep. Kelly took the moment as her opportunity to leave. She wanted nothing more than to go home to her own bed and sleep for days.

▪ ▪ ▪

When she came around the corner and saw the house, her heart sank. She'd forgotten to leave any lights on. The house was dark, and now she had to go in there alone. She almost turned around and went back to Fern's.

No. I'm on my own now. If I'm ever going to grow up, this is the time.

She parked her car, locked it, and walked fast to the front door, suddenly wanting to be out of the night. She turned the key in the lock and turned on the lights in the front hall, which synced to all the downstairs lighting.

Something fell and broke in the kitchen and the back door slammed shut. Kelly ran to the window and saw a dark shape scale the stone wall at the back of the property.

Heart pounding, she dug around the bottom of her purse until she found Detective Antelope's card with a LifeSaver stuck to it. Bless the man, he answered on the first ring.

▪ ▪ ▪

Antelope made good time on the drive to Green River. The second he pulled up to Kelly Ryan's house, she ran outside to meet him.

"Someone broke in," she said, face pale. "They could still be inside."

He grabbed her arm. She screamed and pulled away.

"Get it in the car," Antelope commanded.

"What are we doing?" Kelly asked, rubbing her arm. The detective was the third man to put his hands on her in the last week.

"I just saw a black car tear through a stop sign a ways back. Did you see a black car on your street tonight? Was it parked on the street when you went into the house?"

"No, I don't think so."

"Get in," Antelope said again.

This time, Kelly complied.

He took off after the car, swerved around the corner. On two wheels, the Cadillac rocked, and then slammed down on the road. Kelly fell against the door panel and hit her arm. She let out another scream.

By the time they got to the intersection on West Flaming Gorge Way, the road was empty in every direction. He hit the steering wheel hard with his right hand.

"Did it help?" Kelly asked wryly.

He almost smiled. "No comment."

He drove her back into the neighborhood at a more normal speed and parked in front of her house. "Stay in the car, I'll check the house."

"No way," she said. "He could be anywhere. I'm coming with you."

"Do you have the keys to your car? Get out of here. Go grab a coffee at the travel plaza and wait for me there."

She shook her head. "They're inside. I dropped them on the table when I went in. Habit. As soon as it hit me what happened, I panicked and didn't think to do anything but call you."

"Smart move." He opened his door. "Wait here."

She grabbed his arm. "No way am I staying out here alone."

"Lock yourself in. I won't be long."

"Someone could be watching us right now."

He pried his arm free. "I can't have you with me in there. It's against regulations."

"What if you don't come out?"

He put the keys to the Cadillac in her hand. "If I'm not out in ten minutes, drive away. You've got your phone. Call 911 if you have to."

CHAPTER 54

Antelope heard the locks of his Cadillac engage as he approached Kelly's house.

With his gun drawn, he stood to the side of the front door, reached across, and threw it open as he held himself flush against the house.

"Detective Antelope, Sweetwater Sheriff's Department. Show yourself. Drop your weapon."

Inside the house, there was only silence. He entered the front hallway, moving with caution.

Everything appeared to be intact and undisturbed in the great room, the same in the kitchen beyond, except for one shattered coffee mug on the floor. The large bedroom suite at the back of the house, which appeared to be Kelly's, was also untouched, though he did notice that the window was open.

At the patio door, he hit the button for the floodlights at the back of the house. The yard lit up like a football field. He pushed the slider open. "Detective Antelope, Sweetwater Sheriff's Department. Show yourself. Drop your weapon."

Again, only silence in return.

He closed and locked the slider.

The basement was easy to check: open plan, three walls of shelves, the usual stuff organized in plastic bins, nothing open or otherwise disturbed. Washer and dryer, lids open, clothes in the dryer ready to be folded.

Upstairs again, he latched the basement door and went up to the second floor. A master bedroom and two smaller bedrooms, two bathrooms, a combination computer-and-craft room. Every room appeared to be in order.

Kelly would have to check everything, but it appeared none of the usual valuables had been taken. Electronics, jewelry, prescription medications were all untouched.

He turned off all the lights, collected Kelly's keys, and locked the door.

When he got back to the Cadillac, Kelly unlocked the doors.

She'd found his CD collection; Joan Osborne sang "Heatwave" out into the neighborhood as he slid into the driver's seat.

She turned the music down.

"Whoever was in there didn't stay long," he said. "You must have scared him off when you pulled into the driveway. There's a few things out of place in the living room."

"Could you see where they broke in?"

"Do you always keep your bedroom window open?"

She smacked her forehead. "Damn it. Yes, I do. It's a thing with me. Stupid."

"Especially when you're alone. Especially now."

"What do you mean especially now?"

"Two of your best friends died this week." He studied her face. "Aren't you a little bit scared?"

She looked confused. "Max took his own life."

He thought for a minute, and decided she had the right to know, if anyone did. "That's what it looked like at first. It's listed as the official cause of death. And for our purposes in the investigation, we've decided to let it stand. But—and I'm only telling you this because of what happened here tonight—I think you might be in danger, Kelly. I don't think you should stay here for a while."

"What do you mean?" She shrank into her seat. "How am I in danger?"

"I don't know and I could be wrong. But I have a bad feeling."

"Do you think someone is after me?"

"I don't know. We have two people dead, and you know both of them. It could be you interrupted a burglary in progress tonight, but I don't like the timing."

"It could be Jack. Do you think Jack came here and did this? What would he want in my house?"

"I don't know. It could be Jack or it could be someone else. But my guess is, whoever was in your house tonight thought he would find something that would tie him to Stacey's murder."

CHAPTER 55

They sat in front of the house until the forensics unit arrived from the Sheriff's Department to take prints and retrieve other evidence specimens from the crime scene. Kelly sat in his car with both his jacket and the heater on, listening to Joan Osborne and the Funk Brothers, as he led the forensics team through the house.

Pepper agreed to have Kelly stay at her house for the night. In the morning, Antelope would complete the paperwork necessary to put Kelly in protective custody. The Sweetwater County Victim Advocacy Program would cover the costs of her temporary housing and lost wages for the duration.

As they approached the city limits of Rock Springs, dawn was a bright orange line on the horizon. Kelly, who'd been sleeping soundly on the seat beside him, woke and rubbed her eyes.

"I saw you with him the night of the calling hours," Antelope said. "I didn't know you had that kind of relationship."

"What kind of relationship do you think we had?" she asked stiffly.

"The kiss said a lot."

"We're old friends. He'd had to look at Stacey dead in her coffin for hours. He wanted to feel alive. So he kissed me."

"Tell me the real story of you and Max."

"The real story, huh? What I've said doesn't satisfy you? We hung out sometimes. We got high together. Max always had good weed. We were two of a kind. Both of us stuck here, trapped by tragedy."

He turned off the music. "How about you cut the bullshit?"

"Why would I lie to you?"

"I don't know, Kelly, it's what you do. And I don't get why you don't get it. Two people you know are dead. Lying might get you killed."

"You're trying to scare me."

"If I could scare you into telling the truth, I would. But you don't scare easy."

"Why are you so sure I'm lying?"

"I saw your face the night Max was killed. My gut tells me he was more than a friend. Did you know about this?" He opened his glove box, pulled out Max's insurance policy, and dropped it in her lap. "You don't need to worry about your son's future."

"What do you mean?" She stared down at the papers. "What is this?"

"Your son, Timothy, is the beneficiary of Max Hart's life insurance policy. Max left a half a million dollars to his son."

■ ■ ■

Pepper opened the garage door when she saw them drive up. Antelope pulled in to avoid any early risers who might witness Kelly's entrance. The house was at the edge of a cul-de-sac on a small side street on top of a ridge overlooking Rock Springs—a perfect, out-of-the-way hideout spot to keep Kelly in until he figured out his next move.

The smell of coffee brewing made him feel happier than he had in days. Pepper let them in and seated Antelope at the kitchen table before showing Kelly the way to the guest bedroom and bath. She already had bacon and eggs frying on the stovetop. The table was set for three.

"Nothing beats breakfast when you've been up all night," Antelope said as Pepper reentered the kitchen. "Where's Kelly?"

"She's taking a shower. Want to fill me in?"

He told her about the break-in at Kelly's place and his fear that it was connected to Stacey's murder. Other than keeping Kelly in a secret location under lock and key, he didn't know how to protect her.

Kelly joined them in a white terrycloth bathrobe, her face glowing pink from the hot shower. "Sorry I took so long. Knowing that a stranger was in my private space tonight made me feel like I couldn't get clean enough." She dropped into a chair across from Antelope. "How long are you going to keep me locked up here?"

"I'll be back later today with a plan. For now, I don't want you to be alone."

Pepper nodded her agreement. "I planned to work from home today. I have some psychological reports to write."

"This is serious. You think I'm in danger."

"We could be dealing with the same person who killed Stacey."

"You mean I could be his next victim, don't you?"

"I don't know anything for sure right now. I want you safe. So you'll stay here until I'm sure it's safe for you to go home."

"I have to make a living, Detective. What am I supposed to do about my job?"

"Call in sick. No other information. Make the call now, please."

She made the call, delivered the message into a voicemail box. There would be no one to answer at the Black Tiara at this time of the morning. When she looked at him he saw the fear had returned to her eyes. The magnitude of the situation had finally landed and taken root. That was what he wanted. Kelly Ryan on her own, trying to think her way out of trouble, was likely to cause more trouble for him.

"When are your parents due back?"

"They have the condo in Prescott until Sunday."

"Let's hold off on notifying them of the break-in. Do they check in with you?"

"No, when they're on vacation they don't want to think about things at home. I won't hear from them."

"I need to take your cell phone. It's traceable with GPS."

"I'll take out the battery."

"I can't let you have it here. It's too risky."

"You don't trust me?"

When he didn't answer, she handed it over.

"I'd rather turn it off than remove the battery," he said. "This way I can monitor incoming messages and text every few hours, see if there's anyone trying to meet with you."

"Take care of it," she said. "I've got important stuff saved on it."

He gave her a hard look. "You've got my cell number. Use the house phone to call me for any reason, and don't think you're bothering me. If anyone tries to get in here, use the landline to dial 911. Otherwise, stay off the phone. There's no reason for anyone to call you here. So if the phone rings, don't answer it. Don't answer to anyone knocking at the door, either." He turned to Pepper. "All this okay with you, Doc? I'll call your cell phone when I'm on my way back here. Lock up when I leave. Got it?"

"This is crazy," Kelly said.

Antelope frowned. "I need to know you understand the seriousness of this situation and won't do anything to compromise your safety."

"I got it. Don't worry, I understand."

"You won't get restless and get an idea to walk out of here?"

She lifted her foot up. "No shoes. And seriously, I don't have the energy to walk out of here. I'm going to bed. Those are my big plans for the day. I'll still be sleeping when you get back here."

CHAPTER 56

Kelly Ryan sat cross-legged on the wicker sofa across from me. After Antelope left, she slept for six hours. When she woke up, I served lunch on the back deck overlooking downtown Rock Springs.

I wanted to get Kelly talking about her brother and the accident in Flaming Gorge. I'd gone online earlier and found the website for the town where Todd Bellamy had attended seminary. Still considered a celebrity within the climbing community years later, he held the record for the longest vertical solo climb in the state. I tried to imagine how an experienced climber could make a mistake tying and securing knots. No one had mentioned alcohol as a factor in the accident. Maybe Kelly would know.

"You have a great place," she said. "I love my personal witness protection hideout."

I smiled. "I'm glad you approve."

My house was a cedar shingle small ranch. It was small by neighborhood standards but just right for me with its combination living room and dining room, galley kitchen, two bedrooms, and sunroom-turned-office with a view of the city.

Like many areas of Rock Springs, the subdivision sat in a high-subsidence area. Built above former working mines, the land was in constant danger of falling into an open shaft or tumbling down the hillside. Compared to other areas of instability in my former life, the vulnerable landscape felt perfectly safe to me.

"I trust Detective Antelope and I can tell he's good at what he does," Kelly said. "But I just don't understand why anyone would want to hurt me, especially someone I know."

"Perhaps it would help to think about this as if it were happening to someone else. You know, sometimes we're too close to see things about ourselves because we're right in the middle of them, but if we imagine them happening to a friend, it's easier."

"How do you mean?"

"Pretend you have a friend at work. Her best friend is murdered. What's your first thought?"

"Her boyfriend did it," Kelly said automatically. "And it's funny, that was my first thought when I heard Stacey was murdered. No specific reason. It's not like they fought all the time or anything, and Connor's no monster. But he is insecure and jealous as hell."

"How about now?"

"I don't believe it. He was my brother's friend since they were little kids, and he's my friend too. It's a terrible thing to think about someone you've known your whole life. I would hate it if my friends thought I could be a killer."

"You don't think Connor's capable?"

"I don't know what to think. I started to let go of the idea when I saw him at the funeral, so sad and broken, really suffering."

"All of you were so close, and now it's just you and Connor."

"It's creepy."

"It seems like everything changed the day of the accident," I ventured.

"You're right. Nothing seemed the same after Tim died and Max changed so much."

"I keep wondering how it happened. Father Bellamy was quite experienced and he was supervising the climb. None of the news reports mentioned it, but I wonder if alcohol played a role?"

"I guess the plan worked," Kelly said flatly.

"What plan is that?"

"Our families made a pact to keep quiet about the drinking. They were afraid if people knew the boys got drunk the night before, they would be less sympathetic. But we all knew about it."

"So they were hung over the next day?"

"Yeah. So their instincts and coordination were off. But regardless, the biggest factor seemed to be that the knots didn't hold."

"I'm surprised Father Bellamy didn't check them."

"Supposedly he did, but then they're all readjusting those things as they go along. I guess it was hard to know. And then the weather shifted; it started raining so hard it caused flash floods that closed the road and delayed rescue getting to them."

"It sounds like destiny, all those complicating factors coming together at the same time."

Kelly stared out at the horizon. "I always felt sorry for Connor. He's the only one who got out of it without an injury, but he's also the only one who's had to live with the memory forever. I wish I knew the truth about all the stuff Jack said—seeing him with someone else, a guy no less. You can't trust Jack, especially since he wanted Stacey for himself. He probably made the whole thing up."

"You and Jack dated. What do you think of him?"

"You mean as a killer? Does he have it in him? It's kind of scary to admit, but he definitely has a wild side, and there's passion in him, right under the surface, all the time. And sometimes it comes out in a good way—you know, all sexy and hot—and sometimes it comes out where he needs to hurt someone."

"How long did you go out with him?"

"Too long, but it's always too long with a guy like him. Off and on for a year since I started at the club. I'm done with him now, but honestly it ended before he started up with Stacey, I just didn't know it." She shrugged. "I'm not saying it didn't bother me, because it did. She was my friend, and he didn't get that it made a difference. So screw him. It would never have worked out for him and Stacey. She was too good for him."

"Was Stacey too good for Connor?"

"I used to think they were perfect for each other. But now I don't know. And Max didn't help."

"What do you mean?"

"Maybe he told you in therapy. I know you can't talk about it because of what he says being private. He told me about all the memories coming back in therapy—the old priest molesting the three of them when they were little innocent kids. It makes me sick. I knew a few things Tim told me, but that was a long time ago and after he died I tried to forget about it. It's the new stuff I'm still trying to get used to. I mean, if any of it is true. With Max dead, we'll never know."

"What new stuff?"

"Connor and Father Bellamy."

"What about them?"

"The two of them hooking up."

"So Bellamy was abusing Connor?" Max's dream came flooding back to me. Perhaps it was a real memory after all.

"Not exactly. Max said Connor was into it too, didn't see it as abuse. You look surprised to hear this."

"I am. It's news to me."

"Like I said, *if* it's true. I never thought Max would kill himself, even though he struggled so damn hard all these years. I heard it in his voice: it messed him up thinking about Connor and Father Bellamy. But how could he be sure, after ten years of not remembering anything, that it's true?"

I reached for my phone. "Detective Antelope needs to hear this."

CHAPTER 57

His uncle had taught him everything he knew about women: how to get them, how to handle them, how to let them go when they got to be too much trouble. He wished he could talk to Val now, but his uncle had given strict orders to stay away, saying he didn't want to get charged with murder.

When he went back to Rock Springs the day of the funeral, Val told him the girl had come home and started working again—and, best of all, she hadn't pressed charges. He couldn't afford to catch another domestic case. Three strikes and you're out, saddled with a felony charge.

"Stay away and let things calm down here," Val said. "If you get arrested for anything, who knows what the girl will do—jump on the bandwagon, add the domestic violence charge on top of it."

He'd become what he'd vowed never to be: a man who seduced the woman of the house he worked on. He knew many contractors who took up with the wives of wealthy men who paid them big money to renovate their homes. The fortunate ones escaped without a problem; the affair took place for the length of the job, then the contractor moved on, the woman happy with the work and the husband who paid for it. In other cases, the contractor won the woman over, and she divorced the husband, took his money, and married her new toy. But marriages between contractor and client rarely ended in happily ever after.

What could you expect? Things begun in secret were destined to end badly. So Jack had steered clear of that scenario and focused on his goal of making money and building a reputation.

In a town as small as Rock Springs, you only got one chance. One wrong turn, one bad decision in the construction game, and you were done; a mistake like that could mean the end of business.

Until he met Stacey, he'd turned down every offer of romance that came to him through his work.

Val had taught him women could suck you in like quicksand, seduce you with their beauty and need. Get too close and you could lose your footing and be stuck forever.

The prophecy played out—stuck in a crummy motel in Salt Lake City, eating the same crappy meals every day from the same crappy local places. He kept the truck hidden and he didn't drive because he didn't want to take a chance the license plate would be spotted. But he walked the city for hours in his baseball cap and sunglasses, stopping for coffee, eating out, getting exercise. Like being in prison but without the walls. Funny, since he was doing all this to *avoid* jail.

Boredom set in after the first day. Ordinarily he dealt with boredom by fantasizing about women and masturbating. He tried to picture Stacey—the times they made love in that big empty house, the radio on and the door locked.

No matter how hard he tried, the only image that came: Stacey lifeless on the floor. Never again would he make love to her—or, he realized, get off thinking of her.

He tried not to feel sorry for himself. He could still masturbate while picturing Kelly and Sharnelle and sometimes the two of them together—hot girls both of them, he couldn't complain.

The first few days, he'd come and gone from the motel without too much care. But all that had changed a few days before when he'd noticed the deputies across the street. They were keeping a steady watch on the place—predators tracking their prey.

Since then he'd stayed inside with the blinds closed and the air conditioner going full blast. He watched the news three times a day for updates on the case. Every day the coverage was less, the spots shorter.

Yesterday, the regional news had carried the story of the private funeral of Max Hart, Stacey's crazy brother. She didn't talk about him much, only to say he was a head case because of some accident. He'd shot himself in church after making a confession. People were speculating that he'd confessed to his sister's murder before pulling the trigger.

And something else caught his attention, too. Something of benefit to him in the event he needed a bargaining chip. Was that . . . ?

Yes, he was sure of it now. It was the same guy, the one he'd seen come into this very motel with Connor Collins. He'd been caught on camera right in the middle of the small funeral party.

Jack jumped up, so excited he almost ran out of the room. The exile could end.

He threw his things in a bag and walked out the door.

CHAPTER 58

Antelope listened as Kelly repeated her recollection of the last phone call she'd had with Max on the night he died.

"He said he and Tim had a plan? Did he tell you the plan?"

"No. He was upset but also excited. He couldn't wait to talk to Connor about it."

Antelope looked at me and I gave him a slight nod. Connor had said nothing about this when we talked with him two days before in his apartment.

His phone vibrated and he checked the caller before answering, "Antelope here. When? I'll be there. Reserve the big interview room for six o'clock. Great timing. Helpful to have that going in. Thanks." He set the phone down and looked at me. "The Salt Lake County Sheriff's Office apprehended Jack Swailes this morning and processed the extradition paperwork. Salt Lake City deputies are en route, transporting him to the state line now. Our deputies will meet them and take custody of him."

"How did they find him?"

"They did a stakeout at the Spring Grove. Swailes went to the lobby for the free continental breakfast, bought the paper, and went back to his room. A few minutes later, they had him in custody. He didn't put up a fight. He told them he had some important information in the murder case. Coincidentally, the DNA results from his cigarette came back. They match with specimens taken from the body."

I almost clapped my hands with excitement. "Finally, a break."

"Maybe he's going to confess," Kelly said.

"We'll know soon enough. Meanwhile, I want to set up a meeting between you and Connor."

Kelly frowned. "Why me? I'm not sure I want to talk to Connor. I'm scared. Max met with him and ended up dead. I'm not saying there's a direct connection, but things are getting kind of weird. I don't know who I can trust anymore."

He put her phone on the table. "Here, take a look. Thirteen texts since I left here. I'd like to know what's on Connor's mind and why he's insisting on seeing you. If I bring him in for questioning at this point, I have no doubt he'll lawyer up. But he's got his own agenda here, and I can prepare you to get the information we need from him. Will you do it? Will you help us out, Kelly?"

"Like undercover work?"

"Sort of."

"I'm scared."

"Is this safe?" I asked.

"Don't worry," Antelope said. "We'll be nearby."

"These are the kinds of things people say can't go wrong but they do go wrong. I'm scared." Kelly gave me a pleading look. "What do you think I should do?"

"A few minutes ago you said you didn't know who you can trust," I said gently. "There's one thing I'm certain of, Kelly. You can trust Detective Antelope."

Kelly thought for a minute and nibbled on her right thumbnail. "You owe me a manicure when this is over. All right, I'll do it for Stacey and Max."

"It's a deal," Antelope said, satisfied. He put Kelly's phone back in his pocket. "Sit tight until I finish up with Swailes, and I'll get back to you with a plan. In the meantime, the same rules apply. Nobody leaves this house."

CHAPTER 59

On the drive to the Detention Center, Antelope wondered what Swailes would say. He hoped to get a confession out of him. But Swailes as the killer no longer felt right. He still didn't know why Stacey had died or who had killed her. But the simple explanation Connor Collins had offered the first day—Jack killed Stacey in a crime of passion because she rejected and fired him—sounded overly simplistic now. Sexual energy had certainly given life to the case and maybe Swailes had gotten caught up in it to the point of murder, but something in his gut said otherwise.

He didn't want to be around people, so he stopped at Wendy's for takeout and drove to the edge of the desert and parked. As he ate his chicken sandwich, a freight train came into view, crossed his line of vision, then disappeared over the tracks headed west. The whole thing took less than ten minutes, yet he felt soothed. He realized for the second time in a week that these small, ordinary moments were what got him through the tough spots of his work.

■ ■ ■

Antelope went in angry. The way he saw it, he couldn't feel anything else. If Jack Swailes ended up adding nothing to the investigation, they'd wasted time, effort, and money on searching for him and hauling him back to Wyoming. And if he did know something, he'd delayed and compromised the investigation by running away.

Inside the interview room, the air was warm and sour with the smells of cigarette smoke and body odor. One look at Swailes told him the man was scared; he was slouched in the chair, hands folded on the table, fingernails bitten down to the quick, blue eyes hooded and wary. His attorney, a stocky man in blue jeans and a white shirt with a bolo tie, stood up and removed his black Stetson.

"Hello Detective, I'm Calvin Smithson; I'm representing Mr. Swailes and am here to advise him today."

Antelope recognized him from the halls of the courthouse. Val Campion kept the guy on retainer to handle all his business and legal matters.

"Please have a seat, Mr. Smithson."

Antelope turned on the video and audio, stated the identifying details of the interview, and read Swailes his Miranda warning.

"Mr. Swailes, you are being questioned in relation to a homicide," he said, getting ready to dive in.

"Before you begin your questioning, Detective, my client has some information to share with you which he believes to be pertinent to the investigation," Smithson piped up.

Antelope felt his blood pressure rising. He took a deep breath. It took an arrest for this character to come forward with a potentially useful lead?

"Go ahead."

"We'd like it on the record that if this information proves useful, the Sheriff's Department will reconsider my client's status. Mr. Swailes is currently being held on charges of obstructing justice. When we are assured the charges will be dropped, my client will not hesitate to cooperate."

Antelope contained his rage. "Let's get this straight, Counselor. I'm investigating a homicide. Your client found the body. I instructed him to report for fingerprinting and instead he left the state. It's taken a week to locate and apprehend him—a waste of our human resources and funds expended. No deal."

"Proceed with your questions, Detective." Smithson sat back in his chair. "I advise my client to withhold voluntary assistance at this time."

Jack waved his arms back and forth as if he was flagging down a car on the road. "No, no, stop. You're making things worse for me, man." He shot Smithson a dirty look. "I don't want any trouble. And this thing I'm about to tell you, I didn't know it when I left town. So it's not like I've been holding back or holding you up."

"What information, Mr. Swailes? Whatever it is, it better be worth my time, because it's long overdue."

"I know you got the word on where I spotted Connor Collins with a dude in Salt Lake, because otherwise you wouldn't have known to come looking for me there. Now I know who the other guy is."

"I need a name."

"I saw him on the TV. The news ran a story on the guy who killed himself in church. They said it was Stacey's brother. They showed a picture of everybody at the grave. I recognized him the minute I saw it. It's the same guy who I saw going into the room with Collins. It's the priest."

"Father Bellamy?" Antelope asked.

Swailes shrugged. "Whatever priest was at that funeral, he's the one."

CHAPTER 60

All the way back to town, Antelope kept trying to work out scenarios to get to the truth without anyone else getting hurt. Could it be true Father Bellamy and Connor Collins were involved in an ongoing sexual relationship?

And if they were in a sexual relationship now, did that mean Max's memories were accurate and it had been going on for years? It sounded too bizarre to be true.

The two men were both highly intelligent and skilled in argument and persuasion. He decided the only thing to do was to separate them. Pepper could take one of them and he could take the other.

It wouldn't work to do the interviews at the station. They'd lawyer up and it would be the end of it for the day, maybe forever. He still couldn't say exactly how, but he was sure this was related to Stacey Hart's murder.

He called Our Lady of Sorrows.

"Good evening, Our Lady of Sorrows Church, Sister Julia speaking, how may we help?"

"Hello, Sister Julia. Is Father Bellamy available?"

"Not at the moment, no, but I believe he'll be back soon. Can I take a message?"

"Let him know that Dr. Pepper Hunt will be by later this evening to discuss some new developments in the Stacey Hart case with him, will you?"

"Absolutely, Detective."

"Thank you, Sister."

Pepper was the best person to talk to the priest.

Now, to have Kelly take a crack at Connor.

He drove the ten miles back to Rock Springs under a sky studded with stars. Their distant fire traveled from light years beyond and warmed his heart. An idea burned within him, fueled him for the remaining fight, on a trajectory that was finally moving him toward the answers in this baffling, tortured case.

■ ■ ■

Pepper and Kelly waited for him outside on the deck, under the same sky that spoke to him with its brilliance. They looked beautiful and serene lounging and looking up at the lavish stars.

"You did good, Detective, brought me to the right place." Kelly smiled. "I could stay here forever."

"Someday soon we can do this for pleasure—sit out here under the stars and enjoy a summer dinner together," Pepper said.

His absence had clearly had a positive effect on the women, released them from the ceaseless, buzzing current his work created.

"That's a plan," he said. "But not tonight's plan."

At the same time, they both sat forward and gave him their full attention, ready for whatever came next. Two pairs of intelligent eyes, Kelly's the blue of a robin's egg and Pepper's the color of a new penny. It was the trust he saw there that got to him. What was he leading them into on this summer night?

"Things just got more interesting," he said.

"What did Swailes have to say?" Pepper asked. "Actually, wait. Let's take this inside; it's getting chilly." She gathered up the plates and glasses from the supper they shared and carried them inside. He and Kelly followed her in and the three of them stood at the counter in the small galley kitchen.

"Not what I expected, but it kind of fits," Antelope said.

"He's a liar," Kelly warned.

"He claims it was Todd Bellamy with Connor at the motel." Kelly put both hands over her mouth and gasped. "Oh my God, Max was right!"

"We don't know for sure," Pepper reminded her. "Remember, this is Swailes, who has a lot to gain from trading information with law enforcement."

"That's the card he played. He'll lose any advantage and be in a worse situation if he lied. I'm sure his lawyer advised him of that. It's time to talk to Connor."

Antelope handed Kelly her phone.

"Take a look at this. Fifteen phone calls and texts in the last twenty-four hours. Connor's running scared. Call him and see what he wants. Tell him you want to talk in person and get him to come here."

"Will you be here?" Kelly's voice trembled.

"Doc, let's switch out the cars, hide mine in the garage so he won't get scared off. I'll be out of sight but ready to move in if there's trouble."

Kelly looked at Pepper.

"Call Connor," Pepper said. "It's the next thing to do. We need to know what's got him so wound up."

Kelly reached for the phone and hesitated, looked at it like it was an unknown, possibly dangerous, object.

"Put it on speaker," Antelope said.

She pressed the call button.

Connor answered on the first ring. "Jesus, Kelly, where've you been? Are you all right?"

"Hey, I'm sorry, I've been sort of out of it and sleeping a lot."

"Where are you, though? I've been to your house. It looks like a ghost town. I thought something happened to you."

"Someone broke into my house last night. I didn't want to stay alone. I'm staying with a friend."

"Listen, I need to see you. There's something you need to know."

"Okay. You sound strange."

"That was me the other night at your house. I'm sorry I scared you. I needed to see you and I know it was stupid, but I thought I'd wait inside for you. Then, when I heard a car, I panicked."

"I don't understand. You broke into my house?"

"The window in your bedroom was open. You should close and lock it. It's not safe."

"Connor what's going on? You're freaking me out."

"Where are you?"

"I'm staying with Dr. Hunt, Max's therapist. Can you come here?"

"Are you alone?"

"No, she's here. But we can talk alone."

"Maybe it's better if she hears what I have to say too. What's the address?"

"She's on Hilltop Drive, number 200, the little brown house at the end."

"I'm on my way."

Kelly dropped the phone on the counter, got up, and began to pace. She grabbed her cigarettes and went out on the deck. Antelope went out after her. She had to hold it together for a while longer. He had the feeling Connor was about to tell them something that could bring the case to a close.

"It's almost over, Kelly," he said. "You have to hold on a little bit longer."

"He killed her, didn't he?" she demanded, her voice rising. "And now he's coming here to kill me too."

"I won't let that happen."

"You'll be in the bedroom. It doesn't take long to strangle someone. You won't hear it."

He kept his voice level and calm. "You have to trust me."

"Why? Why should I trust you? I trusted Stacey and she stole Jack from me. I trusted Max and he killed himself and left me alone with our kid. I trusted Connor and he broke into my goddamn house. Now you want me to trust you when you're using me for bait to catch a killer. Leave me alone."

"He's running scared and I don't know why," Antelope said. "Follow the conversation wherever it goes. And don't worry, you'll do fine. You have great instincts and people skills. Connor has a sexual relationship with Bellamy. We're going with that. We don't know when it started or how active it is. We know about this one time Swailes saw them together. It's information we didn't have before, and it's somehow connected to Stacey's murder. Get him to talk about it."

"Did you hear a word I just said?"

"Your life put you here in the middle of this. You have to see it through."

"You're using me, just like all the other men in my life," she spat.

"I'm asking for your help and I'm trusting you to come through. It's not the same."

He'd said the right thing. She looked at him and nodded just as a car turned into the driveway and parked outside, catching her white, frightened face in the slow sweep of its headlights.

CHAPTER 61

Pepper let Connor into her house then disappeared into her study, where Detective Antelope waited. Kelly refused to talk to Connor without smoking. The house was cool with the door to the deck wide open.

When he walked in, goose bumps came up on her arms and she wanted to run right past him out the front door and never stop. She lit up and the smoke disappeared behind her. The room had a weird wind tunnel effect from the currents of air coming up from the canyon below the house.

She sat up straight with her back against the cushions of the leather sofa, legs crossed in a yoga position. Connor sat on the edge of a straightback chair he'd pulled over from the dining table and set at a diagonal to the arm of the sofa.

He leaned forward, his arms resting on his thighs, closer than she wanted him to be, close enough to touch her, large hands hanging down, loose and inert. *Did those hands strangle Stacey?*

"You're going to think I'm crazy, but hear me out," he said. "We both lost two people we loved this week. I don't want to lose you, too. That's why I went your house last night."

"Connor what's going on? I know you saw Max the night he killed himself."

"There's so much you don't know."

"Tell me."

■ ■ ■

"He remembered the day Tim died. He said his death was no accident. I didn't want to listen. Why dredge that up after all this time? For ten years I put it out of my mind. But if he's right, and it wasn't an accident, then Tim was murdered."

Kelly couldn't help it; she was terrified, and she knew her eyes showed it.

"Don't look at me like that!" Connor said.

Kelly jumped up and ran toward the open door. "Oh my God, you killed them both!"

Connor went after her and grabbed her by both arms. "No, no, it's not like that!"

She screamed and Antelope was there in an instant. He pulled Connor away and pushed him onto the sofa, pinned his arms behind his back. "Get a hold of yourself," he said.

Pepper put her arms around Kelly, who cried softly into her shoulder.

Antelope glared at Connor. "Do I need to cuff you or can you keep your hands to yourself?"

"I came here to save her life," Connor said. "I'm not going to hurt her."

"Sit back down over there and finish your story."

Antelope stood in view of Connor, his arms crossed. Pepper positioned herself on the couch between Kelly and Connor.

"I didn't plan to make an official statement to law enforcement."

"Your choice—speak up or I'm arresting you for obstruction of justice."

Connor inhaled a shaky breath, then exhaled. "All right, here it is. Beginning at age fourteen, I willingly engaged in a sexual relationship with Father Bellamy. He didn't coerce me, and I knew what I was doing. The relationship continued throughout high school. At the end of our senior year, Tim and Max learned about it. They wanted to report him to the Bishop in Cheyenne. When we were altar boys, the three of us were molested by Father Kroll. That was abuse. We were little kids who wanted no part of a sick old man who forced us."

Connor closed his eyes and pressed on his eyelids. A few tears escaped and he struggled to hold himself together.

"Tim and Max were my best friends. They believed Todd had abused and manipulated me. They said he was taking advantage of me and my vulnerability from the prior abuse. I couldn't convince them otherwise. I didn't want Todd transferred to another parish and I didn't want him in jail. The man was good to me. I didn't have a father, and he stepped in and filled that role. It was more than sex, but they didn't believe me."

Kelly held her hands to her face. She couldn't believe what she was hearing.

"I didn't know what to do, so I told him Max and Tim planned to go to Cheyenne to meet with the Bishop after graduation. I don't know what I expected him to do—talk them out of it, I guess, show them he wasn't like Kroll; it was just the opposite, he cared about me. Then everything went to hell. Tim died and Max got hurt. I never thought it was anything but an accident. Why would I?"

Connor looked at Kelly. The room was silent. He shook his head.

"He was my priest. I was a teenager, a sexually experienced teenager. Now, in this moment, as an adult, a member of the bar, I understand that his actions meet a criminal standard. But back then, I swear to you, it didn't feel sick or wrong to me." He slumped his shoulders. "After things died down, nothing changed with me and Todd. I needed his support more than ever. Then Stacey and I got close. We were both hurting over Tim and Max. I kept the two relationships going for years—ten years. It seemed normal to me; it was the only life I knew."

"And then?" Antelope prompted.

"And then someone told Stacey I cheated on her. I denied it. How could I possibly tell her the truth? She'd leave me for sure. She wanted to believe me. She went to the church to get some guidance from her priest, the one person she still trusted. But instead, she found me and Todd together, having sex in the vestry."

Kelly's stomach clutched. *Poor Stacey.*

"I thought I'd lose my mind. She told me she didn't want to marry me and tried to give back the ring, but I wouldn't take it. I couldn't say anything. She was right. She walked out the door and left me." Connor's voice trembled. "I broke down and cried like a baby and Todd said he would take care of it and make everything right. He told me to go home and let him handle it. I did what he said, like I always do. The next morning, she was dead. My first thought was Jack Swailes killed her. He was after her and I told her get rid of him. It made sense at the time. It also blinded me to what I couldn't see, didn't want to see." He looked straight at Kelly. "I see it now. Todd killed them both, Max and Stacey."

"That's an interesting story, Counselor," Antelope said without emotion. "The only problem is, it could easily have been you who killed them. You also had a lot to lose."

Connor's phone buzzed in his pocket. Seconds later, Pepper's phone vibrated on the counter.

"Check your phones. It might be important," Antelope said.

Pepper and Connor showed their screens to the group. The texts were from Bellamy, and they were identical:

It ends at Pagan Cave.

CHAPTER 62

For all we knew we would find a dead priest at Pagan Cave, his body crushed at the bottom of a sheer rock wall. Or the text was a setup, an ambush.

Antelope drove my Jeep and the four of us set off for Flaming Gorge. The idea was that Connor and I would talk to Bellamy and attempt to get him to confess and voluntarily turn himself in. Kelly and Antelope would wait within hearing distance, and Antelope would intervene if things got violent. It wasn't a perfect plan, but Kelly was too frightened to wait alone in the Jeep. I had my Beretta, too, and was prepared to use it if Bellamy made any moves on me or Connor.

Antelope had decided that his presence would be problematic for a few reasons. Bellamy hadn't texted him, and he was a man who needed control. If Antelope showed up, he might see it as a direct challenge, and we might not get the confession we were angling for.

When we turned south onto Highway 191, the weather changed. The stars disappeared behind steel wool clouds riding on the back of a loud, fierce wind out of the southwest. A blinding darkness clamped down, black and impenetrable, a desolate, suffocating void. The vehicle shuddered and swayed when the wind slammed into it, first one side and then the other.

Antelope gripped the steering wheel to keep us on the road,

his eyes straight ahead, fixed on our target. Kelly and Connor were silent in the backseat.

When the GPS announced one mile to our destination, Antelope turned off the headlights.

As we got closer, I began to feel afraid. I'd hoped a plan would emerge at some point on the drive down, but no one had said a word the whole time. None of us knew for certain what we'd find.

Antelope cut the engine. Outside, the wind wailed as it spun through the canyon.

Antelope put his hand on mine, warm and steady, and I was grateful for this small human comfort.

We were in an unknown wilderness in the pitch dark with a rogue summer storm ready to strike, on the lookout for a killer.

Thunder boomed and reverberated, bouncing off the canyon walls, and I shivered.

"Once we start walking, stay right behind me," Antelope told us. "It's a straight shot to the base of the climb. When we get there, we'll switch places: Pepper, you and Connor go on ahead, and Kelly and I will hang back."

"It's pitch dark," I protested. "How will you see the trail?"

"Stay close and trust me."

We got out of the car and started to walk. The sound of the doors closing might have alerted Bellamy, but he didn't leap out of the bushes and attack us.

I followed inches behind Antelope, my index finger hooked into his belt loop.

From our right came a low rumble, the slurp and gurgle sound of fast water sliding past the rock walls of the steep canyon.

The first raindrops came down slow, like snowflakes adrift on invisible currents. A minute later, they shapeshifted into hard-as-nails hail that hurt every place it hit. The chips of ice hit the earth with the sound of gravel.

We walked for at least a quarter of a mile. I was chilled to the bone; my teeth chattered. Then the rain and hail slowed down and stopped. Above us, the clouds parted and revealed a huge white moon and, below it, the looming mass of Pagan Cave.

And there he was, standing on a boulder high above us. Even from a distance, it was clear from his stance—arms crossed on his chest, head held high—that Todd Bellamy relished the scene he set in place. He'd summoned us to him, and he knew we'd come.

He had yet to notice us on the trail. Antelope took the opportunity to make himself scarce.

"All right," he said, "this is where we split up."

My heart sank. The thought of going on without him filled me with dread. But there was no turning back.

Connor took the lead and I followed him slowly over the wet rocks, thankful for the moonlight, which lit up every crevice with an eerie, incandescent glow.

Bellamy waited until we were a stone's throw from him to speak. He smiled as we made our way across the top of the boulder toward him. "It's good to see you, Connor. Thank you for coming."

"Why did you bring us here?" Connor said.

"I would think that's obvious. Such an important place in our history. That was quite a storm wasn't it? Just like the last time we were here together."

Connor scowled. "Are you finally ready to talk about what really happened that day?"

"We both know what happened. I did what I had to do. You trusted me to take care of the problem, and I did."

"I had no idea what you were planning to do."

Bellamy's gaze shifted to me. "I'm sorry it didn't work out to meet at the church, Dr. Hunt. I made other plans for tonight. I have a date with destiny that can't be interrupted."

"If I had to guess, I'd say you plan to take your own life," I said.

"This is your area of expertise. And I understand you have an ethical obligation to try and change my mind. But that won't happen. I've been moving toward this moment for a long time."

"This is about your relationship with Connor, isn't it?"

"Everything has been about Connor from the moment I set eyes on him. It's always that way with love, isn't it?"

"Have you thought about what it will do to Connor if you kill yourself?" I asked.

He looked down at Connor. "I'm sorry to say this, my boy, but you have always been weak. It's time for you to deal with life on your own."

"Is that how you managed to keep Connor under your control all these years? Feeding him a story about how he needed you and couldn't make it on his own?"

"He had no father, no male role model. He needed a man to give him guidance. I came into his life at the right time. He was grateful, as he should have been. There was never a right time to break his dependence."

"You seduced him into a sexual relationship when he was a young teen. Is that your idea of guidance?"

"You know what happened. Those boys were sexually abused in the most exploitive way by my predecessor. Connor seduced me. It wasn't the other way around."

"You're delusional and a liar," Connor shouted. "That's not what happened."

"That's your story?" I demanded. "A thirteen-year-old boy had the power to pull a thirty-year-old priest into an unhealthy sexual liaison? You were an adult. You could have stopped what you knew to be wrong."

"Go on, judge me; I expected nothing else. The world judges what it doesn't understand."

"This is the place where Tim Ryan died and Max Hart was injured, isn't it?" I asked.

"It is indeed." Bellamy sounded almost smug. "I came back to complete the circle."

"You made it look like an accident, but you planned on both of them dying. Why did you do it?"

"The two of them thought they were heroes. They were planning to report me to the Bishop in Cheyenne. They were misguided. They thought I was hurting their friend and they wanted to protect him. Connor saw it differently. That's why he came to me and told me what they were going to do." He spread his arms wide. "If they'd gone through with it, it would have ruined everything. I would have been transferred away from Connor. He'd have been left all alone. I couldn't let that happen."

"So you rigged the ropes on the belay line and counted on the two boys falling to their death."

"That was the plan, yes."

"Why did Stacey have to die?"

He looked at Connor again. "You were in a wild panic that Friday night she came to the sacristy and found us together. I promised you I'd take care of it, that I'd talk to her and calm her down and everything would be fine. I sent you home and went to talk to Stacey. Needless to say, it didn't go as planned."

"You must have lived in fear all these years," I said, "always wondering if Max would regain his memory and figure out what you'd done."

"That's right, Dr. Hunt, and he wouldn't have remembered anything if it wasn't for you and your work with him. In the end, it's your fault that everything came back to him. And what was the first thing he wanted to do? Finish what he started ten years ago. That's what he came to tell me at the church. He wanted me to know he was going to the authorities. I refused to be brought down and humiliated by Max Hart." He said the name with contempt. "He thought he understood things he knew nothing about. What Connor and I shared was no common sexual hookup. We loved each other. No one has the right to destroy love."

"You were a priest and Connor was a child when it started," I said.

"Age and time make no difference. I thought you'd understand."

"I tried to end it so many times," Connor said, his voice ragged and raw. "You wouldn't let me go."

Bellamy shook his head. "How could I let you go? You needed me."

"It was *you* who needed *me*." Connor was crying now. "I loved Stacey. I wanted a life with her."

"But it was nothing compared to what we had. She was a useful prop. No one would question your sexual orientation. You could rise to the heights of your career with her by your side. And I wanted that for you. Marrying Stacey was part of the plan. But she ruined it by threatening to do the same thing her brother wanted to do. It was bad enough she wanted to take you away from me. I couldn't believe you were going to go along with that. But that she would expose us both? It would have ruined your career, and mine as well. She had to be stopped."

Connor shook his head, tears running down his face.

■ ■ ■

"Dr. Hunt, I wanted you here because you have the knowledge base to understand what happened, to be able to tell my story, the true story," Bellamy said. "The rest of the world will see me as a sexual deviant and predator who should be arrested and charged. As a psychologist, I imagine you would characterize me as a narcissist. But I'm just a wounded soul. And even wounded souls need love."

"So why kill yourself?" I asked. "You might have gotten away with the murders."

"Connor finally put it all together. I killed three people for him, for us. And instead of getting the love and loyalty I deserve, he's done with me. The love is gone. So what's the point of living?"

"You played God and took lives that weren't yours to take," Connor said. "You came here to do it again. You're going to take your own life because you can't face the consequences, can't face who you are and what you did. You want these people here to tell your story. It's not going to happen that way." He pulled out a pistol and pointed it at Bellamy.

"Connor," I said, inching toward him slowly, "it's not worth shooting him. You didn't murder anyone. You have a life to live."

"I won't shoot to kill, but I'll shoot him in his tracks if he makes a move to go over that ledge," he snarled. "I want him to face it all. The real punishment is knowing everyone knows what you did. You believe what you want is more important than what anyone else wants."

"I did it for *you*—to protect your future!" Bellamy said.

"You can't brainwash me anymore," Connor said. "Everything you did, you did for yourself. You killed Tim and Max and

Stacey because you didn't want to be exposed as a perverted priest. You took everything from me. Put your hands behind your head and walk toward me."

Bellamy did as he was told. I didn't like that he was moving closer to us. I wished that Antelope would show himself and take over. I didn't trust that Connor could keep control over the man who had ruled his life for so many years.

It happened so fast—Bellamy turning and overtaking Connor, grabbing the gun as Connor struggled to free himself, then flinging Connor away. Connor losing his balance, falling, and rolling so close to the edge of the rock I thought he might go over. Bellamy standing above him and aiming the pistol at his head. Connor springing up and going for the gun again.

Then a shot rang out, and both men dropped to the ground.

Bellamy howled and writhed in agony, but it was only a superficial wound to his arm that had brought him down.

Antelope quickly took control. He had Bellamy cuffed in seconds. That done, he examined the wound, made a tourniquet from his T-shirt, and re-cuffed Bellamy's wrists in front of him to keep pressure on the wound.

The way back was easier in the moonlight. Kelly and I followed the three men out, Todd Bellamy inching slowly along the narrow path in front of Antelope, the detective's hand anchored firmly on his shoulder.

CHAPTER 63

In the summer, the Black Tiara set up an outside dining area with wrought-iron tables, cordoning them off from the parking lot with ropes of flowers.

The scene had a Parisian-café vibe until you got up close and noticed the flowers were plastic. The smell of black asphalt from the parking lot mixed with Chinese cooking in the hot afternoon sun. The surrounding lot was overgrown with tall summer grasses swaying in a breeze that would turn into a stronger wind as the afternoon wore on.

After spending the morning at the Sweetwater County District Court, where Todd Bellamy was arraigned on three first-degree murder counts—he would remain in custody at the Sweetwater Detention Center until the trial date in October—we arrived at the Black Tiara for lunch. It was one o'clock, a late hour by Green River's lunch schedule, and the restaurant was empty.

Antelope chose an outside table farthest from the street traffic. He pulled out a chair for me before sitting down across from me. A waiter came out and set water and silverware on the table. Antelope ordered a pitcher of margaritas.

"You were right," he said. "No matter how special Bellamy believes himself to be, as a killer he's just like all the other guys, trying to get away with crime, motivated by concealment."

"He refused to take responsibility for his actions and he wasn't willing to pay the price for what he did wrong."

"Because he never saw it as wrong, because he's a narcissist."

I smiled. "You're getting good at this."

"I've got a good teacher," he said.

The waiter brought our margaritas and we placed our food orders. Antelope poured us each a glass and we clinked them together before taking our first sips.

"If Max hadn't heard about that priest getting arrested," Antelope mused, "do you think he could have gone his whole life without remembering what was done to him as a kid?"

"Absolutely. The human mind has creative ways to deal with what's too overwhelming or horrific to handle. All the defense mechanisms work to protect us. The heaviest hitter is denial. Max's brain injury made it even easier for him to shove those memories out of his head."

"It's an efficient and effective way to deal with the bullshit until a priest is arrested and the denial collapses. What about all the other hundreds of cases like this that have been all over the news for years? Why didn't he get flashbacks when he heard about other priests molesting kids?"

"Max had his own problems with sex and intimacy that made normal relationships difficult and were a result of the abuse he suffered at Father Kroll's hands. Like many victims, he blamed himself for it and felt guilty about it. When the Greybull priest was exposed for engaging in the same sexual acts Max enjoyed, his brain made connections between all those different factors: priests, sexual deviance, sexual abuse. The combination unlocked his memory."

"The one I don't understand is Collins." Antelope shook his head. "Ten years leading a double life hooking up with a priest while making plans to marry a woman. How does that happen?"

"Todd Bellamy is a sociopath who cared only for his own needs. He's grandiose and entitled. Connor Collins shares some of those features, and Bellamy played into his need to feel special. He lost his parents when he was very young and lived with an elderly grandmother who didn't have the energy, physical or emotional, to meet his needs. He fit the description of the perfect victim of a child molester. Kids need love and physical touch. Abusers are keenly aware of this need. They identify vulnerable kids and make their moves on them."

We paused while the waiter set our food down in front of us. I thought what a strange conversation ours must be to overhear as he backed away.

Antelope picked up his sandwich, but stopped short of taking a bite. "Wait, you said kids need *love*. That's not love, it's abuse and exploitation."

I shrugged. "It's complicated. If the abuser isn't violent, the attention and the touch can be experienced as pleasurable. That's certainly not true in all cases, but in some it is. And those kids end up feeling guilty because they enjoyed it. That's what happened for Connor the second time around, right? By then he's older and beginning to get interested in sex, and along comes Bellamy with this deal that includes special attention and sexual pleasure."

"He was too weak to resist."

"He was getting stronger—or at least, he was leaning less on Bellamy. Over time, it seems, he transferred much of his need for love and protection from Bellamy to Stacey. Things might have worked out for the two of them if he'd taken that job in Evanston and gotten more distance, geographic and emotional, from Bellamy."

"He wasn't that strong. He was still turning to the priest whenever things got tough with Stacey. If he hadn't gone to the church that night, Stacey wouldn't have found the two of them together."

"We can't know if he ever would have made the break," I admitted. "He says he wanted to, but he let it go on for fifteen years."

"Then there's Stacey. Why do you think she went for Swailes? That happened well before she knew about Connor and Bellamy."

I'd thought about this a lot. "He was the opposite of Connor— decisive and willing to act. He wanted her and he went after her."

"He's also an abusive, violent guy. That wasn't going to change."

"It seems to me that he was drawn to Stacey because he wanted to be a better man. He thought if he had a good woman, he could become the man she deserved."

"Poor Stacey: two men, broken in different ways, both in love with her and wanting her to change them with her love. But that's not love, is it?"

I tilted my margarita glass toward him. "You're a smart man."

"Just trying to figure out this love thing like everybody else."

"The private clinic in Arizona Connor's going to should help him deal with everything. We both did some research and I think this place has the right approach and the level of expertise to handle his complicated situation. When you think about it, every part of his world collapsed. He still has some money left over from the church settlement and he plans to sell the house. He can't imagine living there after what happened to Stacey. He said he'll spend every penny he has to get the help he needs."

"Can therapy help him? You said he's a narcissist; they're hard to treat, right?"

"He has a lot of work to do. There are the losses to grieve, the trauma to heal, and the narcissistic and passive personality traits that allowed him to remain in the situation he was in. Even as an adult, it can be overwhelming to process the kind of sexual abuse he's suffered. As memories come back, so do the feelings—anger, sadness, outrage at what's been taken from him. He's just beginning to realize that his whole life, not only his sexual life, has been changed by what Bellamy did to him."

Antelope switched topics. "Mrs. Hart and Kelly sat together at the arraignment."

I nodded. "Kelly stopped in to see me last week. She wanted to tell me she finally got around to telling Fern about Max being her son's father. She said they've been spending a lot of time together and Timmy's happy to have a second grandmother. In September, he'll go to Fern's after-school daycare program."

"That's a bright spot." Antelope frowned. "I worried about Fern, both of her kids murdered. How do you live with that?"

"There's no simple answer. The strength of love determines the depth of the grief. It always helps to find a way to continue loving. Fern has Timmy now." I cocked my head to the left. "Have you heard from Kelly?"

"You're asking because of how I couldn't think straight around her?"

"Yes."

"I settled it the night we went to Pagan Cave."

I gave him a puzzled look.

"After all the driving around—getting Bellamy processed into custody, you and Kelly back to your place, Collins home—I was beat and thought I'd crash the minute I hit the bed. But I couldn't sleep. I got in my car and started to drive with no idea where I was going. I found myself driving up your road. I wanted to see you but it didn't feel right to wake you up. So I watched your place, and it felt good knowing you were inside asleep and safe." He smiled. "It was peaceful. The moon came up, high and bright, and the town looked shiny, the way it can when it's at its best. I closed my eyes for a minute and probably would have slept there all night except Kelly opened the door just then and climbed in beside me. I woke up real fast."

I chuckled. "I'll bet."

"We said a few things to each other. You know how it is when you go through something as powerful as this; talking can help give it a meaning you can live with. She's been through a lot in life, and she needed to take a minute to put this thing we'd shared in perspective."

"That makes sense." I was trying to maintain a calm composure, but his words were making my cheeks grow warm.

He stared down into his margarita. "In the end I felt it was important that she understand why I was there, why I drove back to your house that night even though the work was done, the case was closed, and I was dead tired. I needed to be where you were. Kelly knows I came back for you." He lifted his eyes, looked straight into mine. "And now you know, too."

ACKNOWLEDGMENTS

I am proud and grateful to have the second book in the Dr. Pepper Hunt Mystery series published by the stellar teams at She Writes Press and SparkPoint Studio.

Brooke Warner, Crystal Patriarche, and Lauren Wise set an incomparable standard in the publishing industry, and it's an honor to be among the fine authors and books they endorse and present to the world.

I enjoyed working again with Krissa Lagos, whose keen editorial eye and sense of story fine-tuned the manuscript. Thanks are also due to proofreader Chris Dumas for his precise work.

Renowned designer Julie Metz captured the mood of the book with a magically evocative cover.

The contribution of friends and family who read early drafts and shared thoughtful suggestions helped define the scope of this story.

It was easier writing the second book having experienced the unanticipated joy that came from meeting readers who generously told me they loved the first book. Readers are a delight and an enduring motivation to keep writing through the solitary hours.

ABOUT THE AUTHOR

J.L. Doucette returned to Rhode Island after living for many years in Wyoming. She earned a doctorate in counseling psychology from Boston University and has a private practice in Providence.

Author photo by Staceydoyle.com

SELECTED TITLES FROM SHE WRITES PRESS

She Writes Press is an independent publishing company founded to serve women writers everywhere. Visit us at www.shewritespress.com.

Last Seen by J. L. Doucette. $16.95, 978-1-63152-202-4. When a traumatized reporter goes missing in the Wyoming wilderness, the therapist who knows her secrets is drawn into the investigation—and she comes face-to-face with terrifying answers regarding her own difficult past.

Glass Shatters by Michelle Meyers. $16.95, 978-1-63152-018-1. Following the mysterious disappearance of his wife and daughter, scientist Charles Lang goes to desperate lengths to escape his past and reinvent himself.

Water On the Moon by Jean P. Moore. $16.95, 978-1-938314-61-2. When her home is destroyed in a freak accident, Lidia Raven, a divorced mother of two, is plunged into a mystery that involves her entire family.

Murder Under The Bridge: A Palestine Mystery by Kate Raphael. $16.95, 978-1-63152-960-3. Rania, a Palestinian police detective with a young son, meets cheeky Jewish-American feminist Chloe at an Israeli checkpoint—and soon becomes embroiled in a murder case that implicates the highest echelons of the Israeli military.

In the Shadow of Lies: A Mystery Novel by M. A. Adler. $16.95, 978-1-938314-82-7. As World War II comes to a close, homicide detective Oliver Wright returns home—only to find himself caught up in the investigation of a complicated murder case rife with racial tensions.

The Wiregrass by Pam Webber. $16.95, 978-1-63152-943-6. A story about a summer of discontent, change, and dangerous mysteries in a small Southern Wiregrass town.